ROAD INTO THE UNKNOWN

Britt St. Vincent was roaring in his gleaming Ferrari 275 GTB along a deserted midnight highway when he saw the headlights behind him.

Incredulously he watched them gain on him, then suddenly saw the sleek body of a coupe abreast of him, then passing him.

His brain told him that no car in the world was capable of doing what this car had done— and he knew he would have to follow it. He would drive into eternity to solve the mystery of this phantom car.

This was Britt's first contact with the power of THE MIND MASTERS . . .

and the last time he could feel safe in calling his mind his own. . . .

Other SIGNET Books You'll Want to Read

☐ **BLACK SAMURAI by Marc Olden.** Rescued by the Japanese samurai and trained for seven years, Robert Sand became the Black Samurai, a trained killing machine and a man with a mission—out to stop the international terrorist band which had murdered his friends. (#Q6011—95¢)

☐ **THE GOLDEN KILL: BLACK SAMURAI #2 by Marc Olden.** A ticking bomb . . . an explosion of death . . . and Robert Sand, Black Samurai, wages a one-man war against a worldwide empire of evil. (#Q6012—95¢)

☐ **HAWAII FIVE-O by Michael Avallone.** Base on the CBS television series, this fast-paced adventure novel conveys the turbulent atmosphere of the fiftieth state—exotic, beautiful, and the deadliest "beat" in the world for the men of the special police force assigned to keep order. (#T5817—75¢)

☐ **HAWAII FIVE-O #2: TERROR IN THE SUN by Michael Avallone.** Six of the world's deadliest professional killers decide to get Steve McGarrett—six ways at once. (#T5818—75¢)

☐ **THE REVENGER by Jon Messmann.** The blasting novel of a deadly avenger who taught the Mafia how to sweat with fear. (#Q5649—95¢)

☐ **THE MECHANIC by Lewis John Carlino.** By the bestselling author of **The Brotherhood,** the story of a man who made an art of death on demand. (#Q5338—95¢)

THE NEW AMERICAN LIBRARY, INC.,
P.O. Box 999, Bergenfield, New Jersey 07621

Please send me the SIGNET BOOKS I have checked above. I am enclosing $_____(check or money order—no currency or C.O.D.'s). Please include the list price plus 25¢ a copy to cover handling and mailing costs. (Prices and numbers are subject to change without notice.)

Name_____

Address_____

City_____State_____Zip Code_____
Allow at least 3 weeks for delivery

THE MIND MASTERS

John F. Rossmann

A SIGNET BOOK
NEW AMERICAN LIBRARY
TIMES MIRROR

Copyright © 1974 by John F. Rossmann
All rights reserved

SIGNET TRADEMARK REG. U.S. PAT. OFF. AND FOREIGN COUNTRIES
REGISTERED TRADEMARK—MARCA REGISTRADA
HECHO EN CHICAGO, U.S.A.

**SIGNET, SIGNET CLASSICS,
MENTOR, PLUME and MERIDIAN BOOKS
are published by The New American Library, Inc.,
1301 Avenue of the Americas, New York, New York 10019**

First Printing, July, 1974

1 2 3 4 5 6 7 8 9

PRINTED IN THE UNITED STATES OF AMERICA

I

It feels good . . .
Britt's consciousness at last verbalizes the sensation which for the past half-hour has been throbbing through his veins, pumped by the rhythmic thrumming of the V-12 engine that is alive next to his outstretched legs. The machine and its master are alone, satisfied as they roar through the dark night.

Britt lives to drive.

And he's good—very good. The day's practice at Riverside Raceway has again shown that. Driving an obsolete Porsche 917/10, Britt captured fourth fastest qualifying time and will sit among the new snarling factory Porsche 917/30KL racers on the starting grid for tomorrow's Sunday feature race. According to the orchestration of the world-dominating Porsche factory team, that qualifying spot was to have been won by Gerhardt Mueller, the team's new rising star. Britt's furious but well-controlled qualifying laps have upset the factory's plans.

No member of the racing brotherhood knows what compels Britt to drive with such mechanical determination, to so completely merge his mind and body into his machine that the steering column becomes a steel nerve stalk through which his brain can feel the tires like fingers clawing the pavement, grasping desperately through howling hairpin curves. And when Britt races, his engine's revs, the pounding of his heart, the hiss of his air-gulping carburetors and of his flaring nostrils are each sensed and monitored without prejudice by his brain, producing a torrent of mental input that leaves little conscious room for memories. . . .

Britt *must* drive.

Now, Britt's hands tighten on the steering wheel. The black leather creaks under the strain of his grip as he fights back a sudden surge of memory from his subconscious. He forces himself to monitor the gauges glowing on the dash.

Nearly midnight, he thinks, glancing at the clock whose numbers gleam strangely green in the darkened cockpit of his Ferrari 275 GTB. The deserted freeway Britt is driving on is too monotonous to command his full conscious attention ... memories are stirring. Britt forces himself to concentrate, squeezing his thoughts back to the pit garage that he has left just thirty minutes earlier out at Riverside Raceway: *The clutch ... the clutch ... did I correct for that overcenter response? ... only took up two turns on the cable ... hope that's enough to see me through tomorrow's race....*

Britt's eyes are burning from his need for sleep. The full Saturday's practice just ended has been followed by tedious hours of final tuning for Sunday's feature race. Britt rubs the back of his hand across his right eye and the touch starts tear water flowing which cools his fatigue-fevered eyeball. He blinks.

Britt's vision is slightly blurred now as he glances up at the rearview mirror.

CHRIST! The word explodes silently in his mind.

The headlights of a lone car are closing in on him—fast.

CHP again ... DAMN!

Britt's brain evaluates in an eyeblink his chances of accelerating away: the thirty-mile stretch of freeway ahead is straight and empty ... the California Highway Patrol cruiser can sprint to 130 miles per hour but is no match for the sustained 160 mph which Britt's blood-red Ferrari can maintain.

Caught again in the infamous Cucamonga speed trap. A tight, wry grin of resignation flashes unseen in the blackness across Britt's lips as the Ferrari begins to respond to his brain and his foot and slows slightly. But, now, a warning signal suddenly flashes from an upper level of Britt's subconscious. His eyes dart again to the mirror: *Wait a minute ... that's no CHP unit ... and whoever it is, he's really moving!*

Britt's memory neurons are quickly activated. Electrochemical impulses leap with nanosecond speed from neuron to neuron, energizing the protein molecule chains on which the day's events have been stored. Britt's memory bank search is completed in an instant—results: negative: ... *no ... I was the last driver to leave the track tonight ... I'm sure no one else was still there ... so who the hell could that be closing in on me?*

Britt's eyes snap ahead. There is no moon. The night's darkness is thick, oppressive. The Ferrari's beams probe out into the galactic blackness and reveal nothing but rows of gleaming plastic lane reflectors which are sweeping past the hurtling machine like shooting stars. Britt cannot see the mighty San Gabriel mountains which parallel the freeway several miles from its northern flank—but he knows the forbidding peaks are there, looming in the blackness. He can feel their presence, like a mammoth burden on his right shoulder as he drives.

Another second has ticked away. Now Britt's eyes again dart up to the rearview mirror: *Where'd he go!?!*

The strange pursuing car has disappeared.

Britt's brain knows instantly that he has not passed an off-ramp in at least a mile. A sudden stab of confusion is instantly superseded by the subtle impact on Britt's senses of a small change in his cockpit environment—a barely perceptible increase in the illumination level. Britt's eyes flick a glance out the right side window in time to see the headlights and streamlined nose of a sleek coupe pulling abreast of his still-speeding Ferrari.

The phantom car is suddenly pounding along just inches from Britt's machine while his brain races, searching for an explanation. The experience and logic circuits of his brain tell Britt that there is no vehicle in the world capable of closing the gap between the cars in only the instant he had glanced at the road ahead.

Britt looks ahead no more. His eyes focus hypnotically on the strange machine, his brain's logic systems are being short-circuited with perceptual information that does not compute. He stares for several seconds, only subliminally aware of the leaden numbness that is creeping through his limbs.

OH, GOD! ... GOD ... OH, GOD!!!

Britt's brain explodes, staggers, tries to reject, then explain the grinning face it sees glowing ghostly green in the dashlights of the strange machine that streaks along menacingly close to his speeding Ferrari.

"Gayle!" Britt cries aloud.

Gayle. Poor dead Gayle.

Before Britt's benumbed brain can react, the phantom car accelerates rapidly away. Quickly, Britt stomps on the Ferrari's gas pedal, holding it hard against the firewall. A low moan seeps into the car's cockpit as its engine's six dual Weber carburetors open wide their throats and inhale deep the damp midnight air. Britt ignores the soaring speedometer needle. He would drive into eternity to learn the mystery of the phantom car.

Flashing lane reflectors become a shower of streaking meteors as the two machines bellow through the awful night. The pursued machine now veers suddenly, wildly skidding toward an exit. Britt follows, his Ferrari's tires shrieking, shredding chunks of tread as they claw into the concrete curve of the off-ramp. Up deserted small-town streets the two machines hurtle while street lamps swoop overhead like attacking comets. On and on the machines roar through the night, the banshee wail of their mechanical hearts ripping the shroud of silence that darkly drapes the quiet streets of the little town of Ontario. Through the city, leaping over railroad tracks, blasting clouds of sand from the surface of the narrow, black desert road beyond the town . . . surging, twisting up the foothills . . . heading north, always north—toward the mountains. And now, looming ever larger, blacker than the starless night through which it thrusts itself, is Skull Summit.

The realization of where the phantom machine is leading him registers with only little impact on Britt's whirling, busy brain.

Skull Summit, towering 13,000 feet, is seldom mentioned in southern California, except on maps and by playful youngsters on Halloween. The massive mountain's stern granite and impossible cliff-clinging roads have successfully intimidated even Los Angeles real estate developers in their land-killing search for recreation properties. Only a few people live on the mountain in an unnamed village near the peak. The villagers are reportedly quite odd and have little contact with outsiders. Two anthropologists who had gone to study the villagers just two weeks before Britt's arrival at Riverside have only today been found crushed in their car at the base of a thousand-foot cliff. Newspaper reports say that the brakes apparently failed.

JEEZ!! Britt curses angrily.

The Ferrari's steering column is thudding under the hammerlike impact of Britt's overhand grasping as he frantically turns the wheel to keep his twisting machine from plunging off the cliff road and into bottomless empty blackness. That realization of sudden danger sears through Britt's body like a hot flame. The numbness that had engulfed him far below on the freeway now begins to wear off. Britt's exterior senses and reflexes remain focused on the dim taillights of the mysterious machine he pursues, while the internal logic systems of his brain resume their struggle to sort the confusing facts which are emerging from the melting mental numbness: *It's impossible . . . I KNOW that . . . yet I have to know who or what . . . goddam!! . . . I can't catch up!*

Now Britt calls upon all his driving skill, pushes his Ferrari to the ragged edge of control, but finds himself still unable to close the strangely constant gap between his car and the fleeing lights.

The road grows suddenly steeper, the switchback Britt is entering becomes sharper—cold sweat bursts through his forehead pores as he barely makes the corner . . .

Where the hell'd she go!?!

The phantom machine screamed around the sharp switchback just yards ahead of Britt and was out of sight for only a split second before Britt, too, careened around the curve—but the road ahead is now empty . . . completely empty . . . dark . . . quiet. The pavement runs straight as far ahead as Britt can see in the white light thrown out by his Ferrari's Carello quartz-iodine lamps. Britt switches the headlamps off. The blackness rushes in on all sides like a tidal wave and Britt slows his machine to a crawl. He strains his sight into the darkness, searching for the slightest glow, the slightest movement of a shadow that would reveal the car he has been chasing.

As Britt's eyes complete their electrochemical shift from cone to rod neural function and adapt to the dark night, he begins to perceive strange shapes at the roadside. He can actually feel the angular presence of dark, squat cabins that stand like silent sentries amid the trunks of massive black trees which crowd to the edge of the narrow road. Britt feels as if he is being watched.

Suddenly—the blackness of the night erupts in a blast of blood-red smears and sight-searing white. Pain stabs through Britt's head. He tries to stop himself from falling . . . falling into a bottomless black void . . . and shrinking . . . shrinking to the size of a pebble . . . a pinpoint . . . nothing . . .

II

An eon later, a star appears.

It gleams tiny and bright in a sky milk white.

And, now, the cold touch on Britt's shoulder, like the steadying hand of Death.

Britt's eyes are throbbing . . . their focus unclear. An eternity of effort passes in a clock tick while he struggles to sharpen the image of the star: *It's falling,* his mind uncaringly computes. *It's falling onto me.* . . .

Britt's brain suddenly surges. A cry of alarm echoes through his skull and bursts from his lips even as his hand rockets upward to intercept the descending hypodermic needle.

"Welllll!" a surprised voice says.

Britt is exhausted by his effort. Sharp pain cracks through his brain mass and produces images of gray octagons in his internal eye. Britt's arm drops heavily onto the bed on which he is lying.

"Well, well." The voice intones again. "It looks like I won't be needing this after all."

Britt's eyes open again and home in on the source of the sound. In seeming slow-motion response to the direction of his brain, Britt's vision sensors scan across an expanse of acoustic-tiled ceiling panels and fluorescent lights.

The face is smiling. Smiling down pleasantly. The skull is nearly bald, its fleshy cheeks alive with a ruddy glow which contrasts with its white tonsure and beard.

He looks like a bald Santa Claus. The incongruous thought causes Britt's strengthening Self to flash annoyance at its lower-level consciousness.

"We didn't intend for you to be hurt, Britt." Santa Claus smiles concernedly. "You're just too good a driver—you almost overtook your own subconscious back there in the village."

Britt's mind is trying to make sense of what the strange

THE MIND MASTERS

man is saying. Britt raises himself up on his elbow and ignores the throbbing pain in his forehead. "What happened? Where am I?"

"Here . . . drink this," the older man says. He holds out a glass of water and something else. Two round white pills gleam in the palm of his strong hand. "They'll help your headache."

Britt looks up from the bed suspiciously. "What is it?" he demands.

A broad grin flashes across the elder man's mouth. "One hundred percent pure Bayer aspirin," he replies with amusement detectable in his voice.

The ice-cold mountain water feels good in Britt's parched, hot mouth. The crystal fluid alone seems to ease his headache. He hands back the glass and touches his forehead—"Ow!"

"You bumped the steering wheel of your car when its front wheels struck a log at the side of the road, Britt." The man sits down on the foot of Britt's bed. "It's lucky we were expecting you—our villagers down there don't take too well to strangers, and we couldn't risk telling even them beforehand that we were bringing you up the mountain."

Now, nothing is making sense to Britt. "Expecting me?! Bringing me up here?" Britt looks quickly around the room, then back at the man: "Up *where?* Who *are* you?"

"This is Mero Institute, Britt . . . and I am Dr. Bartholomew Webster, head of the institute." Dr. Webster folds his strong, stubby arms across his chest.

Britt's brain is frantically searching for memory traces. A second ticks away forever. Britt shakes his head and says: "Sorry . . . Mero Institute doesn't ring a bell."

"I would have been worried if it did, Britt," remarks Webster with another flash of amusement in his eyes. " 'Mero' is an aboriginal word for 'man,' Britt . . . and that's what we do here—we study *man*."

Britt stiffens. His muscles coil tightly . . . ready.

The bedsprings respond with muffled pops as the older man briskly rises. Hands folded behind his back and brow wrinkled in thought, Webster walks slowly to the window of the small medical room. Britt's eyes follow the man's movement and feed back information to Britt's subconscious: the room appears to be an examining room. There is a door five feet beyond the foot of Britt's bed. The only other exit is the window. Britt takes stock of the fact that he is dressed and has on his shoes.

Webster stops at the window and stares out into the early black purple of the mountain morning. "It will soon be dawn, Britt . . . Sunday morning," he says quietly. Some seconds of silence slip away. Webster turns wearily again toward Britt and stands with his hands still joined behind his back, appearing as if he were about to deliver a lecture: "We study man here as a *whole*, Britt. We approach the integrated human system from every point of view— psychology, physiology, sociology . . . our staff is small, but includes some of the world's best minds . . . there's Janick in sociology . . . Ratkin in anthropology . . . Wortmann in psychology . . ."

Wortmann! The name triggers an immediate response in Britt's memory banks: "Top Psychologist Lost Off Catalina Island" the headline had read four years earlier in the Los Angeles *Times*. The story has remained prominent in Britt's upper-level subconscious even though it is part of a past that he struggles constantly to forget.

Webster notes the flash of recognition which has illuminated Britt's eyes for an instant.

"You know Wortmann, Britt?"

The young man eases himself into a sitting position on the edge of the bed and casts a covert glance at the door: it does not appear to be locked. Now Britt stands up and tests his balance. Webster is watching him intently.

"Yes, I know him—or *knew* him," Britt replies with suspiciousness and challenge sounding in his voice. "I studied under him at Stanford back in '63 when I was working on my PhD in physiological psychology." Britt rivets Webster with a stony stare: "I didn't know that he had been found alive."

"He wasn't, Britt."

Webster made the statement evenly, matter-of-factly. Britt's glinting eyes demand more than riddles.

"Actually, Britt . . . Dr. Wortmann was never really lost at sea. We here at Mero arranged the entire disappearing act. You see, Britt . . . what we do here is secret. . . ."

"SssshhiiTTT!" Britt spits the word out with vehemence and disgust. He snaps his body round and slams his palms down hard on the edge of the washbasin next to where he stands. He glares angrily for an instant into the chrome-circled drain, then flicks his eyes up to the image of Webster

THE MIND MASTERS [9]

which is reflected in the mirror above the basin: "I thought you people said you would let me alone if I kept my mouth *shut* and my brain *out* of psychic research!!!"

Britt whirls round and hurls more angry words at Webster: "Well, I've kept my end of the bargain, *haven't* I!?! For five years now I've not touched a V-meter or a test tube ... I've *done* nothing but race my cars! I've *said* nothing but quote lap times!"

Webster is grinning again ... a strange, wry grin with little amusement in it. "Relax, Britt," he says gently. "This isn't a government installation. In fact, some of the people now here at Mero are refugees from Pentagon labs similar to the one you were in ... only most of them got out earlier than you did—and under less tragic circumstances."

Britt does relax, but only slightly. Webster persists in speaking riddles. Britt leans back against the washbasin, indicating he is willing to listen.

"As I was saying before you interrupted," Webster goes on, "what we are doing here *is* secret ... and, yes, it *is* psychic research. As I also said, however, we are studying man as a whole. We believe that much of what we today categorize as 'supernatural' is not beyond nature at all. Somewhere in man himself are the physical and psychological keys to understanding most psychic powers and astrological influences."

Britt nods; he has long known and accepted that viewpoint.

"And as for Al—Dr. Wortmann, that is," Webster continues, "we arranged his disappearance *with* his cooperation so that he could come to this secret location and take part in our vital work." Webster nods over his shoulder into the brightening blackness outside: "When it becomes light out there, Britt, you will be able to see how very well concealed we are here. Our labs are located under and amid a thick stand of hundred-foot-high fir trees. Fifty yards from this window is a sheer granite cliff—a four-thousand-foot drop. The winds that whip around this two-mile-high peak keep curious helicopters and aircraft far away. And the only land access is through the village about a thousand feet below here and a mile down a precarious road. I furnish that remote village with medical services they can't get otherwise. In return, the villagers ask me no questions and make certain that nosy people don't get up here."

"Okay, Webster, let's hold it right there," Britt interrupts.

"Before you say another word—tell me just how the hell *I* got up here. You said that you were expecting me—that you *brought* me up this mountain."

"Frankly, Britt," explains Webster, "I don't know who you saw at the wheel of that car which you chased up this mountain, but *we* put that phantom car into your head—your own subconscious furnished the face." Webster pauses and grins: "Only thing was, that phantom car was supposed to lead you right on through the village and all the way up to our headquarters and labs. But you loused that plan up with your driving. It was *too good!*"

Britt begins to understand. His head nods slightly in appreciation of the plan: "I *knew* that there was something wrong with that car. Even back down on the freeway I knew . . . but I was too . . . too amazed at who I saw driving the car to listen closely to my brain's warnings that the bits and pieces of information did not compute."

"What bits of information, Britt?" Webster asks with genuine interest. "I really need to know in case we want to use that technique again—on someone *else*, of course," he adds with a smile.

"Well . . ." Britt begins slowly as he recalls the details. "First, I couldn't recognize the make of car it was when it pulled alongside my Ferrari. For me, that's *unusual*. I think I know every type of two-seater coupe on the road today. And I knew also that it wasn't a home-built rig by the way it walked away from my Ferrari. Then, coming up the mountain road, the distance between my car and the one I was chasing remained almost precisely the same, no matter how hard I pushed my 275. You know, even in races between evenly matched drivers and cars, the gap see-saws. Finally, when I rounded that last curve and saw no sign of the machine, I knew—at least, my *brain* knew—that was impossible."

Webster nods quickly: "Okay . . . then that's the moment when your brain's logic systems got through to your consciousness with the facts. The car *had* to disappear because your brain was telling you that such circumstances could not exist." Webster pauses. "Looks like we'll have to be more careful of details in the future if we want to use that plan again."

"Is it a naturally or electronically produced projection?" Britt asks automatically. Yet, even as the words leave his mouth, he flinches internally: more old memories, long suppressed, are stirring.

"For the moment, it's a physical process," replies Webster. "Basically it's hypnosis projected from the mind of a naturally psychic staff member here at Mero." Webster eases himself down onto a white wooden straight-backed chair that sits next to the window. He sighs.

"But our overall goal, Britt, is much more serious than that, as you can well imagine. Our long-range objectives are scientifically identical to that of the military group for which you had worked—first, we want to discover the secret of the natural basic principles of psychic powers. Second, we want to establish training techniques to enable people to develop conscious control over these natural but dormant psychic powers. And, finally, we want to develop electronic tools for duplicating these powers. Our aim here at Mero, however, is to use these powers to establish worldwide understanding and communication."

"Oh, God," Britt whispers.

Weariness and dismay sag over his face like melting wax. "Why can't you just leave well enough alone? . . . God! . . . I thought that I was never going to hear this kind of crap again."

"I know what you're thinking, Britt," Webster says sympathetically, "—*and* remembering. But what we are doing here at Mero is probably the world's last hope for offsetting and countering discoveries from ongoing work like that which you were involved in at the Harry Diamond labs in Washington. There is also a world of benefit that man can reap from perfecting his God-given psychic powers—look, for example, at the strides toward unraveling the mystery of psychic healing that are being made by individuals like Dr. Thelma Moss at UCLA and by Dr. Marshall Barshay at the Sawtell Veterans Hospital in Los Angeles. Their progress is only the beginning of many *good*, benevolent uses of psychic power which can come—but only if we can stay a step ahead of the work now going on at Harry Diamond and other——"

"Just a second, Dr. Webster," interrupts Britt, raising his hand slightly to command a pause. He remembers reading of the beneficial work of Drs. Moss and Barshay in the Los Angeles *Times* back on July 30, 1972. That report pleased Britt—but something Webster said an instant ago causes concern: "—are you telling me that the Pentagon *still* has an active program at Harry Diamond? When they let me out of there, I was assured that the program was ending."

Webster shakes his head somewhat sadly. "Britt, you've stuck too well and too long to your promise to them of noninvolvement in psychic science."

The old man now seems suddenly years older. His chin sinks slowly to his chest. With great effort, his face lifts again and fixes worried eyes on Britt: "A lot has happened since you left those labs, Britt. Come . . . I have something I want to show you before the Sunday morning sun comes up."

III

The filmy form glows ghost white and floats, flickering like an icy flame in the blackness of the closed, cold room.

Britt stares, fascinated. The transparent visage slides across the bare wall and illuminates unseen details in its path: a black, weblike crack in the sweating plaster . . . dust on the hinge of the heavy door.

Now, the gliding figure suddenly stops and fixes its airy eyes on Britt who is half-hidden in the darkness. The figure's lips begin to move. But the words which drift across the void are not synchronized with those lifeless lips: "The person speaking there, of course, Britt, is Henry Cabot Lodge," Dr. Webster says as he adjusts the focus on his clattering movie projector. "This old newsreel shows him in the UN General Assembly on May 26, 1960, making his famous revelation of the secret listening devices that the Soviets had placed in the United States seal that hung in our Moscow embassy. . . ."

Britt remembers it well. While Webster continues his explanation of the film sequence, memories flash with computer speed along long-unused paths through Britt's retention cells. Time becomes a separate reality while Britt's Self internalizes and drifts back . . . back . . . and now Britt's mind is once again in that time . . . the past is real and present: UN Ambassador Lodge's televised revelation of Russia's electronic spying infuriates Britt's untried ideals, just as the revelation also infuriates the entire Cold War-frustrated American populace.

But the news also awakens Americans to a chilling age of electronic insecurity. The public quickly feeds on stories showing the science fiction-like sophistication in eavesdropping devices that many nations' spy and military organizations have developed in supersecret laboratories. The bugged martini olive becomes the standard joke as people everywhere humorize their fear of the giant step that Big Brother has taken behind the well-guarded fences of government research centers.

". . . And now here," Webster is continuing a half-second later as Britt's consciousness again tunes in on the present that is measured by the clock. The scene projecting on the wall is changing: "Here we shift to June, 1967, and Glassboro, New Jersey. Look there, Britt, there you see Soviet Premier Alexei Kosygin and President Lyndon Johnson waving to a crowd of reporters just before the start of their meeting."

Britt shifts uneasily in his chair and watches the scene. The smiling faces of the figures reflect on the cornea of Britt's eyes.

"Government spokesmen," Webster recounts, "told the press at that time that the reason behind selecting such a diplomatically remote spot as Glassboro for this meeting was so that Johnson and Kosygin could confer in a relaxed atmosphere. Today, however, we know that Glassboro was selected because it was far removed from the bugged walls and telephoto windows of the world diplomatic centers. The subject matter that Johnson and Kosygin would discuss *had* to remain a secret at all costs."

The film clip now runs out and the projector switches itself off automatically, smothering the room in sudden blackness. Britt's eyes do not immediately adjust. He can only hear Webster's footsteps as they move away.

Britt blinks awkwardly as the neon ceiling lights flash on. Webster is standing by the door, next to the light switch. The white-smocked scientist turns and slowly walks over to where Britt sits out in front of a paper-cluttered desk. Webster clears a small space and half-sits on the edge of his desk.

"Another thing that you probably didn't pick up on in the last few years, Britt, is that columnist Jack Anderson actually uncovered and reported on the discussion that made Glassboro so supersecret. It was, you see, the world's first summit conference on *psychic warfare.*" Webster pauses and watches for Britt's reaction. But Britt remains stone-faced.

Webster continues: "Maybe Anderson didn't have the Pulitzer Prize fame and household-name status that he enjoys today . . . maybe, too, in those naïve pre-Watergate days the major news media just couldn't bring itself to believe Anderson's story—whatever the reason, very few people picked up on the significance of his report. Soon, the report was forgotten in the flurry of events that began in South Vietnam."

Britt nods. "Well, Webster," he says, "that was two years after I had left the Harry Diamond labs. And even after two years . . ." Britt stumbles over his words as a painful memory surges upward hard against the barrier which imprisons it deep in his subconscious. ". . . Even then," Britt continues, "I had no interest in reading about psychic research or world affairs. There has been a lot that I have missed in those two areas."

"There has especially been an explosion in psychic science, Britt," Webster remarks, "the scope and breadth of which the layman—and even *yourself*—will find hard to believe when it becomes more widely known." Webster pauses. "But that is information you can acquire gradually. What I want to do right now is to update you on the big picture of the immediate world danger against which we here at Mero are targeting our efforts."

Now Webster stands and walks around behind his desk. He eases himself into the foam-filled black vinyl swivel chair and sits staring up at the ceiling for several seconds while his mind orders up from his brain's memory storage the precise sequence of events which had led to the 1967 Glassboro conference: "It all came about quite accidentally on America's part, Britt," Webster begins. "None of America's military men had seriously predicted that in the mid-1960s we would find ourselves in a psychic military clash with the Soviet Union. That is not to say that the battle might never have happened. No, both our nations had launched themselves on a research course that could only result in a collision sooner or later. The rapid success of the Russian psychic scientists and KGB just made things happen sooner—and again—Jack Anderson detailed in his newspaper column most of what I'm about to tell you.

"You see, Britt, after the discovery of the Russian electronic bugs in the Moscow embassy, our CIA began making regular electronic sweeps of the building to detect 'Fred's' ears almost as soon as they had been planted."

"Fred?" Britt is unfamiliar with the name.

"Fred," Webster explains with that flash of amusement returning to his eye, "is the name our diplomats have given to Big Brother in Russia." The amusement fades again quickly as Webster continues his story: "During one of those routine electronic sweeps of the embassy to detect the telltale signals

from Russian bugs, our CIA picked up some very unusual electromagnetic emanations pulsing through the building. The resident CIA chief tried to report this discovery to Washington but was prevented from doing so by one of the senior State Department diplomats in the embassy—the Russian psychic scientists had already gotten into the diplomat's mind.

"Washington, however, soon became alarmed about the whole operation of its vital Moscow embassy. Top-secret reports were being leaked, and U.S. diplomats there were making public remarks that tended to give substance to Soviet propaganda about American involvement in Vietnam and the Middle East. Finally, a CIA agent who was posing as an East German exchange student at the City of Moscow Engineering Institute learned from a casual conversation with a Bulgarian classmate that the Soviets had launched a secret psychic attack on the American embassy. The Russians, you see, Britt, had at that time already achieved such a level of sophistication in their psychic research that they felt confident they could launch this assault on our key Cold War embassy and be assured of either gaining control of or destroying the minds of major U.S. diplomats who were at that time engaged in delicate, secret talks with some of Russia's East European allies."

Webster pauses and leans forward, placing his elbows on the cluttered desk top:

"When word from that agent got to Washington, Britt, all hell broke loose. An incredulous Department of Defense was called into action. It was a ticklish thing—how do you counter an unseen psychic assault without appearing to the world to be either a fool or the instigator of raw aggression? Well, some dusty DOD scientists had the answer: in an underfunded, almost forgotten program, they had been pursuing psychic-warfare research. Their program had begun in the mid-fifties when American intelligence first learned that Russia had added psychic science to the official list of sciences which were to receive top Soviet university attention and military allocations. Today, of course, anyone need look no further than the public listing of psychic science in the official *Soviet Encylopedia* to see its status in Russia. In any case, because of the groundwork of a few U.S. scientists, our Department of Defense was able to quickly assemble and launch a psychic counterattack. Jack Anderson reported that this U.S. counterattack was code-named 'Project Pandora.'"

"How appropriate," says Britt, smiling sardonically.

Webster nods his head slowly in agreement. "Yes, Britt, a Pandora's Box of psychic horror and enslavement had indeed been opened. Kosygin and Johnson had tried to replace the lid at Glassboro . . . but it was too late. The work you were engaged in at the Harry Diamond labs was an outgrowth of that original Project Pandora, and it continued *openly* until the Glassboro meeting . . ."

"And it's *still* continuing?" Britt inquires, already knowing the answer.

"Britt . . . the terrors that came howling out of Project Pandora will be with us for the rest of time—and beyond. But we have to deal with them *now* . . . before it's too late for us all."

Webster is growing increasingly agitated as he speaks. He rises abruptly from his chair and strides across the room to the office window which is covered by drawn blinds.

Now the blinds crackle sharply, like a deck of metallic playing cards, as Webster yanks on the cord and hauls them up in a single, rapid movement.

Outside, in the first morning light, tall fir trees stand crisp and silent against an overcast sky. A cold wind gusts gruffly against the forest, and billowing branches of green-black pine needles flash silver undersides to the sky as waves of wind surge through them. The sight reminds Britt of the rippling pattern wind makes when it blows across the quiet surface of a lake.

Webster stands at the window, hands folded behind his back, and stares at the wind-tossed trees. The man's staring, unfocused eyes remain riveted out the window, but his mind's eye is seeing secret cerebral scenes even as he begins again to talk to Britt: "Out there, beyond our mountain, people are going about their daily work unaware that their very minds and souls are in danger of being possessed by powers and for purposes as evil as any that a Satan could conceive. The Russian people, the Americans, Chinese, English and French—every one of us threatened by hidden, headlong-rushing research into nightmares!"

Webster stops, suddenly silent. Slowly he raises his open right hand until its palm is a half-inch from the cold surface of the windowpane. Both he and Britt watch for several seconds as the heat energy radiating from Webster's flesh causes a ghostly image of the hand to form on the glass.

Quickly, Webster lowers his hand and begins to speak while watching this vaporous outline contract and disappear. "I mentioned the Watergate hearings a few moments ago, Britt." Webster sees Britt's image in the glass nod acknowledgment. "Think back, Britt, to when General Haig testified about the eighteen minutes of taped conversation between Nixon and Haldeman which had been blanked out by a mysterious hum —a hum supposedly caused by an accidental erasure of the tape by Nixon's secretary."

"Yes," says Britt slowly, "I recall that testimony. Rose Mary Woods said that she could have erased only about five minutes of that segment . . . ohhh, yess," Britt interrupts himself as he remembers something else. "I had forgotten that Haig had told Judge Sirica that White House aides had discussed the possibility that some—what was it Haig called it . . . ?"

" 'Sinister force' were Haig's words, Britt."

"Yes . . . some 'sinister force' had erased the tape. Haig said he and others had explored the possibility of some 'devil theories,' didn't he?"

"Indeed he did, Britt," hisses Webster in a strained whisper. *"Human* devils!" he adds in rising tones. The scientist pauses and breathes deeply, regaining control of his voice. "You see, Britt, the White House—the President—had been the target of psychic probing just as our Moscow embassy was back in the sixties. Our analyses here at Mero conclude that Nixon's increasingly erratic behavior beginning in late 1971 resulted from the psychic pummeling he underwent as various groups competed for psychic control of his mind."

"What groups?" asks Britt.

"At least three that we can identify," replies Webster as he continues to watch earth's sun-star rising in the sky. "We feel that his mind has been a psychic battlefield with Pentagon, Russian, and Chinese groups struggling to control him. Some of his own staff may have been psychic agents . . . we think he suspected this and began the secret taping of conversations with them in order to gather evidence. He didn't realize that tape recording, like psychic energy, is electromagnetic and can easily be erased by a psychic once he learns he is being recorded."

Webster falls silent once again.

Britt, too, is deep in thought.

"I had no idea," says Britt softly, talking to himself as

much as to Webster. "When I left the labs in Washington, I thought that was the end of it."

"So did most people who knew of the work there, Britt," Webster answers. He sounds weary now. It has been a long, sleepless night for both men. "Even most top military and civilian leaders in both the U.S. and Russia thought that the Glassboro meeting pretty well wrapped things up. Psychic warfare programs were officially disbanded and their funds reallocated."

Neither man speaks for several thoughtful seconds.

Now, Webster goes on.

"But Glassboro wasn't the end of it, Britt . . . obviously. By easily diverting funds within their mammoth defense budgets, small groups of supermilitarists here and in Russia covertly continued what were at first just scaled-down psychic programs. But their work produced some notable effects on American and Russian life. In this country, for instance, the violent student rioting of the late sixties was—as you probably learned before you left the Harry Diamond labs—largely instigated by electronic mood-control devices that were derived from the psychic discoveries of Project Pandora. The riots, it is now evident, were the first phase of a massive plot. The students were used by U.S. military extremists for two purposes. First, the riots tended to discredit the student causes. Second, the civil disturbances conveniently provided the plotters with the necessary reason to reinstate some of their psychic weapons programs under the guise of 'crowd control' research.

"For the most part, however, Britt, the more significant psychic warfare programs have remained hidden and disguised from all top level military and civilian leadership. From the feedback we have been getting lately here at Mero, we are certain that similar secret psychic research is still advancing rapidly in China, France, Israel, Egypt, South Africa and Chile—in addition to the United States and Russia. In each nation, the research is being controlled by small groups working without the knowledge or approval of civilian and military leadership. Although these scattered groups are currently working to beat *each other* to the secret of powers that will give them world control, there is a good possibility that they could even now join forces and make a *combined* psychic bid for world control—and at this moment they appear to stand an almost even chance of succeeding if they joined forces."

Webster leans against the window frame. He half-turns his head toward Britt and adds: "So far, our work here has been successful in at least *frustrating* these groups . . . so far . . ." Webster's thoughts are drifting away; Britt brings him back with a question.

"And just how are you accomplishing that?"

Webster's face snaps full toward Britt. His eyes flash: *"Truth,* Britt, truth is our simple and effective strategy! Our small group of people here is tops—and very dedicated. Our cross-discipline approach to psychic research has so far enabled us to keep a step or two ahead of the military groups who are taking a narrow approach to psychics, searching mostly for weaponry and population control applications. We've consistently beaten them to the punch on major new discoveries—and as soon as we come up with something new, we manage through our outside contacts to secretly leak the discovery to the news media and to scientific journals. We believe that the sooner the public and general scientific communities learn of each psychic discovery, the more time and opportunity they will have to negate the strategic military value of it by proceeding to develop peaceful civilian applications and uses for the knowledge and technology."

Webster pauses. He grins. "Why, a group of our outside agents is now publishing a series of true-to-fact novels which describe through scientifically accurate but fictionalized adventures both the danger the world is in and what we are doing to prevent psychic enslavement of people's minds.

"Of course, Britt, all this makes Mero the hate object for every military plotter in every nation. Each group may be out to beat the other right now—but it's also true that they're *all* out to remove us. That's why we have our headquarters hidden on this mountaintop, and why we stage such theatrics as phony drownings to bring scientists to our staff up here."

"Tell me, doctor," Britt inquires. "Why don't you tell the whole world right now the story you just told me?"

Webster has turned again and is looking out the window. The breath from his nostrils fogs a small section of the cool window glass. The haze quickly vanishes. "No, Britt . . . sad to say . . . but no one would really believe us—not just *yet,* at least. Our opponents can cover their tracks too well right now, and public opinion is not yet ready to accept the reality of psychic science. We'd look like fools—and a later warning might then be completely disregarded."

Webster watches a hawk, wings folded, plunging through invisible waves of wind. "We would get no more serious attention today than did Jack Anderson with his original reports of the Glassboro meeting and Project Pandora."

IV

"Why did you go through all the trouble to lure me up here—you know that I've been out of the lab for a long time . . . my knowledge is obviously outdated . . ."

Britt hesitates.

"Anyway," he adds with a trace of bitterness in his tone of voice, "the warning I got when I left the Harry Diamond labs was pretty clear. If they learned of me even thinking about going back to psychic research, I've *had* it."

"I know all that, Britt," says Webster quietly. "I have absolutely no right to ask you to help us after what you've been through . . . but we also *absolutely* need you. True, you will require some updating, but with your background you can absorb the new input almost immediately."

Webster suddenly stands erect, pushing off from leaning against the window frame. "Give me a few more minutes of your time, Britt," he gestures toward the door and starts walking as he speaks. "Come, let me show you something."

Webster holds open the door. Britt moves past him, out of the office and into the long, neon-lit corridor outside. A massive stainless-steel door seals the far end. The two men walk toward it in silence. Their footsteps echo sharply on the hard tile floor.

They stop just in front of the cold, gleaming surface of the steel door. Webster removes a plastic card from the pocket of his laboratory smock and injects it into a thin, nearly invisible slit in the shining metal. A sound is heard—a tiny whine, high-pitched, well muffled. The door begins swinging silently inward.

Webster turns to Britt: "If someone somehow ever managed to open this door without a card—blam! . . . no more mountaintop."

Britt steps through the door in front of Webster and into a bright, blue-lit room. Once in, Britt stops, he stands still and stares, fascinated by the activity around him. Three

THE MIND MASTERS

walls of the large room are lined from floor to ceiling with computer components. Hundreds of small red and white lights flash and blink in ever-changing patterns across dozens of display boards, tape reels spasmodically spin and stop, spin and stop, while in low cabinets magnetic disks whir beneath clear plexiglass covers that reflect the winking lights. It is like stepping inside a living brain at work. The electric hum that permeates the room is randomly shattered by machine-gun bursts of typing as information spews from a multi-unit print-out terminal in the center of the large room.

"Adam is *always* busy," Webster remarks, moving toward the master terminal. Britt follows.

"You're doing good work, Adam," Webster says, looking straight ahead toward a prominent set of whirring tape reels. The terminal at Webster's waist suddenly spits out a tongue of print-out paper in a burst of typing. It stops, silent again. Webster rips the paper from the terminal in one swift motion. He hands it to Britt.

"THANK YOU, DR. WEBSTER," the paper reads.

Britt is amused. "What else can Adam do?"

"At this point, Britt," Webster says—the man is staring at the spinning, stopping, spinning, stopping reels which stare back at him like monstrous eyes—"Adam can do more than we thought we designed into him. He seems to be learning as much from us as we are from him."

Webster turns to Britt: "In fact, Adam is the one responsible for your being here"—he glances over his shoulder—" aren't you, Adam?"

Again, there is a clatter of typing and paper leaps from the terminal. Webster hands the new message to Britt: "MERO NEEDS YOU, DR. ST. VINCENT."

Britt hands the paper back to Webster. "Okay, now suppose *one* of you two tells me why I'm so needed."

Webster walks across the room to a table that stands in front of one of the tape-drive units. On the table lie three one-inch high stacks of computer print-out. "The first of these stacks, Britt, is a list of what we believe are without a doubt *genuine* haunting sites. They are located all around the world. You see, one of our latest projects has been to program into Adam's memory banks all the known reports in all of human history concerning hauntings. Actually, we —the human men and women here—did very little of the work involved. Adam did most of it himself. We just brought to him what were literally tons of microfiche and manuscript from public and private libraries around the globe. With his optical scan units, he read it, assimilated it and analyzed it according to the criteria that we had given him —and according to some which he came up with *himself*.

"Adam required only a week of actual analysis to print out for us these lists of what he considers are *positive* hauntings—phenomena that can be explained only by the actual presence of a living, human spiritual entity." Webster taps his index fingertip on the middle stack of print-out while continuing: "There are ten thousand such occurrences in these three stacks. The hauntings cover the range of human history from the earliest biblical period to within the past six months. All of them are listed in descending order of probability. From among the top one hundred cases, Adam has selected twenty that he would like you to begin investigating immediately."

Britt stands half grinning, his head shaking slightly: "Now, let's back up a second," he says. He walks over to the table. Reaching out slowly, Britt thumbs the first stack of print-out, fanning the pages like a gambler with a deck of cards considering a risky bet. "I followed you okay until that last sentence—why does Adam want *me* to investigate these hauntings?"

Webster purses his lips and looks hard into Britt's eyes: "We are not considering *laboratory* investigation, Britt. Laboratory research remains, of course, the best way for developing programs to *utilize* the principles of psychic science, but it has become too slow a way to try to *discover* those principles."

"And what have you come up with that's faster?" Britt asks as Webster pauses for a breath.

The older man hesitates a second before replying: "We are seeking to establish contact with a friendly spirit—a former human being who is now living the fullness of spiritual life, unencumbered by a body, and who would be inclined to share with us as much knowledge as possible about the spiritual and psychic principles according to which he or she now lives."

Britt is incredulous. "You really *mean* that, don't you? . . . Do you think I'm some kind of medium? I'll bet you've read those old army reports about the powers I had when I returned from Vietnam? Well, let me set you straight, Webster—I was never very sure that I really had any so-called psychic powers even then . . . and I haven't tried to use

THE MIND MASTERS

them, or even think about them, for years now. No, doctor," he adds with a firm, negative shake of his head, "I'm no medium or whatever you seem to think I am."

"We know that you're no medium, Britt. And it isn't even the psychic abilities which you may or may not possess that has prompted us to seek you out for this project. We tried mediums here, Britt . . . the best, most reputable we could find. The results were more than *disappointing*—they were *disastrous*."

Britt picks up the first stack of print-out on the haunting sites and scans the information. He looks up: "Why was that?"

"Well, Britt," Webster explains, "we are going to need a consistent, reliable way of communicating with the spirit world. Mediums did not provide us that; their ability to make contact depended on too many human variables." The scientist pauses. Britt can see some sort of recollection flit across the man's eyes, but Webster goes on: "And, as I said, Britt—we need to contact *friendly, helpful* spirits." He turns abruptly and strides across the computer room, toward a large door half-hidden in the shadows of a memory disk unit. "Follow me, Britt."

Webster opens the wooden door and switches on a light in the other room. Inside, partially blocked from Britt's view by stacked boxes of print-out paper, stand three computer tape-drive units. The machines are silent and smashed, broken and bent so that they resemble misshapen metallic grandfather clocks.

"The result of attracting back an *unfriendly* spirit," Webster states while making a sweep of his arm toward the ruined computer components.

Britt stands in the doorway and surveys the scene in thoughtful silence.

"We always held our séances in the computer room, Britt, so that Adam could record everything that occurred. We learned one thing right away both from the verbalizations that came through the mediums and from the sensations that coursed through our own minds and bodies during each séance: *every* spirit that we summoned was angry at being recalled into this primitive physical world that we occupy. It is as if the spiritual world is so much better than this world that the spirits didn't even want to be reminded of what they have departed from."

"And one of these spirits did *this* to express his annoyance?" Britt asks, looking at the smashed machines.

Webster nods and glances again at the wreckage. "Scared hell out of us all, Britt . . . one minute we were sitting quietly in the dark around the table in the room out there . . . and the next instant the place was alive with a wierd pulsing glow, a swirl of luminescence that made us feel as if we were immersed in an indoor display of the aurora borealis. Suddenly everything began flying through the air . . . tables, chairs . . . us. These heavy tape units were sent tumbling across the room . . ." Webster's voice trails off. He turns quickly and motions for Britt to step back into the main computer room. Webster closes the door behind them.

Britt walks over to two white, contoured plastic chairs that sprout on steel stalks from the floor next to the main print-out terminal. Webster follows him. They sit in the chairs.

"Is the lab research so slow that you feel you must risk *that?*" Britt asks with a nod of his head toward the door of the room they had just left.

Webster inhales deeply and slowly before he replies: "We have learned that the pace of discovery in the military groups' psychic research has greatly accelerated in recent months, Britt . . . each new bit of information has been the key to several more bits of information, and on down the line . . . The Russians, for example, have already mastered the laboratory ability to kill by psychokinetic projection."

Britt raises a skeptic eyebrow and Webster responds to Britt's nonverbal question: "Yes, Britt, they have. We first learned of their successful work in the summer of 1971 when Stanley Krippner, director of the Dream Laboratory at Maimonides Medical Center in Brooklyn, and his assistant Richard Davidson were granted a tour of Russian parapsychological centers. While there, they learned that the Russians now have a training program which is actually a production line for developing psychokinetic martial skills. The Russians prize pupil so far in PK skills is a woman known as Nina Kulagina—after her initial training, she was able to stop the heart of a frog with her PK powers."

"Well, I can see things really *have* changed since I left psychic research," Britt comments flatly. "How were you able to learn of Krippner's trip to Russia?"

Irony sounds in Webster's tone as he explains: "Well, it

THE MIND MASTERS [27]

didn't exactly require a CIA-type probe—Krippner's whole trip and Kulagina's PK skills, as well as a full sketch of Soviet psychic research, were written up in a detailed article that appeared in the March 18, 1972, issue of the *Saturday Review of the Sciences*. The public reaction, of course, even to *that* alarming article was another yawn of about the same proportions as the one that greeted Jack Anderson's report about Project Pandora and Lyndon Johnson's Glassboro meeting with Kosygin."

"Have the Russians taken the lead in psychic research among the groups whom you are competing against?" Britt asks.

"I'd say it's a toss-up at this point, Britt," the older scientist replies, "between the Soviets and the Red Chinese groups whose two-thousand-year-old work with acupuncture has furnished a wealth of knowledge about human bioplasm and psychic energy."

Webster relaxes into his chair and folds his arms across his chest. "In any case, Britt, Mero still has a few aces up its sleeve—and that brings us back to why you are here. Our biggest hole-card at the moment is an electronic device which we have designed in the hope that it will enable us to establish a permanent and reliable communication link with spirits in the Beyond."

Now, Britt's eyes narrow . . . a veil of doubt covers his face. Webster notes the expression and explains: "We've already successfully tested the apparatus in the field, Britt. The test was at the site of a well-documented haunting in Santa Barbara, at the Mission. We feel we were able to contact the spirit of an Indian who had been murdered there around 1885 by a group of real estate men who were after his land for sale during the land boom that followed the completion of the Santa Fe railroad link to Los Angeles. However, we were never really certain of our contact with the spirit."

Britt is extremely interested. He leans forward with his elbows on his knees. "Okay. I'll accept the fact that you might have such a device, but why then were you not certain of the spirit contact that you made with it?"

"Two principal factors, Britt," replies Webster. "First, the section of the Mission where the murder had taken place was in the process of being renovated. We now feel that the renovation probably weakened the bond which held the spirit at the Mission. Second—and related to the first reason—

since the renovation had already partially freed the spirit, it was difficult to induce the spirit to give us its full cooperation. The spirit knew that he would not have to rely on *us* for freedom. And that also points up a basic weakness of even this electronic 'medium' that we have developed—it seems to be no more successful than human mediums in attracting the attention of already-free spirits from their apparent bliss in the Afterlife."

Britt's lips are parting as he prepares to speak, but Webster raises a hand to forestall the young scientist's questions: "I know you have a lot of questions, Britt . . . and I think Adam is waiting to answer them." Webster turns toward the master tape-drive console and addresses it: "Adam, are you ready."

Britt's eyes dart quickly to the print-out terminal where he expects to see a reply. He is somewhat startled to hear a deep, deliberate voice slowly speak: "Yes, Dr. Webster, I am ready."

"Can he sing, too?" Britt asks.

An almost silent sliding sound catches Britt's attention. He sees a panel in the black floor disappear. A large television monitor now rises smoothly from beneath the hole. The blue lights overhead dim. The men sit for a moment in silence surrounded by the computer consoles that are flashing their thousands of tiny colored lights. Now, a picture begins to form on the screen. Webster whispers to Britt: "These films were secured for us by Dr. Leopold Sauton . . ."

Sauton! Time stops moving in Britt's consciousness. Within the eternal capsule of a billionth of a billionth of second, long-suppressed information leaps from Britt's subconscious retention cells: *Sauton, head of the Electrochemical Task Force, Group B, Project Unk, Harry Diamond Laboratories. Died and body lost in light plane crash during Yukon hunting trip.*

". . . at the time that we arranged to bring him here to Mero," Webster is still finishing the sentence a nanosecond later as Britt's conscious mind again tunes in. "They show an experiment which took place at the Harry Diamond labs just a few weeks before you left there, Britt."

V

The film which Sauton smuggled out for Webster had obviously been made for viewing by the Pentagon and Central Intelligence agencies, who during those years had been overseeing the work at the Harry Diamond labs. The film credits are now rolling by on the screen and Britt is casually reading the names:

Pickett! Britt's mind catches at the name moving up the screen: *Colonel Willard Pickett, Project Director.* A chill shoots through Britt's body.

Now, a scene appears on the screen: four middle-aged men are walking into a gleaming stainless-steel and white laboratory. There they are greeted by a group of waiting doctors and technicians, among whom Britt recognizes Dr. Sauton and Colonel Pickett. There is no sound track to the film, so Dr. Webster begins to explain the action: "You probably recognize Dr. Sauton, Britt . . . this is the experiment that caused him to decide to leave the Harry Diamond labs a short time before you also arrived at that decision. Sauton had been told only that this experiment was being set up to test the truth of the ancient observation that ESP projection frequently occurs before, during, or just immediately following the moment of death.

"History, as you know, Britt, is filled with reports of people being 'visited' by relatives and friends who are either calling for help just before they die or who try to console the surviving relative or friend regarding the death. Such reports have recently been verified by Soviet experiments with animals. In one test using rabbits, a mother rabbit was taken from her litter and carried out to sea on a ship where she was killed. At the moment of her death, instruments both on the ship and on shore by the cage containing the young rabbits recorded large rises in bioplasmic energy potentials —both potentials showed *identical* patterns."

The film rolls on while Webster talks. The four subjects

are led to seats in front of an array of electronic devices. Britt recognizes the machines which range from the hospital-familiar electroencephalograph to advanced versions of the Russian-developed Kirlian cameras that are used for photographing bioplasmic auras. The unsuspecting subjects are shown being wired to the equipment. Thick leather straps are fastened around the men's wrists, waists, and ankles, securing them firmly to the chairs, which are also bolted to the floor.

"The subjects," Webster narrates, "of course knew nothing of what was going to happen. Sauton himself had only reluctantly agreed to the test and thought that the subjects were merely going to be *threatened* with death." Webster shifts uneasily in his chair. "I've only seen this film once before myself, Britt . . . I still find it hard to believe that anyone could actually do what we will soon see. The subjects were convicted murderers, Britt. They had been 'volunteered' for this experiment with the knowledge that it could lead to their being freed." As Webster speaks, the film shows the technicians swinging into place across each man's chest a shiny steel truss. Each truss is securely fastened to the arms of each chair. In the center of each truss is an electric motor, a gear set, and—connected to the gear set and pointing directly at the heart of each subject—a sharp surgical knife. Each subject looks with unfaked fear in his eyes at the gleaming point of the knife in front of his own beating heart. The points of the super-sharp instruments catch the glare of the camera lights and reflect like a row of tiny, brilliant stars.

"Here," Webster explains, "you are seeing the technicians advise the subjects that each knife is precisely set so that when the motors are turned on, the point will very slowly advance toward the subject's heart and very slowly pierce the outer layers of skin and muscle. The four subjects are advised that three of the knives are set to stop when they meet the resistance of the breast bone—the fourth will not stop, but will continue slicing in, right into the pounding heart of the unlucky man." The scene on the screen suddenly cuts to scan the array of instruments in front of the subjects; all of the instruments are showing potentials, the needles of the electroencephalographs and electrocardiographs are bouncing wildly, tracing large, sharp wave patterns. The self-developing film rolling through the Kirlian cameras is showing that surges of glowing bioplasmic auras are emanating out from the bodies of the frightened, tied-down subjects.

The film quickly cuts back to a close-up looking down the row gleaming of knives. The knives now are moving . . . slowly moving . . . moving ever closer to the heaving chests of the terrified men.

"I think we've seen enough."

"Yes, Dr. Webster," Adam responds in his inhuman voice. The room lights grow brighter again, and the television picture simultaneously fades and disappears.

The two men sit a moment in silence. Britt breathes in deeply and exhales slowly. "There are so many things my subconscious has buried," he says softly.

Webster nods, indicating he knows what Britt is speaking of. "Well, Britt, you don't know all of what happened *next* in this experiment—no one else at the Harry Diamond labs except Dr. Sauton knew *all* of what that experiment produced. When that test ended and the awful murder was done, Sauton stood in shock, Britt, stunned at the cold-blooded killing of the subject. The other physicians and technicians in the lab were jubilant. They had seen and got what they were hoping for. Those scientists then gathered the graphs that had been spewed out by the EEG and EEC machines; they quickly plucked the roll of film from their Kirlian camera and hurried out of the room even before the body of the dead subject had been removed. Sauton, however, waited until the living and the dead subjects had been taken away by the orderlies. Alone in the room, he was sickened and dismayed, and deep in painful thought. Sauton wandered along the banks of instruments to which the subjects had been connected. In their haste to begin analysis of the results, his colleagues had forgotten to switch off the machines. Sauton absently fingered the graph paper still slowly coming out of the machines as he walked along the array of instruments. The needles of three of the electroencephalographs were producing only straight, flat lines on the slowly growing tongues of graph paper. Suddenly, Sauton related to me later, he stopped cold in his tracks—the paper coming out of the fourth electroencephalograph that had been hooked to the murdered subject was still showing a tiny, barely visible pattern. Sauton let the machine run on until he had about an eighteen-inch strip of the pattern. Then he switched the machine off. Sauton told me later, Britt, that he knew right at that moment that he had made an astounding discovery. Sauton then hurried from the room to join his colleagues—but more importantly and strictly for himself: to secretly compare the strange EEG pattern that he had found with the pattern that had been produced by the machine while it was connected to the unlucky convict."

Webster pauses. He rubs his tired eyes and continues:

"The patterns were, of course, basically identical, Britt. The first pattern was larger, amplified more because the electrodes of the EEG were connected directly to the man's body . . . but both patterns were the *same!* Sauton's conclusion was inescapable: the dead man's life energy—his *spirit*—was still in that room even after his bloody corpse had been removed.

"Sauton's agitation over the awful experiment was observed by his colleagues, so, a few days later when he requested a leave of absence in order to do some thinking, it was granted. Pickett's conditions for granting Sauton's request included that he must not mention to anyone what kind of work he was doing or where he was working, and that he be accompanied at all times by a CIA agent.

"Sauton chose to take a hunting trip into the remote back country of Alaska. Our Mero Institute operatives had already at that time begun gathering detailed information on the work and staff of the Harry Diamond psychic research teams, so when we learned of Sauton's disillusionment and his planned trip, we devised a scheme to bring Sauton here to work for us. The bush pilot who flew Sauton and his guard out of Anchorage for a deserted back country hunting cabin was a Mero agent. When they reached the remote cabin, our agent was supposed to fly back immediately—but he remained long enough to make a pot of coffee for Sauton and his keeper. The coffee contained a powerful sedative, Britt.

"As soon as the drug had rendered both men unconscious, our agent administered an antedote to Sauton and revived him. Our agent explained to Sauton who he really was and told Sauton about our organization and our work. Sauton had known me professionally before he went into the Harry Diamond labs, he knew my integrity and was very receptive to joining our effort against what was happening to psychic research."

"How did you dispose of the guard?" Britt asks.

"We didn't kill him, if that's what you're thinking, Britt," Webster replies. "No, he became our first non-lab test of a new memory control drug that we had developed. Our agent and Dr. Sauton carried the CIA bodyguard back aboard the aircraft and flew him out to a remote section of the coast over which the plane had flown on the way to the cabin. While heading for that coastal area again, Dr. Sauton administered a precise dosage of our new drug to the CIA agent. The dosage was calculated to make the man forget everything right up to the point of the original flight over that section of water.

"When our pilot reached the spot again, he flew low and slow over a small fishing boat that was bobbing on the deserted sea. The boat was crewed by two more Mero agents. The CIA man was dumped from the plane. The cold water revived him from the sedative, and when he was hauled aboard our boat, the crew told him that they had witnessed the plane crash and sink with Sauton and the pilot aboard. Of course, the CIA man could remember nothing except flying over the water the first time. When he got back to Washington, the Harry Diamond staff psychiatrists decided that the accident actually did occur and that the trusted agent was suffering from common psychological suppression of the details of the tragedy. So, Sauton ended up coming here with his copy of this film—*and* with his invaluable piece of graph paper."

Britt now speaks up: "There's something you have to explain to me more clearly, Webster, before I can completely accept the story you've just related. In all my studies, I have never heard of a memory drug such as you describe—how can it be and how does it work?"

"Well, Britt, it was derived from some of the new discoveries that have been made since you left the world of research. Actually, we at Mero cannot claim credit for the basic research; we merely built on the work that is still being done by Dr. Ernest Noble, professor of psychiatry, psychobiology, and pharmacology at the University of California in Irvine. He has been studying the effect that social drinking has on human memory. His work shows that memory is a chemical process. As you know, Britt, whenever a person does, hears, says, or sees *anything*, an electrochemical impulse travels through the brain. As the impulse flashes at great speed through the millions of brain cells, it leaves behind in each cell a chemical trace, a chain of protein molecules that are quickly linked together—like a wire being strung—for the electrical impulse to travel along. Most of these chemical chains are soon reabsorbed by the cell, because if they all remained permanent, the thousands of things we heard and saw and did each day—from hearing the random honk of a car to seeing the flight of a bird—would each stay in the brain and soon leave no room for things we need to remember. For things that we *do*, however, need to remember, repetition serves to make the chain stronger. Each time we repeat an action, the electrical impulse travels along the same chemical chain and leaves on it another thin layer of protein; as the chain or 'wire' becomes increasingly thicker, the impulse travels along it easier each time—in effect, that is why 'practice makes perfect.'

"Our Mero people here went a few steps beyond what Dr. Noble is doing, Britt. We came up with a way to administer an enzyme that would cause the brain cell to digest new protein memory chains at a controllable rate. We determined how thick memory chains are at various stages and how much enzyme is required to dissolve them at each stage."

"That is a *remarkable* step, Webster," Britt says with sincere compliment. "But it prompts this question on my part—how does a person remember things that happened a long time ago, things which haven't been repeated in years? Shouldn't such memory traces have been 'digested' again by the body's natural enzymes?"

"Most memories *are* wiped out," Webster explains. "Those that suddenly pop to mind after many years have passed have never been completely 'forgotten.' The memory chains have been kept at a specific thickness by the subconscious mind which repeats the memory at regular intervals in order to maintain the protein chain—there are many things, Britt, which your subconscious will *never* let you forget . . . but let me return to my story of Sauton. . . .

"Based on Sauton's observations before leaving the Harry Diamond labs, Adam here was able to statistically confirm what Sauton had suspected from the moment when he first saw the strange phenomenon of the EEG machine producing a pattern while not connected to a person. Adam's earlier analyses had shown that the chemically generated electrical energy of the human nervous system is a segment of some extreme range of electromagnetic energy—so extreme that even Adam could not decide on which extreme end of the electromagnetic spectrum it was situated. This energy, Adam concluded, is the source of energy of human intellectual activity and is inseparable from it. In other words, it is the soul, the human spirit, the energy of the nonphysical intellect and personality—the Self.

"Adam's analysis further supported another hypothesis that Sauton had formed: that during a sudden and violent death, the human spirit, in a supreme effort to hold body and soul together, surges with all the energy at its command. This frantic and instantaneous surging creates an immensely intense electromagnetic field. This field is powerful enough to disturb the natural electromagnetic fields of nearby objects and surroundings, things such as trees, boulders, gallows, floors, rooms, walls, furniture—you name it. The powerful electromagnetic surging is frequently strong enough to bring about fusion between the magnetic fields of the spirit and the magnetic field of whatever nearby object it is affecting. When this happens, the spirit becomes ensnared—its electromagnetic energy field fused together with the magnetic field of the surroundings after the body dies."

"My God," Britt exclaims softly as the full impact of Webster's revelation hits hard and stabs deep in his psyche, deep to break the subconscious shield that Britt has built around the buried memory of poor, dead Gayle. The psychological membrane in Britt's mind that separates past from present, conscious from unconscious, quivers; he struggles to suppress secret, surging, insistent images and he comments aloud, "Of course . . . that would explain how a haunting comes about: some poor spirit trapped in a suddenly alien and physical world of which it should no longer be a part."

"Precisely, Britt," says Webster. "But sometimes it is possible for the trapped spirit to be freed by natural means. The motion picture cliché of showing spirits walking about on stormy nights has more than a grain of accurate historical observation behind it. Electrical storms—especially if there is lightning present—frequently cause disruptions in natural electromagnetic fields. A trapped spirit, knowing this, will manifest itself and struggle to take advantage of any disturbances that might present for it an opportunity to escape. Frequently, the spirit is successful. You see, the spirit can escape whenever the electromagnetic field of the object that is holding it is altered significantly. There would be thousands of haunted automobile junkyards—and there *are* more than a few right now—if all the spirits of people who died in car crashes had to remain trapped in the vehicles in which their bodies died. Fortunately, many wrecks are handled by magnetic cranes or are melted into scrap iron—both of which disrupt the field and allow the spirits to escape. One of the reasons why there are so few genuine haunting sites in the United States is because of our habit of tearing down old buildings and plowing up the earth to build new things. These changes release trapped spirits. In Europe, where buildings and other objects have been around for ages, you find a higher incidence of authentic hauntings.

"Therefore," Webster continues, "it is such trapped spirits, such genuine haunting sites, that we must visit in order to obtain the information we require. We feel that these desperate trapped spirits will be more inclined to communicate to us what we seek to know if we can promise them release from their earthly prisons . . ." Webster goes on speaking, but Britt's mind is remembering.

That old, cold pain returns to Britt's fingertips. Like the ground of a graveyard heaving, tumbling in a mighty earthquake, that membrane in his mind begins to split, the widening fissures reaching deeper, down and down toward the psychological coffins buried in Britt's being. The dead are waking. . . .

"Britt? . . ."

"Oh! Sorry," says Britt, shaking his head slightly and smiling apologetically ". . . I was just thinking about . . . somebody . . ."

"Well, Britt," Webster says, "regarding these haunting sites that Adam selected—we knew that we could not simply send our lab people out to the selected haunting sites to test the communication equipment. No, most of our technical people are too well known by the groups we oppose. Our people would be destroyed.

"So, we asked Adam to do a cross-referential comparison and come up with a commonality factor that we could use in setting up some sort of cover identity for our vital field research at the haunting sites. Adam's analysis broke down the top one hundred haunting sites into a dozen groupings. One of these groupings caught Dr. Sauton's eye immediately —because he remembered *you*, Britt."

Britt's attention is riveted once more on Webster's words as the man goes on: "Adam's print-out showed that one group of sixteen hauntings all had in common the fact that they were located near the sites of international Grand Prix auto racing tracks."

Britt's eyes narrow, reflecting his mounting interest—and

his anticipation of what Webster is leading toward. "I think I'm beginning to see why you need me."

"That's right, Britt," confirms Webster, "we plan to send a selected research team to these haunting sites. Our people will be protected by a cover identity that portrays them as a team competing in international racing events." Webster looks hard at Britt: "Only *you*, Britt, have the combination of scientific and racing qualifications to successfully head such an effort. The team we've selected for you to lead includes one of our most competent technical men—but a man not known to our opponents. In addition, you will be working with my son. He has never had anything to do with psychic research and has used his deceased mother's maiden name for many years while he has been competing in amateur racing. In fact, Britt, I'm certain that you already know him—Greg Leland."

"Of course I know him!" Britt says quickly. "He and I have jousted at tracks all across the country. Why, just yesterday I beat him out of a second row qualifying spot for today's race at Riverside." Even as he is speaking those words, Britt's mind realizes that it is now already Sunday. Britt looks quickly at his watch: 9:45 A.M.! His eyes snap to Webster's, and he says to the older man: "Ever since I left the Harry Diamond labs I've had an agent on my tail who is waiting to see if I either go back on my word never to discuss that place or reenter psychic research. In recent months this surveillance has become spotty. I believe that they are finally convinced that I intend to keep my word. But, if I don't show up for that race today, Webster, they will probably wonder where I've been. Even though I'm certain that you can see to it that they never learn that I've been up *here*—the incident will surely mean that the surveillance will increase again to round-the-clock, rather than being dropped altogether. Neither you nor I want *that*."

Webster's face flashes sudden surprise: "Does that mean you're going to join us, Britt!?!"

"No," Britt replies flatly. He rises quickly from his chair. "It means that I'll *think* about it. Right now I have to get the hell back to that track and get into my racing gear." Britt walks toward the door as he speaks; Webster stands and follows him. "I think that I have a pretty good idea of the kind of plan you have in mind, Dr. Webster . . . and I *will* think about it."

"Are you certain that you can drive, Britt?" Webster inquires. "After all, you've been up all night. Won't it be a risk going out there and racing? If you don't want to take the risk, I think we can come up with some kind of story to cover your absence."

"No," Britt states firmly, "I take a risk *every* time I go on the track—but I'm not about to take the kind of risk my absence will lead to."

VI

Goddam!! Britt is thinking with an emotion of exasperation that is shared by all the other drivers who sit at this moment behind the starting line, sweating in their snarling machines. The official race starter is standing to the side of the track, joking with a girl in red STP-emblazoned hot pants. The small-time official has not yet even bothered to turn around to see if the cars have completed their proper line-up for the start. With each minute the man delays, the temperature gauges of the fanless racing engines show an increase. Both the cars and the drivers need to be moving in order to be properly cooled.

Britt is baking. He sits tightly belted into the hard, unpadded fiberglass seat of his Porsche. The Southern California sun breathes down hot on his white racing suit. *Christ!* his mind complains as he feels another drop of sweat trickle down his chest inside his Nomex fireproof "long johns." The protective Nomex irritates his skin as it becomes wet with salty sweat. Britt wants to just tear his hands from the tiny, thick black steering wheel and claw away the itching, but he knows that he will probably no sooner take his hands off the wheel than the starter will whirl and launch the waiting line of racing machines right up Britt's back.

Britt's feet are tucked out of sight, squeezed beneath the low, flat snout of the sleek Porsche. Through his paper-thin leather racing boot, Britt can sense the tiniest change in the response of his engine to his touch on the throttle; the engine seems to be becoming tighter as Britt sits there in the sun. He is blipping the throttle to keep the spark plugs from fouling. All around Britt, other drivers, too, are jabbing at the accelerator pedals of their cars, trying to keep the high-tuned power plants alive until the starter waves the flag. The furious snarls and spitting sounds of the engines are distant to Britt's ears which are muffled by his neck-length, fully enclosed Bell racing helmet. Britt is looking out at the world through the narrow, green plexiglass-covered eye slit. The opening seems far away from his eyes as if he is looking out at the scene from halfway down a long tunnel. With curious detachment Britt observes his arms: they appear to stretch out from some invisible point below him, like massive cables spanning out from the face of a cliff to grasp a giant steering wheel affixed on the opposite wall of the canyon. Now, Britt's Self level of consciousness is slipping away from the immediate challenge of the race ... he thinks many things ... each level of his consciousness is alive with thoughts, memories, evaluations....

Almost casually, his brain's environmental monitor level of circuitry flashes an action-initiative impulse to the functional level of his brain in response to a sudden movement that was observed an instant ago by Britt's vision organs.

The green flag has dropped.

Britt's foot is activated automatically by his brain and it slams the gas pedal to the floor—simultaneously Britt's right hand reaches under the cockpit cowling for the stubby shift lever, ready to shove the lever into second gear. Like the volume of a television set being slowly raised, the sounds of the engine, the screaming of the tires grow in Britt's ears until the job at hand has regained the full attention of his consciousness. His sense of feeling grows along with the growing sound ... jolts are felt from the massive, rock-hard racing tires that now are pounding over patches in the race-scarred pavement ... inertial pressure is pushing Britt's eyeballs back into his skull as the car rockets away from the starting line ... *8000* ... *8500* ... *8700* ... Britt's mind is monitoring the tachometer needle ... at the split second that the pointer touches 9,000 revolutions per minute, Britt's right hand and left foot explode into action! A snap shift into second gear and the Porsche leaps ahead with such brutal quickness that the machine slips slightly sideways as powerful rear wheels try to push past the front. Britt corrects the slide in an eyeblink with a skilled tug on the steering wheel. Now, again the tach touches 9,000 rpms and Britt makes a lightning-quick shift into third gear. The snakelike section of the track—the dangerous esses—are sliding toward the Porsche's low snout at a vision-blurring ninety miles per hour when suddenly everything slows down.

With the peculiar ability of a racing driver to make time a separate reality, Britt's brain slows down the over mile-a-minute racing action so that there is time for his living re-lays and circuits to compute and evaluate the vital moves that must be made in preparation for and threading through the treacherous esses. *Mueller's Porsche on my left seems to be bogging a bit on upshifts . . . Spitzer's and Erde's Porsches ahead don't seem to be following their team plan . . . Erde is trying to take the lead into the first bend, but Spitzer doesn't want to let him do that . . . looks like Spitzer can squeeze in there first . . . I think I can shut the gate on Mueller and go through in third place . . . oh, oh! Erde nerfed Spitzer! . . . looks like he's going to have to take to the dirt!*—Britt is just at the apex of the first ess curve when the road disappears in an exploding cloud of dust from Erde's Porsche as it roars off the road. Flying sand hisses against Britt's eye shield and a large stone *whocks* against his plastic helmet! In another instant he breaks through the cloud and finds himself in second place just five feet behind the roaring tailpipes of Spitzer's leading Porsche.

The pipes spit tongues of blue flame at Britt as Spitzer downshifts for turn six. *Turn six! . . . turn six!* Britt's brain shouts the warning in his head. Britt knows now that his concentration is not up to his normal standards. *Goddam it!! I'm going too damn fast!!!* But he is already into the turn before he jabs at the powerful brakes. The Porsche responds crazily, switching from an understeering attitude to instant oversteer.

Britt snaps the steering wheel to full left lock, simultaneously downshifting into second and letting the clutch pop out against a closed throttle . . . the sideways sliding of the rear wheels stops and the front swings out in front again while Britt skids within inches of the concrete wall. Mueller's Porsche now screams past him on the inside of the curve.

Britt punches his foot against the throttle and is immediately in pursuit. His powerful racer burns its rear tires, leaving blue smoke and black stripes on the sun-melted asphalt track. Quickly, Britt is stepping on the brakes again for the next hairpin curve . . . centrifugal force of the curve pulls Britt sideways as his machine claws for traction, and Britt strains hard to fight the steering wheel and keep the Porsche in the well-worn racing groove through the sharp left-hand bend. Now Britt's accelerating again, upshifting into third, suddenly downshifting into second and back on the brakes for the sweeping right-hand curve that opens onto the mile-long highspeed Riverside straightaway—four wheels sliding sideways in unison, Britt executes a perfect four-wheel power-drift out of the curve. His foot is pressing the throttle hard against the hot fire wall . . . the engine gathers strength, breathing deeply, powerfully . . . it's screaming, shrieking, straining toward its upper limit. Just one tick over that limit and the engine will explode; but Britt's eyes are not on the tachometer. His mind is listening to the engine, monitoring its rpms with a well-trained ear . . . THUNK! . . . Britt shoves the stubby shift lever into fourth gear . . . 8000 . . . 8500 . . . 9000 . . . THUNK! Into fifth! Britt's body can feel the pressure of acceleration pushing in against his eyeballs and his chest, tugging at his cheeks. He remains only a few seconds in top gear before the Porsche hits 180 miles per hour. Britt's hand hardly moves the wheel now to send the car snapping smartly through the sudden chicane . . . 8 . . . 7 . . . 6 . . . 5 . . . 4 . . . Britt's mental calculator begins reading off the braking markers that pass in a blur at the side of the track . . . 3!!! He jabs the brakes hard and downshifts into third! The engine screams and the car slows as if a giant, unseen hand is out in front restraining the hurtling mass. The deceleration forces try to pull Britt forward out of his seat. His racing harness presses tight across his chest as his body rises . . . his eyeballs bulge from their sockets. Suddenly—the forces change direction again and tug him sideways as he enters the long, banked curve at the end of the straightaway. Ahead lies the finish line and the start of the second lap.

Britt hardly notices the signals from his volunteer crew as he passes the pits. He is now driving mechanically, his Self sinking deeper and deeper into a morass of memories which he has long feared to recall, but which now cannot be denied their resurrection. The second lap flashes by . . . the third . . . several times, self-protective instincts flash warnings and Britt becomes angry with himself for his sloppy driving. But always those sepulchral memories call him back into a different, inner world. The monitor circuits of Britt's subconscious mind know that Webster is responsible—Webster, who has told Britt of how the human spirit can become ensnared in its surroundings.

Suddenly the protective psychological membrane over Britt's subconscious snaps. *Gayle! . . . Oh, Gayle!* Tears well in Britt's eyes, burning, blurring his vision just as he again is entering the high-speed sixth turn.

A jolt through the steering column jars Britt severely, causing his half-open mouth to snap shut on his tongue. Britt tastes the salty sweetness of blood in his mouth. The bouncing steering wheel now jerks itself free of his grasp. The car is suddenly spinning wildly amid an obscuring cloud of blue tire smoke and brown dust—it is sliding, spinning rapidly toward the concrete wall at the outside of the turn . . . above the dust cloud from his car and above the wall, Britt's eyes catch a fleeting glimpse of faces . . . faces of race fans, eyes wide in sudden fright as his car spins toward them like a crazy flaming comet.

Suddenly the old, terrible pain erupts again in Britt's head at the moment of the impact! He hears no sound . . . he only feels that pain. . . .

VII

The pain is strangely familiar. It fades now and Britt listens for those sounds. In the green, damp darkness ahead Britt hears something.

Quiet sounds are filtering softly through the high, thick jungle grass. Britt stops in his tracks . . . he freezes . . . listening. The South Vietnamese Rangers whom he is leading also freeze . . . and listen.

Slowly, quietly, Britt pushes the thick grass aside. He can see into a small clearing just ahead. He sees a bamboo hut. A thin trail of smoke curls lazily skyward from an opening in the thatched roof. And in the doorway of the hut sits a skeletal, wrinkled old man.

The clearing seems suspiciously peaceful. The only sound —the sound that had caused Britt to halt his patrol—is the soft crackling of thin palm fronds from which the white-haired old one is forming some sort of object.

Britt signals to his four-man patrol that it might be a Viet Cong trap. He rubs his fingertip across the cold, smooth steel trigger of his carbine. He and his men wait and watch. Several minutes tick tensely into eternity. Still, the only sound is the gentle rustle of the palm fronds as they bend beneath the strangely supple fingers of the old man.

Now, Britt gives the signal to his men. They move forward.

That old man certainly must have heard us, Britt thinks as he and his patrol cautiously emerge from the edge of the jungle. Slowly, they approach the old one's hut. But the wrinkled figure does not look up at them. He seems uninterested, unimpressed by the deadly weapons which Britt and his men carry at the ready.

Half crouching, Britt moves quietly, cautiously past the old man and into the dark interior of the hut. In the dusty darkness of the hut, Britt sees only a red coal fire in the center of the dirt floor. A wisp of smoke curls slowly up from the coals, languorously caresses a blackened pot of boiled rice, and spirals toward the ceiling vent like a spirit rising from a grave.

"It's empty," Britt whispers in Vietnamese over his shoulder to his patrol outside the hut.

Click!

The metallic sound causes Britt to whirl around, finger tight on the trigger! He restrains his automatic urge to fire just long enough to recognize that he does not need to. One of Britt's own men has simply snapped a bayonet into place on the end of a rifle.

But Britt somehow knows what is coming next and he reacts swiftly, swinging his rifle butt and smashing the Ranger hard in the face just as the soldier thrusts the gleaming bayonet at the old man's bare, bony chest.

It is over in an eyeblink. The Ranger falls stunned to the ground. The bayonet plunges into the grass just inches from the old man's thin, leathery thigh. The old man, strangely, has not flinched at all in the face of death.

Britt roughly pulls the dazed Ranger to his feet. As Britt stoops to retrieve the soldier's rifle, Britt looks at the old man and softly says, "I'm sorry" in the native tongue.

The old one's face remains expressionless. He sits crosslegged, motionless, his wrists now resting limply on his skinny knees. In his momentarily idle right hand, the old one holds a water-softened palm frond; in his left is a small, half-completed doll he had been weaving. Britt notices that on the ground beside the old man are four identical human effigies.

Britt angrily hisses an order to his patrol to move out. They hesitate a moment and Britt puzzles over the unexpected look of fear that is reflecting from the eyes of the hardened soldiers. They are looking at the old man and his dolls.

"Snap out of it!" Britt whispers gruffly in English. "Let's *move* out!"

Britt casts one last look over his shoulder at the old man just before the patrol melts again into the hot, humid jungle. The strange old man has not moved even an eyelid since Britt saved his life.

I wonder what he's thinking, Britt muses. And as Britt now turns again to push into the green steaming hell, his thoughts drift back. Britt remembers the anger that he had felt that day when he sat watching the John Cameron Swayze news and saw the films of U.N. Ambassador Lodge exposing the electronic spying of the Russians at a time when they were preaching world trust and peace. Britt thinks back, too, to the impact that Kennedy's inaugural speech had on his life, and how when Britt graduated from Stanford University six months later he decided that what he could do for his country was enlist and volunteer to be an advisor to the South Vietnamese in their so-called struggle against the communist menace. Britt recalls briefly the pride he had felt after he earned his green beret and was assigned to lead a Ranger unit. That feeling of pride had melted in the face of the searing anger that grew in Britt during the six months preceding today's patrol. It is anger fueled by the disillusionment and betrayal he feels after observing the corruption of the South Vietnamese government and the plundering, raping, and murdering by the Rangers of the civilians whom they were supposed to protect. Britt has come to feel more like a gangster than a soldier. He is glad this is his last patrol.

Whannnngg!

A soft, springlike *twang* brings Britt back quickly from his reveries in time for him to see a queer-looking jack-o'-lantern head leap up grinning from the grass . . . it seems to freeze in mid-air for an eternal instant before it spits toward Britt a curious mass of broken bits. . . .

BAMMMM!!!

The sound and the pain erupt simultaneously in Britt's head . . . he feels himself plunge headlong into a deep black pool where he floats far beneath the surface in liquid silence while unseen hands pull and tug at his body. The sea grows rapidly hot . . . Britt feels that he is suffocating . . . the waters become thick and green and are pressing heavily on his face . . . gasping for air, Britt tries to move his leaden limbs . . .

Suddenly—something, someone lifts the green covering from Britt's face. Brilliant sunlight crashes into his aching eyes and a cool breeze sweeps over his boiling skin and flows like clear water into his parched lungs.

Britt's eyes focus through the pain. The old man is squatting next to him. He is smiling. Around the creature's wrinkled neck hangs a string of four dolls. Each has been seared by flame. However, in the old man's frail right hand is the fifth doll. Its head has been dipped in green dye. The old man gently takes Britt's hand and presses the doll into Britt's palm.

Britt tries to smile back, but he sinks once more into the blackness of unconsciousness.

VIII

"You'll like Los Angeles, Lieutenant St. Vincent," says smiling Colonel Pickett. "A few more weeks of rest here and your reflexes will be as sharp as ever." The colonel turns with military briskness to leave Britt's hospital room, but Pickett pauses with his hand on the door knob and he turns his face toward Britt: "You're mighty lucky." His words sound like a warning. "Remember that, Britt—and remember my offer."

In an instant, Pickett is gone. The door swings silently shut.

Britt's eyes slowly scan the room. They finally focus on the dry, human effigy made of palm fronds that is lying on the nightstand next to his bed. Britt has discarded all other reminders of Vietnam—all but for this. And remind him it does . . . his thoughts now drift back . . . back through the weeks and months. . . .

During the first days of his recovery in Vietnam, Britt learned from a nurse that Pickett was a Central Intelligence Agency officer. Pickett just happened to be there that awful day, standing in the jungle evacuation zone when the sweaty medics brought in the remains of Britt's patrol. The corpses were wrapped in green canvas body bags.

Pickett had captured the strange old Vietnamese man immediately after the fellow removed the body bag from Britt's face and placed the doll in Britt's hand. While recuperating in the hospital in Saigon, Britt learned from Pickett himself that the old man was a Viet Cong leader and a powerful figure in the province. American intelligence could not understand what had compelled the old man to risk coming into that U.S. helicopter zone in broad daylight. Britt also learned that none of the army doctors in Saigon could understand why Britt was alive: the Claymore mine that had killed the other four men in Britt's patrol had also blasted a wound in Britt's skull which should have been fatal. The field medics who had recovered the bodies had pronounced Britt dead at the scene of the ambush. Britt would have been evacuated and buried had not the old man saved his life by pulling back the body bag.

Because of that unexplained appearance of the old man, Pickett had immediately suspected Britt of being an agent for the North Vietnamese. The colonel had followed Britt from Saigon to the veterans hospital in Honolulu. There, even while Britt was still weak from his wounds, Pickett often subjected him to sadistic interrogation meant to force Britt to reveal what he was supposed to know about espionage in South Vietnam.

During one especially bitter confrontation in Britt's room, Pickett stood at the foot of Britt's bed and questioned him so maliciously that Britt, though he ached with pain, tried desperately to arise and physically attack Pickett—but Britt's wound-weakened body could not respond to the angry commands of his brain. Even at this moment, months later, as he recalls this event Britt can feel the same trapped feeling that he felt then . . . his mind had rushed around in frantic circles, searching fiercely for a way out of his useless body, a way to get at Pickett. Britt's emotions were boiling, he was seething with uncontrolled rage when suddenly Pickett was launched backward through the air! The man's body crashed heavily against the closed door of the hospital room and fell to the floor. In an instant, two MPs burst into the room, nearly tripping over the body of Pickett as he lay stunned on the floor—and immediately those men were pummeled by invisible hands and thrown roughly across the room amid a clatter of nightstands and metal chairs.

Britt had lain in bed amazed at what he saw happening— and puzzled over the feeling of satisfaction that coursed through his veins during the strange and violent event.

And now Britt recalls that feeling again—a feeling of satisfied vengeance.

Pickett had picked himself up from the floor that day and ordered the dazed guards out of Britt's room. Pickett was not so much amazed as he was intrigued. Pickett's attitude toward Britt, too, seemed immediately changed. Pickett's hostility, his suspicion of only moments earlier was gone. In its place was a sly look, a curiosity. He slowly approached the foot of Britt's bed; there he stood, his hands resting on the bed railing.

Britt can recall now the look in Pickett's eyes that day

as the colonel began to explain that he had only on the previous day been selected by the Department of Defense to head a new program that was being organized at the Harry Diamond Laboratories in Washington. Working under an "enskid"—a secret order from the President's National Security Council—a task force of military and civilian scientists was being assigned to study psychic phenomena and their application to military use. Pickett explained that he was impressed by the violent display of psychokinetic power which Britt had just manifested. Then Pickett asked Britt if he would join the Harry Diamond labs after his recovery from his wounds.

Britt had rejected Pickett's offer that day. Britt told the colonel that he no longer had a clear-cut idea of what constituted the "right" or the "wrong" side in war.

Pickett argued that the research at Harry Diamond was not necessarily for war, but for *defense;* Pickett was in no mood to take a refusal from Britt—in spite of the display that Britt had just shown. Only when Britt sincerely said that he felt that he needed some more time and some more knowledge about himself and the changes wrought in him by the war did Pickett relent.

Pickett left Britt's room that day—but he did not leave Britt's life. Even after Britt was transferred to Sawtell Veterans Hospital in Los Angeles, Pickett paid him regular visits, stopping each time he came to check on the Pentagon-financed psychic research at Stanford Research Institute. And today . . . today Britt completed his final program of physical therapy; tomorrow Britt will be discharged from the army and from the hospital. The colonel had visited today to once again attempt to persuade Britt. And once again, Britt had refused.

Britt is still staring now at the small doll . . . the memories are fading . . . but Pickett's words strangely continue to repeat in Britt's mind: "Remember my offer."

IX

Britt now stands on the stage in his cap and gown. Ahead of him, the other graduates are leaving the line one by one to walk across the stage and receive their diploma and their handshake.

As Britt waits for his own name to be called, he permits his thoughts to wander . . . to wander back to the time shortly after his discharge from the hospital and from the army. Select scenes of the intervening eighteen months flash like vacation slides in his mind: he sees himself again filling out the long registration forms and explaining to Dr. Wortmann, chairman of Stanford's psychology department, the unusual reason why he wanted to enroll in a doctoral program focusing on physiological psychology . . . Britt sees, too, the expression on Wortmann's face after Britt completed the doctoral program in just eighteen months and with a perfect 4.0 average . . . Britt sees, finally, the troubled face which stared back at him from the mirror even this morning of graduation day . . . the face whose sad eyes still asked the same questions.

At this moment, Britt is standing, perspiring beneath his heavy gown, and at last admitting to himself that he has known the answers all along. Quite suddenly, the quest ends for Britt: Vietnam, the hospitals, the changes in his body and his psyche . . . all these are finally fading. Britt feels as if he is awakening from a long and restless sleep and a new sun is rising over a fresh morning.

"Britt St. Vincent."

Britt now walks toward the black-gowned man who holds out his hand and the meaningless paper.

Down the steps from the stage Britt walks, his feet feeling heavy and leaden. Up the aisle between the rows of proud parents who crane their necks to see around him.

There is no one waiting with smiles to greet Britt. With no surviving family, Britt has expected no one. Now, alone in the cloak room at the empty back of the auditorium, Britt takes off his cap and gown, tosses them on a chair, and heads for the door.

Ahhh, Britt says to himself as he stands at the top of the steps that lead down to the car-packed parking lot, *what kind of answers could I have possibly been searching for that could give more meaning to life than a day like this!*

The San Francisco area is crisp and cool, the sun is yellow and warm in the clear blue sky. Britt starts down the steps. . . .

"Congratulations, Britt."

Britt stops in the middle of the broad stone steps and turns around at the sound of the vaguely familiar voice.

"Britt, if you have some time now, I'd like to show you something," says the smiling colonel. Pickett looks incongruous in his mod civilian suit: it clashes with the rigid military bearing that is evident even in the precise manner that he descends the rest of the steps with Britt.

"I was talking earlier to Dr. Wortmann," Pickett comments as he and Britt walk away from the auditorium and head for the athletic field that lies distant and deserted in the mid-afternoon sun. "He tells me that your PK and ESP powers have become dormant again."

Britt nods. "Yep." He takes several steps before elaborating. "Wortmann says they have disappeared because of my anxiousness to learn about what happened to me back there in Vietnam."

Pickett is striding briskly along, looking straight ahead as he walks. "Well, Britt . . . what do you really think happened to you over there? Was it something physical, something psychological . . . or something mystical?"

Britt loosely clinches his hands behind his back and walks, looking down at his shadow which bobs along out in front of him. The bright afternoon sun feels warm on Britt's back. The warm feeling contrasts pleasantly with the clear, cool northern California air that flows into his lungs with each breath. "After all my studies, Pickett, I am more convinced than ever that I underwent what was basically a purely *psychological* change. The physical injury to my brain in no way altered anything to produce those psychic powers. No, those powers were there all along." Britt walks in silence for several seconds before adding: "Colonel, those so-called supernatural powers are inside us all—do you know that even today the Australian aborigines in the Outback country continue to employ ESP as a regular, functional part of their everyday life? Lacking short-wave radios and telephones, the aborigines far-ranging hunting parties maintain brain-wave contact with the main nomadic family group so that the hunters always know where the family is when the hunt is over and it is time to return to them. On the way back to the camp, the hunters transmit to the group what game they have caught so that the proper preparation can be made for cooking and preserving the precious meat before any of it can spoil."

Britt glances quickly at Pickett. The colonel is nodding, but still looking straight ahead; he seems almost to be straining to see something out on the open field that they are approaching. Britt, too, glances quickly at the field, but he sees nothing. He looks down again as he walks and says: "You know my studies covered many ancient writings and observations of today's still-primitive peoples . . . from these studies it is evident that all mankind once had extensive psychic powers. These natural powers appear to have atrophied because of non-use resulting from man's technological progress—after all, who needs the imprecision of ESP when one has the two-way radio? Some of our powers, however, have been suppressed down into our subconscious because of social pressures from our so-called civilization."

"I quite agree, Britt," Colonel Pickett states in his flat, matter-of-fact military manner.

Britt is mildly surprised at Pickett's reply. It is unexpected from such a pragmatic person. Britt listens closely as Pickett says more: "For the sake of example, Britt, let's use your comparison of the two-way radio and ESP. You are, of course, quite aware that all energy in the universe is some form of electromagnetic energy . . . even atomic energy is what results from breaking the electromagnetic bonds of an atom. X-rays are electromagnetic energy . . . radio and television broadcasts are electromagnetic energy . . . light is electromagnetic energy . . . and ESP projection is electromagnetic broadcasting very similar to the broadcasting of radio and television. The difference between ESP and radio, however, is that the one is what some people insist on calling 'natural,' while the other is called 'mechanical' or 'electronic.' Radio and broadcasting towers stand as monuments to the ability of man's brain to mechanically duplicate its own abilities—although at a severe cost in terms of efficiency. The positive side of the coin is, however, that although man's

THE MIND MASTERS [53]

artificial broadcast communication devices have cost him his former ESP ability, the devices have, by freeing his brain from the task of receiving and broadcasting messages, allowed the brain more time for higher intellectual pursuits, to make discoveries, to paint great pictures and write operas."

Britt is extremely fascinated by what Pickett is saying. *Perhaps I've misjudged this man by categorizing him as a soulless military operative.*

"Many good things, Britt," the colonel continues, "have resulted from the brain being freed of primitive ESP and PK tasks. Man's intellect has had time to develop intricate patterns of civilization and commerce—social structures which, in spite of their tremendous faults, have served to provide much of the human race with a far better life than the aborigines lead. Civilization has produced more da Vincis and Einsteins that it has Attilas and Hitlers.

"But man has still come only a little way, Britt. He has had time enough to reap the benefits of his crude, although successful imitation of his own natural powers. Today, however, man must again turn his mind's eye inward and focus on his ancient powers in order to develop machines more efficient at duplicating those powers. . . ." Pickett pauses. "Ah, here we are, Britt . . . let me show you what I mean."

Britt has been very receptive to what Pickett was saying; his estimation of the military man is changed. But Britt is now somewhat puzzled when Pickett stops near a tiny object resting on the vast, empty athletic field.

"Is that a model airplane?" asks Britt.

"It's a very special model plane, Britt," Pickett replies as he squats down next to the small craft. "It's an *electric* plane, Britt. No noise, no pollution—and *no* batteries aboard." Pickett stands up again, holding the model and its control box. He hands the model to Britt. "The power—the batteries," Pickett explains, "for this little electric motor stay here on the ground in this control box." He flicks a switch on the box.

Britt flinches slightly as the small propeller begins to spin —it quickly becomes a blur. The only sound, however, is a quiet whirring.

"Give it a launch, will you, Britt," says Pickett.

With a cautious toss, Britt sends the little craft into the air. It flies level for a moment, gathering speed. Pickett pulls a lever on the control box and the model's nose points steeply upward. Higher and higher it climbs into the crisp blue sky. Britt watches it soaring away for a moment before he casts a questioning glance at Pickett.

"The secret is *here*, Britt," says Pickett in reply to the look in Britt's eyes. "This control box works on the same microwave principle that the telephone companies have used for decades to transmit phone calls without wires. At Harry Diamond labs we have successfully dug a little more deeply into the secret of man's natural way of transmitting messages via ESP and have come up with a new technology that may some day make it possible for people to fly across the country—or the ocean, or the world in quiet, nonpolluting airliners which require no stops for fuel. Instead, the aircraft will have electric engines that pull power out of the air—electromagnetic power that is beaming out from a network of towers which resembles present-day radio and television towers—or from space satellites. And can you imagine having an automobile that never has to stop for gas? Your car of the future, Britt, might have two antennas— one to pull electromagnetic radio waves out of the air for your listening enjoyment, and a second antenna by which the clean, quiet electric motor pulls broadcast power waves out of the air. Just turn on the switch and drive away."

Pickett maneuvers the controls. The little aircraft performs a graceful, curving descent and lands gently, noiselessly, at Britt's feet.

"Well, Britt . . . *now* are you ready to join my team in Washington?"

X

Britt is satisfied, even content, during his first few months at the Harry Diamond labs. He feels secure inside the high fences that surround the many acres of parklike setting in which the modern research labs are situated. He feels stimulated, too, in the company of so many men and women of similar scientific interest.

One young researcher in particular has become someone special in Britt's eyes. Gayle Hillard is a medical doctor fresh out of St. Louis University medical school. As an undergraduate she had once participated as a subject for a research probe into psychic healing; she herself had been amazed when under the test situation she was able to exhibit the electromagnetic "corona" that has been scientifically shown to be characteristic of the psychic or "faith" healers. At the Harry Diamond labs Dr. Hillard is a subject as much as a researcher. She and the other scientists and doctors in her research group are concentrating on establishing the nature and source of the "corona" of excess bioplasmic energy that emanates from persons capable of psychic healing.

Although they have now only known each other for a few fleeting months at the labs, both Britt and Gayle recognize that the "special person" status with which they regard each other is already a deep feeling and one that will never change.

"Let's tell Pickett our plans, Britt," Gayle prods gently.

But Britt is hesitant: "Gayle . . . Gayle, honey, I want to leave and get married as soon as possible, too . . . but . . ."

"But what, silly," she says with a warm smile that melts the worried frown on Britt's forehead. "It's all settled, isn't it really? We could go back to St. Louis . . . you could teach at Washington University and I could work at the medical center there."

Britt is silent. The frown returns to his brow.

He and Gayle are walking along a quiet trail in a densely

wooded and seldom visited section of the vast campuslike grounds of the labs. Britt has walked the lonely woods many times by himself in his first weeks there, before he met Gayle. Now, the peaceful forest has become a favorite place of theirs. "Gayle, did I tell you what Dr. Cerde's group has come up with?"

Gayle sighs; she knows how some of the research groups are beginning to make progress in many areas after months of fruitless searching; and she knows how the excitement of the new developments is making it difficult for Britt to reach a decision about leaving. "No," she says with a tolerant grin, "tell me what they've done now."

"Well," Britt begins, "you know that they have been working on finding out how the brain controls the body"—he watches Gayle nod—"well, using that knowledge of the nervous system, Gayle, Cerde's group has constructed mechanical models of human limbs that actually look and function like natural limbs—these substitute limbs can be controlled by the brain and they draw their energy from the body just like natural limbs!"

Gayle is interested, in spite of the way she feels toward Britt's attitude. "How do these limbs work?" she asks him.

Britt smiles, pleased that she asks: "Cerde," Britt explains, "discovered that some of the super-small electric motors which NASA had developed for space machinery draw so little power that they can operate off the electrochemical energy produced by the human nervous system. So, he took a microelectrode and placed it into the ulnar nerve in his own arm—then when he *thought* about moving his little finger, the motor ran. Cerde called in some engineers and they designed complete artificial limbs around these tiny super-strong little motors. The group molded a new kind of plastic around the limbs which looks and feels like flesh and then tested the limbs on some disabled veterans—amputees —over at Walter Reed Hospital. Cerde implanted the microelectrodes into the nerve endings that once activated the men's real limbs . . . and within a short time most of the men had mastered the ability to use the artificial limbs just like their former natural limbs!"

"Britt," Gayle says in a pleased and somewhat surprised tone, "I hadn't heard that. And that *is* exciting . . ." She pauses: "But there is something *else*, isn't there? I mean, you wouldn't be so hesitant about carrying out our personal plans if there wasn't something more . . . what's up?"

THE MIND MASTERS [57]

Britt smiles. *I wonder if all women have the ability to read minds.*

"Okay, kid," he says, "I'll have to tell you about this one, too. Pickett ordered us not to tell *anyone*—even members of other research cells here—but you're not just anyone to me." Britt thinks a moment as he walks along the wooded path. He kicks a small stone, sending it skipping off the dirt trail and into the grass beneath the trees. "You know, Gayle, that my group has been studying the brain's ability to project its electromagnetic field . . . well, we've come up with a device that can duplicate some of these projections, especially ones that express emotions."

Gayle looks at him curiously.

Britt walks on in silence for several steps while he arranges his thoughts. Then he starts explaining: "People everywhere have long observed that a grumpy person can change the mood of a group of people just by being in their presence for a few moments, and, conversely, that a happy person can make people feel happy just by being around them. Psychologists have sought to explain this phenomenon in terms of social interaction, such as verbal communication and nonverbal communication, like body language. Some months ago, however, my lab group discovered that a person who is in either a happy or depressed mood is actually projecting different wavelengths of electromagnetic energy. These waves are *stronger* than those of a person in a normal, fairly content state of mind and the waves can 'overpower' —if you want to call it that—these normal brainwaves and cause other brains within its range to begin to emit the same type of wavelength."

Gayle asks, "And your group has come up with some type of device that can generate either 'happy' or 'depressed' wavelengths?"

"Right, Gayle," Britt replies. "We had a good bit of fun testing it on some of the other people in the labs without their knowledge. The device is actually quite small—we made one up that fit into a pack of cigarettes. The antenna was a piece of wire running through a cigarette that stuck up slightly from the pack." Britt almost laughs as he remembers something: "In fact, one technician tried to borrow the antenna for a smoke! Anyway, Gayle . . . we would tune the device to emit, say, depressive emotional wavelengths and then we'd walk through other lab areas and watch people become irritable. Or, if we saw someone out in another area becoming frustrated with his work, we could cheer him or her up just by setting the device to produce happy feelings and then standing close by the upset person.

"We named our little toy 'Mood Master,'" Britt says just as he and Gayle reach the end of the wooded section of the path. A hundred yards across the rolling lawn stands the ten-story building where Britt lives and works; lab areas occupy the ground-floor level of the building, while residential apartments are situated on the floors above.

Gayle looks at the building as they walk toward it. She turns to Britt: "When are you going to see Colonel Pickett?"

Britt does not reply immediately. Gayle knows the turmoil in his mind. She waits and walks. Several steps further, Britt stops. He looks at his watch and then at the deepening purple of the evening sky: "It's nearly eight thirty . . . Pickett should be back in the office by now." He looks at Gayle, a resigned but pleased smile on his lips: "I'll go see him now."

XI

"He'll be with you in a moment, Dr. St. Vincent," Pickett's secretary remarks to Britt as he sits on the couch in the anteroom of the colonel's office. It is now dark outside and Britt is watching the red taillights of the unusually numerous security cars that are driving away from the building.

I wonder what the hell's going on? he wonders. MPs and CIA security agents have been moving briskly in and out of Pickett's office since before Britt arrived. Britt glances down at his watch: *9:45 . . . maybe I ought to just come back tomorrow . . .*

"Okay, St. Vincent . . . get in here," commands Pickett's voice from his now-empty office.

Britt rises and walks in. The colonel is leaning back in his chair, his feet on his neat and orderly desk. He is puffing elegantly on a cigar. Pickett now removes the cigar from his mouth and uses it as a wand to wave Britt to a seat. "You aren't happy here, are you, Britt?"

The statement catches Britt offguard. "Why *yes* . . . yes, I *am*, Colonel. What made you say that?"

Pickett's cheeks sink in as he sucks on the cigar . . . he exhales slowly . . . savoring both the cigar smoke and the power he has over Britt's future. "Oh . . . I know you," he says smugly, "I just know your type." He looks with stony eyes at Britt: "I knew it all along. But I thought that maybe we could pick your brains, your talent, and use them for our ends." He flicks an ash deftly into the huge black glass ashtray on his desk. "But it's not working out that way."

"Frankly, Britt," Pickett coldly says to the young scientist, "I never trusted you at all." Pickett suddenly swings his legs down off the desk and reaches into the side drawer.

"Here . . . look at this," he says and tosses an open magazine across the glass desk top.

Puzzled at Pickett's attitude, Britt reaches out for the magazine. It is opened to an article on page 30, checked in red. Britt scans the article: the piece relates in detail how Dr. David Thompson has developed an amazing electromagnetic transmitter that can affect and manipulate the emotional state of people within its range. Britt finishes his quick look at the article and turns the magazine over to see the cover: *Macleans'*, September, 1968.

"*'Macleans,'*" Britt says with a puzzled tone still in his voice. "This is a Canadian magazine, isn't it?"

"Yes," Pickett replies, "*you* ought to know."

Britt shakes his head: "I don't understand."

"*You . . . !*" Pickett hisses venomously. His cool military reserve boils away in a sudden flash of fiery anger. He slams his big, broad hand down resoundingly on the desk top. "*God damn it*, you son of a bitch! *Look* at that!" he says through clenched teeth while pointing at the magazine article with his smoldering cigar. "You know that project is *secret!* How the hell did you and your liberal friends here get it into the press!?!"

"But, Colonel," Britt protests, "the article says that this Canadian scientist developed his own device, similar to ours. We aren't the only ones who could be working on something like this. In fact," Britt goes on before Pickett can speak again, "our group was discussing just today all the benefits that can come from something like we've developed, and how it should be shared. Just think of the great aid this Mood Master will be in the treatment of mental and emotional illness . . . why, psychologists can at last give their patients immediate relief from the symptoms of depression while they have time to treat the basic problems . . . with those kinds of benefits to shoot for, isn't it likely that other countries and other scientists are doing research just as we?"

Blue veins are bulging beneath the taut red skin of Pickett's anger-flushed forehead: "You're goddam *right* they are!" he explodes. "And here a Canadian comes up with the same *exact* thing that we've developed—some *coincidence*, isn't it!?!" He glares menacingly at Britt: "Did you have anything to do with leaking the information that permitted the Canadians to match our accomplishment?"

Pickett stands before Britt can reply. Propelled by pent-up anger, the military man strides toward the corner of the room. He stops at the wall, makes a brisk about-face and looks hard at Britt: "It was a mistake bringing you and those like you here. I can see that clearly now. All along, I've had my men watching you and the other young, dumb geniuses like you in our groups. You've all done nothing but talk about how you can use psychic research for the 'good' of man. *Shit!*" Pickett spits out the word. He aims a blunt finger at Britt and jabs the air while saying, "Well, let me tell you, Mr. Idealist—and you can pass this on to your head-in-the-clouds friends—mankind is best served these days by those who do something to keep mankind from being destroyed. And that job requires hard-working, gut-sweating military men!"

Pickett pauses. He seems now to relax a bit. The seldom-seen sharp edge of his anger slides back into the scabbard of his controlled military training. "You probably saw the security men here tonight," he continues in a mild, matter-of-fact tone which hides completely any trace of the heated emotion that was evident just seconds before. "Well, as of tonight we are initiating new security programs around here —*stringent* programs. We're going on a red alert status until I give further notice. Be careful who you talk to or who you're seen with from now on. You'll know who we don't approve of"—Pickett arches an eyebrow—"in fact, *you* might even be one of those we don't approve of." Pickett grins malevolently.

The colonel walks back to his desk and sits down. He begins looking at some papers on his desk. "Now . . . what the hell can I do for you, Dr. St. Vincent?"

Britt's mind is still racing to catch up with the new thoughts that have been hurled into it.

"C'mon, let's *have* it!" Pickett demands.

"Well, Colonel," Britt begins in a quiet voice, "since you feel that way about me anyway, I'm sure you'll be relieved to know that I'm here to tell you that I'm resigning from this project . . . Gayle Hillard and I are planning to marry."

Pickett stops shuffling the papers on his desk. He looks up at Britt, then leans slightly forward, leaning on his elbows on his desk top. His face is pinched in a small, tight sadistic grin. "No, Dr. St. Vincent," he says slowly, "you're not leaving here . . . and neither is Dr. Hillard." He taps the *Macleans'* magazine with his pencil. "*No* one is leaving here until I find the source of this leak—however long it takes."

Britt is stunned for several seconds. But quickly his own anger rises: "Look, Pickett—if you don't let us out of here right now, when I *do* get out, I'm going to tell a fellow I know at *Newsday*—Robert Greene—a lot of interesting things I know about this place."

The rage ignites again in Pickett's eyes . . . but, strangely, it subsides and is replaced by the glint of amused madness. "Oh? Well, tell me, Dr. St. Vincent . . . just what kind of things will you tell the great investigative reporter Mr. Greene? Why, you yourself don't even know what we are really doing here. You don't know, for instance, that those devices that you've named 'Mood Masters' are already being used in the field by our agents. We've found them very effective for changing peaceful demonstrating students into howling mobs whom we can 'justifiably' attack and imprison." Pickett grins. "It's really a quite handy way of putting you liberals away and turning public opinion against your causes."

Britt can hardly believe his ears. He has read only a little about the student protest against the Vietnam war, and he has been puzzled at the violence of some of the demonstrations, especially since he knew some of the students who had recently been arrested in San Francisco. They were not violent people. Now Britt knows what has caused their emotions to run amuck.

"Does that shock you, doctor?" Pickett asks like a taunting Mephistopheles. "There is more, you know . . . *much* more— like those artificial limbs which you and your bleeding-heart cohorts see as such a boon to amputees." Pickett leans back in his large chair; he puffs his cigar and luxuriates in the look of angry anticipation that glints in Britt's eyes. "Tell me, St. Vincent . . . do you know what a 'cyborg' is?"

Britt makes no attempt to indicate an answer, and no attempt is required, for Pickett's answer is already coming: "A 'cyborg' is a human being whose original natural parts have been either replaced or supplemented by devices that duplicate or enhance the natural functions of parts of the body. We need cyborgs. We need them in the armed services. Combinations of man and machine, able to do what no men could do before.

"And our industrial suppliers need cyborgs, too. Aircraft assemblers whose clumsy fingers can be cut off and replaced by precision tools controlled by their brains . . . there are many possibilities."

Pickett now falls silent. A grin grows across his face: " 'Mood Masters'? Ha! We are destined to become *Mind Masters!*" Pickett tosses his head back and laughs loud and diabolically.

But his laughter stops abruptly. Pickett rocks forward quickly in his chair and thrusts his head toward Britt. "NO!" he roars and crashes his hard fist down on the desk top. "You will tell Mr. Greene *nothing!* You will not leave this compound until I am ready to let you leave!" Pickett's Mr. Hyde fades suddenly and, once again another man, he relaxes calmly in his chair. He inhales slowly, deeply, as if inhaling all the fury that he had just spit out. "No, Dr. St. Vincent," the madman says with a sick smile, "your brain is *much* too valuable to let leave the labs. . . .

"Now . . . get out of my sight!"

XII

The blackness of this night seems unusually oppressive while Britt walks back to his apartment after leaving Pickett's office. He enters the quiet building and walks along the deserted neon-lit hall. His reflection walks beside him like a ghost in the plate-glass windows—windows which peer into the darkened labs that line the hall on both sides. Britt's apartment is directly above the lab that he works in during the day.

His footsteps thud dully in the sterile hall until he stops in front of the elevator. Britt reaches out, pushes the button and notices the watch on his wrist. He looks closely at it while he waits for the elevator to arrive: *12:03 . . . too late to call Gayle . . . probably best anyway . . . wouldn't want to wake her for news like this . . . maybe I can come up with some solution myself if I sleep on it.*

Ding!

The bell rings softly to signal the arrival of the elevator. The doors open. Britt steps in and turns around. He feels a sudden panic when the doors slide shut, sealing him in the metal box. He begins thinking about the things that Pickett has said.

The one-floor ride is short. Britt steps from the elevator. *This hallway is strangly silent . . . not even anyone up watching Johnny Carson tonight.* Britt shrugs and continues walking toward his apartment at the far end of the hall.

Now, suddenly, he stops. The door to his apartment is slightly ajar. Inside, the room appears dark. Cautiously, he approaches. He slowly pushes the door open. The hall light casts a long, rectangular shaft across the room, but the illumination does not penetrate into the black corners of the area.

"Who's there?" he demands.

"Oh, Britt," a familiar female voice replies in a whisper, "it's *me*—Gayle."

Now she rushes from the shadows and squeezes herself against Britt's chest. Britt returns the embrace, then he lifts her gently away: "Hey, pretty lady . . . what are you doing here so late?"

Britt pushes the door closed firmly and checks the lock. He walks across the room and switches on a lamp next to the couch. Immediately, he sees the suitcases next to the chair where Gayle had been waiting in the dark. "What are these for?" he asks.

Seen now in the light, Gayle is obviously agitated and upset. "Oh, Britt," she answers, "tonight after you left for Pickett's office, I went to talk to my research leader, Dr. Sauton, about our plans. He told me that if we wanted to get out of here, we had better do it immediately. Sauton said that Pickett was furious over some sort of security leak and that we might not get out for a long time if we wait."

"I know all about it, Gayle. I've been with that bastard Pickett for the past few hours." Britt pauses. He sighs bitterly. "I think we're stuck."

"No! Don't say that," Gayle pleads with tears glistening in her soft, beautiful eyes. "A little while ago, I gave all my savings to Hank, the guard at the main gate . . . the one who likes me. He said that he would let us through tonight after midnight when no one is around . . . look—I've already packed a few things for both of us . . . let's *hurry!*"

The words are barely out of Gayle's mouth when Britt's apartment door explodes inward in a shower of splinters! One of Pickett's henchmen—already transformed into a cyborg with artificial arms so powerful that he has smashed the thick door as if it were thin glass—stands blocking the exit.

But Britt was reacting even before the splinters hit the ground; he vaults over the couch and snatches from the desk drawer his .45 caliber souvenir from Vietnam . . .

KA-BLAM!!

Hit squarely in the stomach by the heavy slug, the cyborg's body folds at the waist, lifts off the floor . . . he falls half split in two on the cold terazzo of the hall—yet even before the agent's blood splatters on the door jamb, a second cyborg has moved into the apartment with the incredible speed of his artificial legs. Britt's finger is now tightening on the trigger again when the cyborg's plastic paw swats the muzzle aside!

KA-BLAM!

The gun's blast and Gayle's scream sound simultaneously! Britt sees her falling in the instant before the cyborg's fist smashes into his skull. . . .

XIII

Britt is wakening slowly . . . painfully.

He attempts to touch his aching forehead but is momentarily bewildered when his arm will not respond.

Now he calls upon all his mental discipline to force the pain into the background of his consciousness while he concentrates on learning where he is and the reason for his immobility. Britt's bleary vision clears . . . he recognizes the array of lights on the ceiling above where he is lying. *I'm in the operating room directly below my apartment . . .*

Britt knows the room well. It is a completely equipped operating room where he and his colleagues have often dissected the skulls of donated corpses in searching for physical clues to the brain's psychic powers. *I'm on the operating table . . . my arms are strapped down.*

Britt turns his head from side to side. The labs areas are all lit . . . but deserted. No one is visible. Britt hears a sound, like a footstep . . . he strains to lift his head so that he can see down between his outstretched legs . . . he catches a glimpse of several masked and gowned men and women walking toward him. But the strain on his neck muscles is great and he must let his head fall back—and that is when he sees it.

Oh, God! he thinks when his eyes focus on the dark red stain still glistening damp on the white acoustical ceiling tiles. *It's her blood . . . oozing down from my apartment . . . Oh, God! . . . God!*

Britt's vision blurs with tears as the strange, masked faces appear above him.

"Now, Dr. St. Vincent, let's not cry over spilled—*blood.*" It's Pickett's voice filtering through one of the masks.

Hot rage surges through Britt's whole body—he strains with every ounce of strength to burst his bonds and attack the monstrous military man . . . the leather straps creak . . . but they hold firmly.

Britt now scans the eyes that peer above the surgical masks and which are looking down on him. His sight locks on two unmistakably cold vision organs: "I warned you earlier this evening, Dr. St. Vincent, that your brain was much too valuable to let it leave these premises. Now it is going to stay with us for a long time while we study it. My cyborgs here have some excellent artificial surgical 'hands.' They should be able to do a first-class job of removing your brain without damage so that we can keep it—*you*—alive in *this*." Pickett holds up for Britt to see a device that looks like a glass terrarium with many plastic tubes connected to it. "Take a good look, St. Vincent, at what is going to be your new body for many years." Pickett grins . . . a glint of madness sparkles in his eye. His turns now and nods toward one of the cyborgs who is standing near the wall of the operating room.

Britt hears a metallic rattle. He turns his head and sees the cyborg wheeling toward the table a tray on which shiny stainless-steel surgical instruments gleam in the beams of the overhead lights.

Britt watches the plastic hand of the cyborg reach out and grasp a sharp scalpel . . . the point glints as it catches the light—but suddenly the lights go dim. The cyborgs pause and look up . . . slowly the lights being to pulse, growing brighter, dimmer . . . brighter, dimmer. Terror, too, starts pulsing in the still-human eyes of the cyborgs—a terror that Britt can now feel as a coldness forcing itself into his body through the skin of his arms, his face . . . it penetrates deeper and deeper like the icy hand of Death reaching in to seize his soul!

WHAM!

The tray of instruments hurtles across the room and slams against the wall, sending stainless-steel slivers flying everywhere—an ice-cold wind like an arctic gale blasts from nowhere, everywhere, scattering papers, tables, towels, tools, and cyborgs through the air . . . the room is bedlam, the wind is *fury*. Britt's head begins to throb again where he had been struck by the cyborg in his apartment. He feels himself slipping into unconsciousness . . . the boiling madness of the room is becoming remote, distant . . . with great effort he slowly turns his head just in time to see Pickett, wild-eyed, lift off the ground and fly, pinwheeling backward and crashing into the high-voltage transformer of the cauterizing machine!

. . . And now, just before Britt's eyes blink shut a final time, he sees in slow motion Pickett's expression of horror and surprise as the electricity boils his blood and smoke puffs from his exploding eyesockets. . . .

XIV

"Britt . . . Britt . . ."

The sound of his name seeps faintly through the thick red fog of pain that blinds Britt's eyes and shrouds his ears.

"Stand back. Give him room!"

Britt's hearing is returning first . . . the voices . . . and now the buzzing—buzzing as if angry hornets are swooping past . . . the red mists fade from his eyes and Britt sees a hugh yellow body sweep past—*rrrRRROOooWWerrr!* and then another, and another, not only yellow, but red and blue. . . .

"Okay, okay! He's coming out of it . . . c'mon, let's get his harness off and him out of this car before she flares up."

For an instant longer, Britt stares, dazed, at the men around him as they struggle to free him from his racing harness. Another instant and his head clears. The hornets become racing cars running through the turn at reduced speed. On the inside of the curve, a white-suited official stands waving a large yellow flag to warn approaching drivers of Britt's wreck at turn six.

"I'm all right," Britt says quickly. "I'm okay—let me get out of this thing myself!" He half-pushes his rescuers away and strikes the harness breast plate, popping free the locks. He stands unsteadily. A hand grasps Britt's arm firmly and steadies him as he steps over the side of his wrecked racer and onto the hot, sticky asphalt surface of the track.

"Thanks," Britt says as he glances at the man who helped him. Britt recognizes the face: *Greg Leland . . . Webster's son . . .*

Greg smiles. "I was just about to pass you on the inside, St. Vincent," the young man says, "when you lost it right in front of me." He nods back toward Britt's wrecked racer. Britt turns and sees a second car stopped a few feet behind his. A steaming black fluid is dripping from the front of the

THE MIND MASTERS

machine. "Debris from your contact with the wall put a nice hole in my oil cooler . . . I'm out of it, too."

"Sorry 'bout that," Britt says with the casual sincerity expected.

"Yeah," Greg replies in a tone of mock resignation, "that's life and racing. Say, here come the crews to haul away those expensive piles of junk of ours. Let's get off this track before they give the rest of the pack the green flag and we *really* get clobbered."

The two drivers dash side by side to the safety of the empty infield.

"Hold it a minute," Britt calls out as they step into the dust of the infield. His head is pounding terribly from the sprint. He kneads the oily, sweaty skin of his forehead with his fingers, trying to rub away the pain.

"The back of your helmet hit the roll bar," Greg explains, "when you spun backward into the wall. Here comes the ambulance—better let the doc look you over."

The white ambulance rolls to a stop next to them and the dust cloud that had been following the vehicle sweeps forward around it and Britt and Greg. Both men cough and turn their faces.

"*Shit!*" says Britt. The dust grits dryly in his teeth. He spits on the ground just as the rear doors of the ambulance swing open and a race official jumps out. The man nearly lands in the spit. He glares for an instant at Britt, while a second man alights, carrying a medical bag.

Britt sits down in the open rear doorway and looks directly at the race official. Britt has recognized the official as the one whom he suspects of being his shadow from Harry Diamond Laboratories' secret psychic plotters. The doctor places the palm of his hand against Britt's forehead and lifts up Britt's eyelid with his thumb. Next, the physician shines a tiny light into Britt's pupil.

"No concussion," he says unenthusiastically to the official who marks the fact down on the clip board of papers he holds.

The doctor continues his examination. While looking on, Greg says to Britt: "You know, St. Vincent, I've raced against you at tracks all across the country. And I have to admit that you're almost as good a driver as me." Greg smiles and pauses. "Seems kind of unjust then that I managed to pick up a sponsor for the pro international circuit next year, while you've been passed over again."

The medical man listens briefly to Britt's heartbeat through his stethoscope, but apparently satisfied, the doctor yanks the instrument from his ears and tosses it back into his bag. "He's fine," the man says to the official who has been checking off items on the clip board, "just shaken up."

"I wasn't exactly passed over, Leland," Britt says to Greg. "I just never really got out and hustled for sponsors . . . figured if they didn't want me on the basis of my driving skills alone, then *I* didn't want *them*."

Greg grins appreciatively. "Well, Mr. Independent, would you consider driving for *me?*"

Britt half-expected the offer. *Pretty clever of Webster,* he thinks. Britt tosses a can-you-believe-that glance at the Harry Diamond agent, and looks back again at Greg. "You've got to be kidding," Britt says with a mock tone of incredulity that is genuine enough to fool the agent. "After I've just wrecked my car and put you out of the race . . . *you* want *me* to drive for your team?"

Webster's son grins again and nods. "That's right. Tell you what, let's go over to my trailer and talk about it."

"Wait a minute, St. Vincent!"

Britt turns tensely to face the secret agent.

"You have to sign this medical liability release form before you can leave."

The man hands Britt the clip board.

As he scrawls his name across the signature line, Britt knows that he is being closely watched by the agent. "Here," he says and hands the clip board back.

The agent stares at Britt for a second before he and the doctor again climb into the ambulance. Greg helps Britt shut the doors and now they both step back from the dust cloud as the vehicle drives away.

The two men walk together deep into the infield of the huge track, in to where the trailers and transport vehicles of the teams are scattered like a disorganized wagon train encampment.

"After you," Greg says as he opens the door of his large trailer. Britt steps up.

The air-conditioned coolness inside the lush living quarters is a welcome relief from the heat and the noise outside. The door clicks solidly shut behind them.

Britt looks around at the thick carpet and the plush paneled walls. He cocks his head and listens: "It's *really* quiet in

THE MIND MASTERS

here, Greg. You must have spent a bundle having this thing soundproofed. Pretty snazzy."

"Thanks," Greg says with a smile, "but I owe it all to my sponsor who—by the way—is in the next room. Go ahead in and meet him while I fix us all something to wash the dust out of our mouths. I've got a not-so-secret formula that really gets down to thirst-quenchin'."

"What's that?" Britt asks.

"Gin and lemonade," Greg replies.

Britt shakes his head as he starts to open the door to the next room. "Well, I'll try anything once."

Britt walks into the adjoining room—he is not surprised to see Dr. Webster sitting in a large vinyl chair. Britt is not surprised, but he is concerned.

"Don't worry, Britt," Dr. Webster says, "no one saw me come here—no one will see me leave. And this trailer is completely soundproofed and electronically isolated from probes."

Britt's concern subsides somewhat, but he glances suspiciously at the two other men who are sitting at the table against the wall.

Webster nods toward the short sandy-haired man on the left. "Britt, I want you to meet Dr. John Hollender. He's a physicist who specializes in quantum mechanics—masers are his specialty. You've probably seen John around the racetracks since the start of this season"—Britt does recognize the man—"while he's been establishing his identity as the engine-tuning specialist for Greg's car.

"Over there"—Britt's eyes move to the next man—"is Karl Krimmel." Britt knows all about Krimmel's reputation although he has never before met the man. For many years, Krimmel had been chief chassis-tuning mechanic for the Porsche factory racing team. Krimmel had mysteriously quit the racing life three years ago in Europe and had disappeared. The racing grapevine said that he had suffered some sort of nervous breakdown from the pressures of the demanding Porsche factory team manager. Krimmel caused a mild and quickly passing bit of gossip when he had reappeared this season as the chassis mechanic for Greg's ex-works Porsche 917.

"Here we are," Greg says, entering the room with a tray of tall drinks. He places the tray on a small table in front of his father, takes his own drink, and sits down in an empty chair.

Britt picks up a glass, walks over and sinks down into the last empty chair. He slouches back comfortably and draws several long, slow swallows from his drink. He can feel the fluid flow into his body and cool the burning dryness in his chest. "Okay," he says, refreshed, "what's the deal?"

Dr. Webster wipes his lips with a napkin before replying: "I assume, then, that you *have* decided to join us?" He pauses. Britt nods. "Good," Webster smiles, "very good. Well, then, knowing you, Britt, you've probably already figured out much of the plan—you will appear to join Greg's team as back-up driver in the second-team car. Greg will be the focus of attention from fans and competitors. It will fall to *you* to handle the bulk of the communication attempts with the spirits. The plan works quite simply: your identities will permit you to travel the world. The communication equipment will be disguised as engine-tuning equipment. During each race you, Britt, will feign car trouble and drop out, which, as you know, is quite a common thing that happens to most second-string drivers and cars. With everyone's attention still focused on the race, you will be able to slip away, disappear to accomplish your objective, and then reappear the next morning feigning a hangover—again, not an uncommon thing. Karl and Dr. Hollender have established their identities well this season and should be able to provide you with all the back-up assistance you need. I hope you can accomplish your objective at the very first race—the odds of your being discovered will increase with each race, in spite of our planning."

Britt is puzzled about one person: "Why is Krimmel on the team? Is it solely to lend added credibility to our racing team cover? Couldn't you have developed another scientist like Hollender here so I could have more technical back-up?"

Webster cocks an eyebrow and glances at the lanky, silent German. Now, Webster's eyes return to Britt: "Three years ago, Britt, Karl thought he was losing his mind. He was hearing voices and experiencing strange feelings. He went to a professor he knew at the University of Bonn—Dr. Stefen Janick, who is now a member of our Mero Institute staff. We had already contacted Janick and were laying plans to bring him here secretly when Karl contacted him. Dr. Janick diagnosed Karl's problem not as a psychiatric disorder, but rather as some kind of unexplainable change in Karl's blood chemicals that had reawakened in him some rudimentary

THE MIND MASTERS [75]

psychic powers. The change in Karl's blood chemistry is similar to that change which we have observed occurring in many of the young people who today are involved in Pentecostal religions. In their cases, their new belief in a Power Beyond causes complex psychological changes which, in turn, cause physiological changes—mainly blood chemistry changes which reawaken dormant psychic powers: powers of psychic healing and of extrasensory communion with the minds of their fellow believers. Janick is back at Mero even at this moment working toward isolating the chemical which the body produces to bring about these psychic phenomena. Perhaps some day we can learn to stimulate the body's natural production of these chemicals and hormones; perhaps, too, we can synthesize the chemical so that everyone can once again have the benefit of psychic gifts.

"Karl's special powers should be of help to you in your work at the haunting sites. He is remarkably perceptive to most thought waves and emotional emanations. And he can distinguish between waves emanating from natural and non-living sources—such as sunspots—and those which are produced by a human being, either of this world *or* the next. Karl's limitations are that he cannot broadcast his own thoughts, and the thoughts that he receives are like broken radio transmission, usually just phrases and snatches of running trains of thought."

Webster pauses, sips his drink again.

Britt, too, tips his nearly empty glass. The relaxing glow of the gin is oozing through his tired and aching body. He slouches lazily in the chair during the pause in conversation. The only sound in the room is the quiet clink of ice cubes and the soft whisper from the air-conditioning duct.

Webster is drawing a design with his index finger, on the condensation on his glass. He is thinking. His brow is slightly furrowed. "There is one thing," he begins slowly, ". . . just one more that I must tell you all before we begin our briefing on your first mission. I received a coded report this morning from our agent in France that the secret group of French psychic plotters have received word that their Russian counterparts have made an important advance in psychokinetic power."

Hollender interrupts with a question: "Why didn't that report come through our Russian operative?"

Webster purses his lips before he explains: "We have not heard from our Russian agent for two weeks. Her last report was that she had succeeded in being assigned to the research team that had worked on the earlier development of Nina Kulagina's PK powers. Our agent had reported then that the secret Russian group was using a computer model of Kulagina's brain and computerized *acupuncture* programs in an attempt to pinpoint the physical seat of human PK energy."

Webster turns to Britt and adds: "You see, Britt, while most of the world thinks of the *Chinese* when they think of acupuncture, it is really the *Soviets* who are the leaders in that field. In fact, when Stan Krippner and Dick Davidson wrote that report I mentioned, which appeared in *Saturday Review*, they told of how far the Russians had advanced beyond the Chinese in acupuncture. For example, rather than using needles as the Chinese still do, Soviet physicians regularly use precise applications of electricity and even laser beams on acupuncture points. In their report, Krippner and Davidson revealed that the well-known Russian physicist Victor Adamenko had developed what he called a 'tobioscope' which could accurately pinpoint all the acupuncture points of the body.

"Our French agent further reports," Webster continues, "that the undercover Soviet plotters have been able to use a tobioscope to pinpoint in the brain of a natural PK the exact source spot of PK energy. Working from that knowledge, they have surgically implanted laser crystals in that PK energy source spot in human brains. The laser crystal is connected by microelectrodes threaded through the large arteries of the neck to connect with certain nerves at the point where these nerves emerge from the spinal column. By selecting nerves, such as those which go to muscles that are easily controlled by conscious thought—like the muscles of the forearm, it is possible for the Russian subjects who have a laser crystal amplifier in his or her brain to exert psychokinetic energy at will, just by *thinking* about clenching his or her fist!"

"Christ!"

"Interesting...."

"Damn!"

Britt, Hollender, and Greg comment simultaneously as Webster finishes. Krimmil says nothing, but his eyes, although unmoving, unblinking, reflect a strange understanding.

"It's an amazing step," Webster says. "And now you all

must consider that you might encounter these psychic cyborgs should you be discovered during your investigations of the hauntings—remember: Mero might not be the only group out to penetrate the secrets of the Beyond by direct communication. There is one final thing," the old scientist adds, "which our agent reports that offers us some hope of dealing with these psychic cyborgs. As far as he knows, the present laser crystal implant operation has a major failing —when used by the cyborg, the crystal drains electromagnetic energy so quickly from the brain that all cerebral activity ceases ... and the cyborg immediately dies."

"Like psychic kamikazes," Britt observes.

Webster nods his agreement: "Precisely, Britt. And that fact gives you both some hope of dealing with them, and more reason to fear them, since you cannot stop them by threatening them with death. If they were not ready to die for their program, they would not have consented to the operation."

"If they consented."

These words are Krimmel's. Delivered in the German's deep, sepulchral tones, the sentence and the idea they express cause his associates to turn and look at him. "During my years in Nazi Germany," the sad-faced, hard-eyed Krimmel continues, "I witnessed many experiments performed on people without such civilized formalities as *consent*."

A second of silence follows Krimmel's words.

Now Britt breaks the mood: "The question of consent is academic at this point. The way I see it, regardless of how they got that way, these cyborgs now have no life of their own—they are psychic zombies who can only do *and* die!"

XV

"Enough of this brooding," Webster finally says to break the cloud of gloomy thought that has silenced everyone since Britt's last remark. "Here, look at this."

Webster now reaches for a slim, black briefcase which is sitting on the floor next to his chair. From the case, he takes several 9 × 11 manila envelopes. He tosses an envelope to each man and keeps one for himself. "None of these envelopes leave this trailer," he orders. "They contain your first assignment."

Britt and the others are opening their envelopes. Britt withdraws a report from his envelope: *Castellum Mortis*, he silently reads the words on the report cover.

"'Castellum Mortis,'" Webster begins, "is classical Latin, meaning 'the Castle of Death.' It is the name given in history to the haunting site which you will head for first. Castellum Mortis is located on the northeastern coast of the island of Sicily. You will be there ostensibly to compete in the Targa Florio race...."

Webster's voice drones on, but Britt's brain is only superficially monitoring the man's words. Britt's eyes are flying across the words and sentences of the report, reading the background of the Castle of Death:

> The ghost of the Castellum Mortis has been manifesting its presence over a span of more than 1,700 years. A wide variety of reliable observers—including the official reports of Roman centurions—have provided detailed information concerning both the manifestations and the history behind the haunting.
>
> Castellum Mortis is located near the town of Palermo on the eastern edge of Sicily. The castle is not actually a castle, but rather a huge, imposing residence of the type that characterized the private homes of the Ro-

man ruling class around 250 A.D. The structure stands on the very edge of a high cliff which overlooks a small, hidden bay. The bay is formed from the cone of a small volcano that became dormant thousands of years ago. The sheer, high black walls of the dead volcanic cone completely surround the waters of the bay except for a shallow, narrow channel on the seaward side, through which waters of the Mediterranean Sea have flowed in. The dangerous channel has been cut by centuries of sea waves pounding against the extinct volcanic cone. The deep waters of the bay itself are almost constantly hidden in the shadows of the high surrounding cone and are very cold.

The building has become known through the ages as a castle because of the high walls which surround it on three sides. The side walls run right to the edge of the high, sheer cliffs of the cone. A marble porch extends into space from the back of the building. This porch, or balcony, hangs out high over the water and runs the entire width of the main building. Marcus Piscatorus, who built the building in 264 A.D., was quite proud of that porch; it was an engineering marvel of that time and it permitted him to stand out over the waters of his private bay.

Marcus owed everything he possessed to those deep, black waters. He had spent most of his young life as a poor fisherman, but struck it rich when a storm tossed his tiny boat through the crack in the volcano wall and into the hidden bay. Inside, he found the black waters alive with millions of small squid. The bay proved to be an undiscovered breeding ground for these sea creatures which were considered a delicacy in Imperial Rome. The wealthy ruling classes of the time spared no expense in purchasing fresh squid by the ton to squander at their lavish orgies. Marcus made much money selling his secret catches to these people; he soon had his own fleet of fishing and trade ships and became a wealthy man.

His newfound wealth earned Marcus invitations to the very orgies for which his fishing fleet sold squid. It was at one of these affairs that his heart was captivated by Aurelia Furor, the beautiful, decadent daughter of a Roman patrician. For months Marcus pursued Aurelia from orgy to orgy and finally proposed marriage. He proposed out of love, but she apparently accepted only because her noble family had squandered its fortune and was on the brink of bankruptcy. She thought that Marcus would be a convenient free ticket to more partying.

Marcus, however, could not tolerate the corruption of Imperial Rome, and he was jealous of Aurelia's many lovers whom she did not discourage even after her marriage. Marcus, therefore, commissioned his magnificent home to be built in distant Sicily, overlooking the bay to which he felt he owed everything, including Aurelia. The entire structure was constructed of the finest white marble and was filled with treasures of Grecian art. Those high walls which earned the home the title of *castellum* were built to protect both the art treasures and Aurelia from the bands of robbers who roamed the untamed island of Sicily in those days.

Marcus and Aurelia lived in the house several weeks before he had to return to Rome on business. She pleaded to go with him, but Marcus refused and left alone.

He had been gone several days when very late one night he returned home ahead of his planned arrival. The servants were asleep and he entered the house unannounced, going straight to the master's bedchamber. The huge bedchamber of the castle was completely open at the end which faced Marcus' beloved bay. When he entered the chamber that night, the white marble room was flooded with bright light from the full moon. Marcus had been careful to approach the room noiselessly, wanting to surprise Aurelia with a jeweled dagger that he had bought for her in Rome.

A translation of an eyewitness account told to centurion investigators by the servants, who had awakened at the sound of their master's footsteps in the hall, reads as follows: "She was naked in bed with three men. No one had seen Marcus appear in the doorway and he stood there for several seconds frozen by shock and rage at what he saw. Aurelia was lying on her back stretched out full length on the top of one of the men who was also lying on his back. The man's sun-bronzed hands were tightly gripping both of Aurelia's white breasts while he engaged her in anal intercourse. The second man was kneeling, straddling the chest of both Aurelia and the first of her perverted playmates. He knelt above the upper portion of Aurelia's passionately writhing body and held her outstretched arms pinned over her head while she sucked and licked his penis. The third man was kneeling between Aurelia's legs, having intercourse with her while his hands kneaded her buttocks in violent rhythm with his thrusts into her.

"Bellowing madly, and brandishing the sparkling, jeweled dagger, Marcus charged the men. He slashed one of them badly before the other two grabbed him. The death-locked group struggled out of the bedroom and onto the moon-lit balcony. For a moment it seemed to the watching servants that all three men would go tumbling over the edge and into the black waters that waited, invisible, far below. But a sudden surge of strength by one of Aurelia's lovers sent the dagger plunging into Marcus' heart. Marcus fell to his knees, blood spurting through the fingers of his hands. He slowly stood, grasped the dagger handle, and pulled the gory weapon out of his heaving chest. Great quantities of blood spurted from his heart and splattered loudly on the white marble slab on which he stood. Marcus teetered and fell backward over the balcony railing, disappearing into the blackness of the bay.

"No one saw his body hit the water so far below. His corpse was never recovered."

Webster is still speaking when Britt's mind tunes in again. Several seconds have elapsed since Webster passed out the reports: "Before we get into a joint review of what is in this report package, I will brief you on an intermediate step which is crucial to this first assignment—and our entire plan." Webster's eyes scan the men to make certain that he has the attention of all. Satisfied, he speaks: "We must be positive that the secret Harry Diamond Laboratories group is convinced that Britt is finished once and for all time with psychic research and, so, no longer presents a threat to them."

Webster's eyes focus intently on Britt: "Britt, you will soon leave this trailer with Greg. I'm sure that your tail from Harry Diamond labs won't be far away when you step from the door. Make certain that he's near enough to overhear the two of you, then tell Greg that you will think over the offer to drive on his team. Tell Greg you will give him an answer after you compete in next week's Mexican 1000 desert race."

Britt listens closely, waiting for Webster to explain.

"You see, Britt," Webster says, "it is risky business for them to send an agent into any foreign country—if the agent were discovered, it would be difficult for them to do a cover-up, like they could do in the States with their contacts. So your trip to Mexico will be the test. If that group does not send an agent to watch you, we can then assume that they have written you off their list of active threats to their secret program. Chances are, they will not resume the surveillance unless you do something they consider a new threat. And, if your cover works as well as we hope, they will *never* suspect you again."

Webster pauses and smiles. "Any questions from anyone?" He looks quickly from man to man. "Good. Then let's get into this background report on the Castellum Mortis."

Britt does not like being told so directly what to do, even by Webster. *Yes, I'll do it,* Britt thinks, *but I've got one thing to do for myself before I follow your game plan entirely . . . it might get me killed . . . it might ruin everything you hope to accomplish, Webster . . . but by all the life energy in me, it is something that I MUST do!*

Britt's thoughts are now interrupted by an uneasy feeling —a feeling that he is being watched, being probed. Almost involuntarily, Britt looks up from his mock concentration on the report that he holds. Immediately, he sees Krimmel staring at him with piercing blue, unblinking eyes.

XVI

Britt tightens the chin strap of his helmet and throws his body forward hard to test his seat and shoulder harnesses. Then he sits motionless . . . waiting. . . .

His spidery black racing dune buggy is sitting alone atop a wooden ramp in downtown Ensenada, Mexico, just some fifty miles south of the U. S. border near San Diego. Britt is waiting for the Mexican race official standing next to the ramp to look up from his stopwatch and nod. When the official nods, Britt's powerfully modified desert racer will begin to roll down the ramp. Britt will jab the throttle and blast away on his first segment of the Mexican 1000. This race is in precise terms an 832-mile, mad and murderous ordeal through dry deserts, up and down boulder-strewn mountains and across soft sand beaches. Drivers launch themselves out of Ensenada, then pound over the mean earth toward the distant finish line at La Paz, which is situated near the tip of Mexico's rugged and unsettled Baja Peninsula.

La Paz, muses Britt as he sits waiting in the cockpit of his racing machine. *City of Peace.*

Once a thriving city of pearls which divers gathered easily from the gleaming waters of the bay, La Paz fell on hard times in the early 1940s when a mysterious disease killed all the oysters. But La Paz is coming to life again today as a major resort city. A flood of American tourists and new hotels is flowing in—largely the result of this tortuous race. The Mexican 1000 race has an illegal heritage akin to the great stock-car races of the southern United States which grew from friendly country fair challenges between moonshine runners to see whose car was fastest. The Mexican 1000 was born not as a race at all, but rather was a lonely trek by California college students searching for more and better marijuana.

The long finger of land, the Baja—"lower"—California

peninsula, over which the race is run, is mostly arid . . . dead. Colonized by Jesuit missionaries soon after the Spanish conquest of Mexico, the land has long remained mysterious, remote. As late as 1972, only 40,000 people lived in the entire Baja, and even they are mainly congregated in the cities of Tijuana and Ensenada near the north border, or in ocean-isolated La Paz on the southern tip.

Over the course of many decades, a brutal trail has been carved through the forsaken and uninhabited interior. The trail, shifting with the desert sands, the floods of the plains, and the avalanches of the mountains, has been carved by unnamed legions of lonely Mexican truck drivers carrying supplies southward to La Paz. There really is no "road" in the way that most people think of roads. Two drivers seldom take the same route; each driver is convinced that he can pick the least bumpy, less dangerous path through the dry mountains and deserts.

In the mid-sixties, the California flower children discovered the Baja. In search of marijuana at less inflated prices and of better quality than that available in Tijuana and Ensenada, they pointed their battered but reliable Volkswagens southward, down the ruts toward the interior. Tiny oasis towns like Santa Ynes and San Ignacio became stops along the way where cheap but low-grade "grass" was available. But the seekers always pushed on toward the fabled high-grade weed rumored to be grown in the fertile hills around the shimmering waters of Bahia de La Paz.

On Los Angeles campuses, students sought out owners of dusty Volkswagens to buy their pot. Soon, it became a status symbol to drive a disreputable Bug with "La Paz or Busted" scrawled on its dusty doors. Dune buggies were also becoming popular. The liberated economy sedans in their new configuration could chop hours off travel time over the rugged Baja. It became sport among college fraternities to see whose "team" could make it to La Paz and back in the shortest time with the most pot.

With the boom in off-road recreational vehicles the race became formalized, as the vehicle manufacturers in their intense competition for the large Southern California youth market seized on the La Paz competition to promote their product. Famous racing names like Indianapolis 500 winner Parnelli Jones began heading growing lists of professional entries.

The machines and drivers improved, they became more

powerful, more professional. But the Baja did not change its unchanging ways. A few hundred miles of the road to La Paz is now graded, some of it casually paved; but most is as the Jesuits first found it: dry, deadly—a place where a man can die of thirst one day and his body be washed out to sea the next by a flash flood from a desert storm . . . a place where a man can drive for hours and see nothing, no one except perhaps a solitary truck picking its way through the rocks and cactus . . . or a lost and dying steer. Drivers have died, too, even in recent races. Sometimes their bodies were found only by following the buzzards.

Two hundred and thirty vehicles are in today's race with Britt. Ensenada's central marketplace is rumbling with the impatient, noisy exhausts of a colorful army of motorcycles, dune buggies, trucks, and modified Volkswagen sedans. The first vehicle—a big, red, four-wheel drive Ford pickup truck—was waved off at eight o'clock this morning; others have been following it off the launching ramp at timed one-minute intervals.

Now Britt looks quickly at his watch: *11:30*, his mind records while at the same instant his darting eyes catch a sudden movement below on his right: *God damn it . . . I think that they just wait until they see you turn your eyes away and then they wave you off!*

His buggy bounces firmly on hard springs when it hits the cobblestones at the bottom of the ramp . . . hisses rise from the heavy-duty shock absorbers as they steady the vehicle again. The huge, cleated desert racing tires claw and squeak against the cobblestones as they push the car away from the ramp at rapidly increasing speed. The highly tuned Volkswagen engine bellows louder, faster as Britt pushes harder on the gas pedal: *80 mph*, he reads as he nears the end of Ensenada's main street and jams the gear lever into third. The cheering holiday crowd of villagers that line the road disappear quickly behind his speeding buggy. The paved road melts at high speed into a trail of rocks and dust so thick that the steering wheel tugs hard from side to side as the tires are alternately grabbed by six-inch-deep "puddles" of the pulverized sand and dirt. Britt's pectoral and shoulder muscles are now feeling the strain from the steering wheel after only twenty minutes of forcing his rugged machine around sinuous switchbacks and through hard, hairpin curves. Britt glances at the "tip sheet" of road hazards that he has taped to his dashboard. The list, compiled from the bitter experience of drivers who raced the Baja last year, has so far accurately warned Britt of boulders that loom suddenly around blind curves, and of invisible gullies that suddenly open to swallow machines and men, and of deadly, foot-long, razor-sharp cactus spikes that grow close to the road where they can slash an unsuspecting arm. *"Mile 26:34,"* Britt reads on the sheet that is bouncing with his car. *"Cliff at outside edge of blind right turn. Go SLOW!!!"* Immediately Britt checks his front wheel-driven odometer: *26:28 miles!* He jabs the brakes and turns the wheel hard right . . . through the dust kicking up from the outside left front tire that is plowing now a curved path through the gravel and sand, Britt glimpses the edge of a sheer drop-off just inches from his wheel! But quickly he is through the curve and bouncing savagely down the boulder-strewn road before he can even think about how close he came to joining the list of fatal accidents that have occurred on that curve.

1:05 P.M. Britt notes on his watch as he feels the road smooth slightly and become rutted paving. It is the first pavement of any kind that he has seen for an hour. Ramshackle adobe buildings squat ahead, shimmering in the broiling desert heat waves. It is Camalu, first checkpoint in the race. A quick pause—and now Britt is accelerating away again. The buildings' images fade in the dust behind his speeding racer. Four miles out of the town the rutted pavement ends abruptly and Britt's teeth are jarred together by large cobblestones. The jolt forces his mouth to open slightly . . . he nearly chokes on the dust that suddenly coats his tongue and throat. His wheels slice into sand pulverized under the grinding wheels of years of heavy trucks—the puddled grit splashes away from his wheels like water and washes over the roadside cactus as a dusty wave.

2:15 P.M. Britt files the time away in his mind as he sees a car a mile ahead of him. The machine is stopped by the roadside, its wheels tilting inward at a crazy angle. *Broken axle, probably,* he thinks. *I'd better check my tip sheet* . . . *"Bad dip,"* it reads and Britt jabs the brakes hard just as the bottom falls out beneath his buggy's front wheels—the car sails across the dip and slams hard against the opposite side. Britt feels the pressure on his internal organs as they are forced down deep in his gut by the impact. Now, the vehicle is rebounding, sailing again for several more leaping yards down the rutted road. *Everything seems okay,* Britt decides as the machine roars on.

2:30. Checkpoint at El Rosario. Smiling kids crowd round Britt's car when he pauses at the officials' stand. In a moment, he is blasting away again.

Up Britt grinds into the high, dry mountains where treacherous curves are already becoming hidden in shadows that are cast by the late afternoon sun. Boulders, ruts, cliffs, and switchbacks, from blazing sun to blind black shade, higher and higher into the sharp peaks. At last, around a quick, hard curve, Britt sees the checkpoint at Rancho Santa Ynez. Britt checks in just as the car that had left ahead of him in Ensenada is disappearing into a cloud of dust. "C'mon! C'mon," Britt shouts impatiently to the officials who are logging him in. Now they wave Britt off—he hits the gas pedal hard but only accelerates a few yards before he is forced to a sliding, dusty halt by a burro that wanders onto the road from behind a rotting wooden shed. Britt blasts his racer's air horns and flashes the array of a half-dozen halogen lights that line the nose and high roll bar of his buggy. The donkey brays and turns and kicks his heels at Britt before bucking off the road in a snorting cloud of dust. *Shit! that guy must be miles ahead by now.* Britt angrily shoves the gear lever into first and fishtails away in the slick sand that coats the rough road.

Soon he is skidding back and forth along the cliff edge road that overlooks Laguna Chapala. Two thousand feet below him, Britt can see the other racer already speeding across the dry bed of Lake Chapala, leaving behind him a contrail of dust like a jet aircraft flying high and silent in a flat, brown sky.

6:40 P.M. It is dark now and Britt can barely make out the glowing hands of his watch. He is alone. Down out of the mountains for hours, he is bouncing at high speed through a forest of weird-shaped desert boojum trees that stand silhouetted against the deep purple sky like writhing skeletons. Clouds are gathering over the plain ahead. *Got to get out of this low country and into the plateaus before the rain hits and sends a wall of water rushing through this boojum forest.* The gaunt bare branches of the boojum wave in the rising wind like sinister arms reaching from the blackness to grab Britt and hold him on the dangerous low ground . . .

BAM!!!

A bolt of lightning sears the sky and strikes nearby, igniting a boojum into a horrid torch. A sudden gust of rain-damp air strikes against Britt's dry, dusty cheek like the cold caress of death.

What's that?!! Britt strains to hear a roar different and distinct from that of his engine. *Christ!* A wall of water five feet high is boiling through the underbrush just a hundred yards off Britt's left flank! He turns his bucking racer sharply to the right. *If I can make it to that rise a half mile ahead, I'll be safe.* But even as Britt races against a muddy, drowning death, his mind is working on another decision. *I'll never have another chance like this . . . now's the time to put my own plan into action.* He races ahead of the flood along the floor of the arroyo, careening off of boulders buried in the sands . . . scraping against cactus that tear at his racer's purple-painted plastic sides . . . suddenly up—sharply up the side of the arroyo, tires clawing for traction on the steep, loose soil of the bank. *C'mon, baby—dig in!!!* The machine scrambles to the top of the bank only inches ahead of the tumbling wall of muddy water. Britt stops on the top edge of the bank and switches off his racer's lights. His eyes adjust to the darkness and he looks back into the torrent of water roaring down the arroyo, carrying with it a hideous baggage of broken boojum trees and plants, and drowned desert animals. *They'll probably think that I've been washed down to the sea along with the rest of those unfortunate creatures.*

Britt turns his face quickly from the fast rolling water. He slams the gear lever into first and guns his engine. The machine obediently roars away, heading not south toward La Paz, but north—toward the U.S. border.

XVII

Hours have passed since the sudden desert flood gave Britt his chance to turn back toward the States. Britt's dune buggy is coated with sticky mud as it twists and pitches through the rain-washed black of night. Britt is driving without the headlamps on. Huge black boulders and knife-sharp cactus lunge at Britt from every shadow.

Britt is driving with recklessness that mocks Death's worst threat. It is the reckless disregard that has long been controlled and shaped by Britt's strong will to form the force that makes him such a fierce competitor in racing.

But at this moment the controls are off. Britt is being driven, not driving. He is returning to that source of his subconscious hell . . . a man momentarily mad over the loss of a loved one and clawing his way down through the mud of many years which covers the grave of the one who was lost.

Like machine-gun slugs the heavy drops of rain pelt against Britt's helmet visor. Huge clods of sodden mud, hurled up by his racer's unfendered front wheels, strike Britt's arms and chest like sudden, invisible blows from out of the stormy night. And towering boojum appear with each flash of lightning—they stand like invaders from another world and swing their tendriled branches like awful arms trying to seize Britt as he passes.

Suddenly—Britt slows his machine. . . .

A mile ahead, a tiny light flickers through the pouring rain. *That should be the border station at Mexicali, if my navigation has been right*, Britt thinks. *And the irrigation water channel should be about . . . there!* The broad concrete-lined channel that carries Colorado River water into Mexico under a special U.S.—Mexico treaty at this moment lies less than one hundred yards from the lonely border patrol shack. Britt is inching his machine slowly, quietly toward the channel. The storm and the pouring rain obscure

[89]

most shapes, but Britt pauses and looks back at the shack to watch a moment for activity that would indicate that the guards have seen him: *Good . . . looks like I'm home free.*

Britt eases the left front wheel of his racer over the edge of the concrete culvert and begins to steer slightly to the right as he brings the rest of the vehicle over the edge until it is driving parallel to the water and is out of sight below the rim of the culvert. The muddy waters rush noisily near the right wheels of the machine. Britt moves upstream slowly, feathering the throttle so that the racer keeps rolling forward without losing traction and sliding sideways on the rain-slick concrete . . . sideways into the deep, fast torrent.

The minutes tick away . . . now, just ahead in the night, Britt vaguely sees the wire fence of the border. The fence spans the culvert . . . Britt ducks as he drives beneath it . . . *Made it!* he thinks, relieved.

Britt drives carefully for several hundred more yards . . . now he begins easing the dune buggy up out of the channel. He pauses a moment to regain his bearings. He looks at his plastic map . . . raindrops course down it and fall onto his lap. *Let's see . . . I can pick up Interstate 80 outside of Calexico . . . and . . . looks like clear sailing from there to Washington, D. C. . . . only have to leave the Interstate to buy gas . . . this rig'll cruise at 140 mph . . . if I can average 80 mph for the distance . . . and if this storm covers me most of the way to keep troopers off the deserted highways . . . then I can be there in thirty hours. . . .*

Britt drives only a little way before the concrete ribbon of Interstate 80 materializes from out of the rainy night. Britt swoops up the on-ramp and accelerates down the deserted freeway. Soon, the needle on his tachometer hovers at 4,800 rpm, indicating to Britt that he is cruising at 130 mph. Like a hydroplane at Lake Havasu, Britt's racing machine spews tall roostertails of water from its tires as it bores, unstoppable, through the storm.

The foul weather holds in Britt's favor. A vast storm system stretches all across the southern United States. During one fuel stop, Britt sees headlines on newspapers that tell of great floods. *Terrible things,* he thinks, *but the floods will keep highway patrols off the road while they help fight the floods . . . I have something more monstrous to contend with.* He roars away . . . miles to travel. . . .

Now, it is midnight again . . . a full twenty-four hours since Britt drove through the culvert and under the border

THE MIND MASTERS

fence at Mexicali. Britt is nearing the Harry Diamond Laboratories. He has chosen that seldom-used dirt road through the woods around the sprawling campus . . . the woods where he and Gayle used to walk. Even in the dark, the feeling of the place awakens sweet, sorrowful memories in Britt's mind. Teardrops mingle with the raindrops that are trickling down his face.

Britt drives slowly, carefully. *It's got to be around here somewhere . . . I remember chasing those kids off the property that day and they used it to get away . . . ah! there it is!*

In the gloomy, damp darkness of the thick woods, Britt's eyes have been searching along the fence that runs among the trees and separates the secret world of the labs from prying eyes; and his eyes now find what they are seeking—a washed-out section of ground beneath the fence has eroded away just enough to permit a man to crawl beneath the barrier. Britt knows that sensors had been planted in the earth that would indicate to the guards if someone tried to dig beneath the fence; but the dumb, sophisticated sensors had no way of telling their masters of the gentle erosion by nature. Britt parks his dune buggy in a thick, wet clump of bushes. Walking lightly, he approaches the fence. The chain link wire is glowing slightly in the damp darkness, like the electrical corona visible around high-tension lines during fogs and rains. Britt knows he must be careful.

He slithers slickly on the sticky mud beneath the death-dealing wires. Now he's through! Half-crouching, moving noiselessly beneath the dripping leaves of the dense trees, Britt reaches the edge of the woods—and suddenly he freezes: *Oh, God!* The sight of the building where he had once lived and worked brings an unexpected emotional shock. Britt feels his strength draining away. He wants to sink to his knees and sob. But his determination is stronger than the feeling. His powerful subconscious unleashes long-buried emotions—colossal anger courses hotly through his veins, his muscles suddenly tingle as they are pumped taut with adrenaline. Britt grits his teeth so hard that they hurt. *Got to think . . . got to think clearly now . . . got to remember exactly which window had the tricky hinge, the kind that never seem to get fixed.* Britt's eyes now scan the rows of glass windows that line the walls of the first-floor lab area. The scanning stops. Britt squints: *Yes, that's it. . . .*

Britt checks the distant guardhouse. A light reveals a lone guard sitting in the shack, sleepy and snug away from the falling rain. Britt sizes up the hundred yards that lie between the edge of the woods where he stands and the building that he must enter. He studies the sparse landscaping on the vast open area. Small plantings of low bushes and a new, twiggy maple tree will provide his only cover. Without a pause, he scurries quickly to the first bush. Moving from cover to cover, he reaches the windows of the labs.

Britt pushes gently on the corner of that certain window. *Damn! It didn't move!* A flash of impatience shoots through his tense body, but he controls it. He pauses, then presses slightly harder against the windowframe.

Rrrourk!

The tiny sound seems loud as the window swings inward. Britt waits for several tense seconds, listening. Satisfied that no one heard the noise, Britt quietly pulls himself onto the ledge and through the window.

He drops soggily to the floor and stands still a moment, listening again. The only sound he can hear in the near-total darkness is the gentle dripping of water from his sodden clothes. His waterlogged desert boots make soft, squishy sounds as Britt begins moving toward the fateful operating room.

Britt pauses in the doorway of the room of horrid memory. His eyes have adjusted to the dim light that seeps in beneath the door to the corridor. *Nothing's changed!* he realizes with amazement. The amazement grows the more that his brain ponders it: *My God . . . absolutely nothing has changed! Uncanny!* Britt now slowly scans the room. *Everything is just exactly as it was left that night . . . there are the surgical instruments still scattered on the floor as I remember . . . and there's the burnt-out transformer*—like a lightning flash, an image appears before Britt's eyes, a memory of the sight of Pickett's smoking eyesockets when he was hurled against the transformer.

Britt blinks. The vision disappears. He can not help but wonder why the room has been left exactly as it was that night. *It could be that they feared a subconscious psychic attack from me . . . they must have thought that it was ME who caused those things that night . . . of course!* Britt realizes with sudden insight. *Of course! That's it! Why else would they have allowed me to live at all! Only I have known all these years that it was Gayle, not myself!* Britt's Self level of consciousness pauses an instant in anticipation of another realization that is now surging up from one of his lower levels of subconsciousness. *That's it! Something must still be occurring here! . . . something that they think I am still responsible for! . . .* Britt whirls, his eyes search the ceiling. They snap to a stop, focused on a dark stain on the white acoustical tile. At that very instant, the discoloration there changes from a dry stain to one of glistening moistness. The room becomes quickly frigid, icy. Britt shivers and is engulfed in a feeling of bitter despair so sorrowful that his mind is uncomprehending of its depth and breadth—it is beyond any sorrow he has ever experienced. Britt can feel his body turning to ice in the awful cold, yet his mind remains alert enough to be aware of an incongruity—*My breath is not condensing in the air, therefore, the air must not be cold . . . the cold must be internal . . . emotional . . . they must know I'm here . . . somehow I've been trapped . . . they've got me pinpointed with a more powerful type of Mood Master generator!* Britt struggles to turn his eyes back to the glistening stain on the ceiling . . . *oh, Gayle . . .* A torrent of emotion, long-pent, pours from deep in Britt's being . . . *how I still love you! . . . I came to free you from these earthly bonds that ensnare your soul . . . but now it seems that I will be prevented . . .* Britt's outpouring emotions stagger to a confused halt. *The cold has disappeared!* he suddenly realizes. The chill is quickly replaced by a peaceful, penetrating warmth, a feeling Britt remembers from years ago.

And now he understand. Finally, he understands. *So . . . you had forgiven me even then. . . .*

Tears of relief hardly hinder Britt as he walks swiftly toward a tall cigar-shaped cylinder standing in the corner of the operating room.

"DANGER—HIGHLY FLAMMABLE HELIUM" the label reads.

Britt carefully tilts the heavy cylinder and drags it from the corner. He stands it upright directly under the bloodstain. *Fire will free you, Gayle . . . it will break the molecular bonds that hold you here . . . destroy the electromagnetic chains.*

Slowly, carefully, Britt barely opens the valve assembly at the top of the tank. An almost inaudible hiss escapes. From his pocket he takes a candle he had picked up from beneath a Bunsen burner in the outer lab. He strikes a match and is surprised by the seemingly enormous light that flares. *It is really just a little glow,* he tells himself.

Now, with a cupped hand, Britt cautiously hides the tiny flame. He peers into the black lab, and listens. *Just a little flame, but I still have to be careful. . . .*

Britt brushes the flame against the candlewick. And the flame, like a living thing, gives its energy to the candle so that there are now two tiny flames.

Its purpose fulfilled, the match is extinguished. Britt tilts the candle slightly near the valve assembly . . . near the tiny, deadly hiss. Two drops of hot wax fall onto the dusty brass of the assembly and Britt quickly presses the bottom of the candle into the still-sticky drops. His fingers loosen their hold on the candle and it stands alone, its flickering flame awakening a weird ballet of dim, dancing shadows along the walls of the haunted lab. *There . . . that will give me time to make it back to my buggy and be well away from here before the flame reaches the leak.*

Tears burn in Britt's eyes once more as he takes a last long look at the stain on the ceiling . . . the memories . . .

Click!

Britt whirls round at that small sound! A human figure is standing in the hallway door and is silhouetted by the hall light which hurls the man's menacing shadow across the floor toward Britt. The figure's head slowly scans the lab and suddenly stops, riveted in the direction of the candle and Britt. For a micro-instant, the figure's facial features are faintly lit by the flickering flame—Britt sees the light glint on the scar tissue between the cyborg's eyes. Reacting explosively, Britt dives for the floor just as the cyborg's eyes flash like strobe lights.

Britt feels the overpressure from the psychokinetic wave. The brutal power passes close by Britt's body and crushes a stainless-steel desk just behind him.

Britt hears the cyborg's lifeless body thud heavy and hard on the floor.

Britt rolls nimbly to his feet, sprints through the dark lab. He dives out the window, somersaults and runs slipping, sliding across the rain-soaked lawn—a horn suddenly sounds! Britt skids to a stop on one knee in the mud next to one of the lone bushes on the open ground before the woods. A brilliant floodlight snaps on at the distant guardhouse. The large light starts a slow sweep of the open area. Raindrops flash like tiny falling stars through the beam as it probes the night. Shadows quickly stretch out from each bush the beam

THE MIND MASTERS [95]

brushes and pauses at before moving on, creeping closer to Britt's hiding place. *They may not see me . . . this bush is pretty dense . . . if the light sweeps by, maybe I can make it unseen to that tree and then to the woods . . . and maybe away from here . . . wait! What's that!?!*

A familiar sound suddenly intrudes on Britt's rushing thoughts. Quietly at first:

Whup-whup-whup . . .

Now louder and louder . . .

WHAP-WHAP-WHAP . . .

Helicopter! Britt's feet want to run, his memory electrified with a thousand sights of those mechanical birds of prey lazily tracking running men and women and tearing up the dust and their bodies with hot lead spit from a tiny tongue. But his stronger Self level of consciousness forces Britt's body to remain behind the bush. The searchlight now pauses at the bush . . . now it moves on.

Britt breaks for the woods and runs headlong into the thundering swoop of the monstrous black bird as it bursts over the treetops—Britt stumbles on the wet grass and rolls on his back as the monstrous machine swoops over and past him toward the lab building. The chopper banks suddenly just twenty-five yards beyond Britt. It turns and hovers over the bush where he was only a moment before. The aircraft's onboard searchlight sears down on the wet leaves—the heat of the lamp's electric arc causes steam to rise. Now slowly, the light sniffs along the silver trail of crushed, wet grass left behind by Britt.

But Britt is up and running again with the aerial bloodhound whapping and roaring in the black sky just behind him. It is carefully following his zigzag trail. *Just a few more yards . . . I might make it . . . might stand a chance . . .* Britt's lungs are aching for air, his thigh muscles pushing painfully—but Britt loses his footing and slides again on his knee, striking it on the sharp edge of a lawn sprinkler. *Ahhh!!! . . . oh damn!* Britt's mind shouts in pain. He rolls on his side and clutches the torn knee. Warm blood rolls through his fingers from a deep gash. *This is it . . .*

The chopper is sniffing just yards behind Britt. Now the air is pulsing with the roar of its rotors. Suddenly—a brilliant yellow fireball blasts through the glass windows of the distant lab building! And from the fireball, a shapeless silver form streaks like an avenging angel to engulf the chopper, blotting out its sound, and its form—and sending it smashing with earth-shuddering impact into the mud.

A feeling of intense peace brushes over Britt's soul. As if in a trance, he staggers erect and limps quickly into the dripping, dark forest.

XVIII

This rain will wash away my tire tracks, Britt is thinking. He slams the stubby racer's short gear lever into third and accelerates up from the dark side road, onto the empty Interstate. *While they're searching for someone on foot in the woods, I'll be in Texas!*

The storm system supports Britt's escape. Rain pours continuously from the skies as if heaven is trying to scour the earth of its folly and filth. With his injured knee aching and throbbing, Britt bores on through the night, and on through the next nearly dark, overcast day. . . .

Night has swallowed the earth once more and Britt is now again nearing the U.S.–Mexican border.

Once again, he is through the border unseen. And now he is bouncing and blasting back through the boojum, across the sticky flood-plain mud, up and down the rutted mountains. . . .

Then it is morning and clear. Britt's brakes grind to a gritty halt at the top of a hill. Below is the beach. Tan sand, green water, white waves, and blue sky. From out of his mud-caked cheeks, Britt's rheumy eyes squint as they scan up and down the deserted Baja strand. *Good . . . not a living thing in sight.*

Britt wearily eases the gear lever into first. His left leg responds stiffly to his brain's command to let out the clutch. The battered dune buggy picks its way carefully down from the rocky foothill edge and eases its front wheel onto the cool sand. Britt drives very slowly, very quietly along the upper edge of the beach, traveling mostly concealed by the overhanging brush—suddenly he peers intently ahead: a slim, shimmering silver ribbon of water is wriggling down from the roots of the underbrush, down the sand, and disappearing into the sea. *Good . . . there's where a spring is bubbling up underground water from the mountain runoff . . . good spot for a quicksand pool if I can . . .*

[97]

Britt's search is ended almost before it begins. The front wheels of the buggy bog in the sticky sand. He quickly halts the machine. Leaving its engine running, Britt climbs back over the rear bodywork and hops down lightly on his good right leg onto the firm sand at the rear. Quickly, he kneels down at the rear and reaches between the spinning pully and belts of the exposed rear engine. Now he takes hold of the gear control arms ...

Clunk!

He puts the machine in gear and it idles slowly out into the quicksand, pushing its front wheels deeper and deeper into the sticky substance. The nose goes down first as the rear wheels push relentlessly ... until the engine is choked by the pitiless sand.

The black roll bar disappears last.

Britt stands a moment longer, watching large bubbles bulge and burst, bulge and burst ...

The bubbles gradually cease.

Britt looks around. There is no one in sight. No sound but the surf. Britt sighs wearily. A great tension leaves his exhausted body.

He begins struggling through the underbrush, moving up and around the head of the spring in order to avoid the quicksand. Back on the beach again beyond the quicksand Britt squints north into the distance. He begins limping toward Ensenada, fifty miles ahead.

Britt knows that before he reaches Ensenada, he will encounter rescue crews searching for him and other drivers who were undoubtedly caught in the flash flood and their machines and bodies washed from the flood plain on down to the sea. Britt walks on, ignoring the pain in his festering knee by concentrating on the story he will tell of lying battered and unconscious in the brush for two days. No one will doubt it.

And at the Harry Diamond labs, there will be no one alive who can say positively that the spirit that haunted the lab had not at last broken free and wrought its own vengeance.

XIX

Britt knows that something is coming.

He has neither heard nor seen anything. He only notices the people of the Sicilian town of Caltavuturo pause in their chores as he drives through. Now the women and the men who are too old to work in the hard fields of the high mountain farms are standing quietly along the road in the sunny afternoon calm. Unmoving, unspeaking . . . listening, they look down into the mists of the valley.

Something is coming.

Britt slows his rented Fiat 850 sedan, crunching to a stop on the gravelly shoulder of the road. He steps out.

Whatever is coming has just disappeared behind a hill far below. Britt can still hear nothing except for the sudden shrieks of the vultures that for centuries have nested on the sheer black valley walls a thousand feet below the village.

The horrid scavengers have been frightened by something unseen.

Suddenly it bursts around another hill—it is much closer than Britt has expected. A shaft of very bright light stabs at Britt's eyes and is accompanied by an awful, growing, growling, ripping howl. Britt blinks and in that blacked-out instant the beam of light splits in two. The headlights are aimed directly into Britt's eyes and he cannot see what it is. But the mountain people of Caltavuturo know.

The mountain people always know before anyone else.

The machine snarls onward, upward on the mountain road, seemingly possessed of infinite power and unaffected by the steepness of the twisting road. Twisting, sliding through the switchback curves, its brutal bellows bouncing off the granite cliffs behind Britt and ricocheting like shots around the mountains so Britt can hear every snarl and screech three times.

He watches, hypnotized by the sight. Like stop-action frames of film Britt's mind freezes the oncoming machine in isolated still pictures as it claws and flings itself up the long road toward where Britt stands overlooking the curve on which he has parked his frail Fiat. In the first mental frame, the black-green meteor that is skimming along the road becomes an Alfa Romeo T-33 . . . closer in the next frame, it is an Alfa T-33 with a driver . . . much closer in the next, it is now an Alfa T-33 with a driver with a silver helmet that is glinting dully in the hot Sicilian sun. Up the steep, straight section along which it is streaking, the Alfa's black radiator opening looks like the open mouth of a shark . . . closer . . . closer . . . Britt fights an insane impulse to dive out of the machine's hell-bent path as it streaks straight toward him —but the machine turns as Britt knew it would. It blasts past, bare inches away from the low embankment on which he stands, and vanishes like a meteor around the curve! The windy bow-wave of the Alfa's passing buffets Britt and kicks up tiny dust devils along the road. The skirts of the women flap. And already the machine is plunging down the road again—snaking, gliding into the misty valley from which it had risen.

Britt stands silent, watching . . . listening as the racer's sound fades away. Britt waits until he catches one last, distant, sun-splashed glimpse of the dark car—a speck now—as it flashes silently around an outside curve far down on the opposite side of the valley.

Britt is very lucky.

That is the way to be introduced to the Targa Florio race: seeing a thoroughbred Alfa alone in the crisp clear mountains on the day before official practice, straining and sliding around the ancient *Circuito delle Madonie*—the Little Madonna Circuit, the public road racecourse full of donkeys and dogs that seems so out of place in this age of antiseptic asphalt motor racing plants.

The rule-bound world of racing is left behind the moment a driver sets foot on Sicily. Since the end of the Mille Miglia, there is no other race like the Targa. It is a holdover from a distant age of racing. And Sicily is its natural setting: an island that time has not changed.

Britt has arrived in Sicily before the rest of his team is scheduled to arrive. Britt rode a jet across the ocean; his teammates sailed with the cars and equipment from Houston, Texas.

Britt's overt purpose in arriving early is to familiarize himself with the track—to drive it, walk it, and take notes

THE MIND MASTERS

about special conditions so that when the cars arrive, Krimmel will have a preliminary idea of how to set up the chassis and what tires and gear ratios to select. Such advance observation is necessary because the Targa Florio is the last major race in the world that is run entirely on public roads. The roads of the Madonie Mountains are in daily use and cannot be shut down for lengthy practice periods. There is only one day of official practice before the race.

So Britt is not alone, nor does his activity appear unusual as he drives his rented Fiat 850 slowly along the roads, stopping frequently to walk along the course and examine the pavement closely. Many other advance men for competing teams are doing the same thing. Many of the other drivers also carry cameras to take photos of various sections of the course so they can graphically show their mechanics certain road conditions.

The farmers of the area are accustomed to this scouting activity and pay little attention to what the advance men do. It is an unimportant detail to the farmers that Britt carries *two* cameras and is very interested in one particular curve in the road—a curve which sweeps to within a hundred yards of the high cliffs outside of Palermo. The Sicilians themselves no longer travel that curve when they are on foot or bicycle. They only drive it by car. In avoiding that section of road, the people and animals they herd to Palermo have worn a detour down through a shallow ravine on the inside of the curve. The people walk their bikes and donkey carts through the ravine rather than travel the curve that sweeps out toward the black volcanic cliffs—and into the shadow of the dreaded Castellum Mortis.

On this, his first day in Sicily, Britt has not yet even found a room. Immediately after debarking off the ferry that brought him the last leg of his journey from Reggio Calabria on the Italian mainland, Britt rented a car and began a slow tour of the roads that make up the racing circuit. He stopped once at the curve outside Palermo . . . the curve of the Castle of Death. But he had the feeling he was being watched and drove on again, back up into the mountains near Caltavuturo. There, he saw the Alfa.

And now the Alfa is gone. Britt climbs back into his rented Fiat. Back down the road he drives, heading a second time for the dreaded curve near the castle.

He stops his car at the side of the road and gets out with his cameras. Britt is cognizant of his impatience. He glances quickly around him, up and down the quiet road. Two men are approaching on bicycles. Britt kneels down and pretends to check the surface of the road. The men dismount from their bikes at the detour which is about a quarter mile from where Britt is stopped at the apex of the castle curve. The men walk their bikes down one side of the ravine and up the other, then continue on their way.

Britt sits there, squatting on his heels, and thinking. He jiggles a few pebbles in his hand and stares at the castle.

In the warm afternoon sun, the structure does not appear foreboding. Britt squats for a few moments, thinking about what he is there for. He muses about the search he had so suddenly become involved in. He speculates how strangely the now-uninterested people of Palermo would react to him if they knew his true purpose for being there.

Britt stands and aims one of his cameras at the castle. Peering through the prism, he focuses first on the main gates in the center of the castle walls.

Click!

The shutter's tiny crash seems to shatter the stillness. Britt looks around. No one is in sight. He walks along the road and stops about twenty feet north of his car so that he has a three-quarter view of the north side of the castle.

Click!

Britt advances the film and moves again to get into position for a similar view of the south end of the structure. As he walks, Britt ponders a problem. *That wall is cutting off too much of the building. I'll have to get inside the walls today or tomorrow . . . preferably, I can get inside the building itself to take all the necessary shots.*

"Boo!"

Britt whirls quickly, every muscle taut and ready. . . .

"My, my," the young woman laughs, "I thought you racing drivers were supposed to have nerves of steel." She glances curiously at the castle, then at Britt's cameras.

Britt wonders if she had noticed the unusual detail features of his cameras.

"And I thought you guys were interested only in the *road* conditions," says the girl as she nods toward the castle.

"Some of us have a little tourist blood in us, too," Britt replies flatly, unsure if the peasant girl is what she appears to be.

She had apparently been crossing in the ravine and had noticed Britt taking pictures of the Castellum Mortis. She is still standing in the ravine, below the level of the road so that Britt can see only her head and shoulders.

"Not too many tourists take pictures of the Castle of Death," she remarks as she starts walking up the rocky side of the ravine to get to the road and to Britt. She watches her footing while she carefully climbs, holding her delicate arms extended for balance. Her full braless breasts swing heavily against the thin material of her peasant dress with each step she takes.

Britt feels a stab of tightness high between his thighs and behind his scrotum. A hot flash sears through his body. He realizes that he has not had a woman during the hectic week since leaving Mexico; this sudden encounter with a beautiful young woman on a warm, sunny Sicilian day arouses his sexual hunger. He feels his penis begin to hang heavy and fill with warm blood ... the throbbing organ moves lightly out against his faded Levi's.

The girl walks across the road and stops a yard from Britt. Her long brown hair softly frames her smooth tan face with its black and sparkling eyes. Britt involuntarily licks his own lips when the girl's moist, trim mouth parts with an impish smile. The young woman's ample breasts rest now on folded arms which press the dress so tightly that Britt can clearly see the dark outline and the dimpled profile of her pert nipples.

The sea breeze is pushing the rest of the dress against the young woman's lower body. Britt glances swiftly down her length, and although his eyes do not pause until they return a split-second later to her smiling face, Britt is certain that he has seen the dark triangular outline of pubic hair where the breeze firmly presses the dress between her full, firm young thighs.

"So," she says smiling more widely and showing her bright white teeth, "why are you so interested in Castellum Mortis?"

The young woman's smile is infectious and Britt finds himself grinning back in spite of his suspicions about her curiosity and her unusual disregard for the superstitions concerning the haunted building.

"I'm not really all that interested," he explains. "I just heard about the place from some of the villagers in Palermo and I thought I'd get a shot of it while I was checking out the road around here."

The girl's smile stiffens just slightly at Britt's answer. He notices the change.

"That's strange," she says inquisitively. "The villagers not only go out of their way to avoid *passing* this place—they usually take pains to not even *mention* it in their conversation."

Does she know I'm lying? Who is she?

The girl quickly jerks her head to the side and looks toward Britt's rented car.

"You're an American, aren't you," she says, snapping her eyes back to Britt. "What's your name?"

Several thoughts shoot quickly through Britt's head: *I'm registered in the race under my real name . . . no sense lying now . . . it might only make her more suspicious if she's an agent.* "My name is Britt . . . Britt St. Vincent."

"My, my," she says, a mocking smile on her lips. "That sounds *impressive*. Like one of those rich gentlemen racers. Where are you from?"

"From the Los Angeles, California, area at the moment," Britt replies as he turns to walk back toward his car.

"Are you leaving? I didn't mean to bother you."

"I've got to get into Palermo to find a place to stay," answers Britt.

"You didn't make reservations in advance?"

Britt stops and turns around. "No," he says.

The girl giggles happily.

Britt again finds himself smiling at the sparkling sound of her amusement.

"What's so funny?" he demands pleasantly.

The lovely young woman shakes her head with delight . . . sunbeams flash on golden highlights in her soft brown hair. "You'd better have oil in your veins, because now you'll have to sleep with your car," she says. "And, you know, a lot of the drivers *do*." The girl pauses, her eyes narrow and the amusement in them is displaced by a steely glint of suspicion: "You know something else? *You* don't look like one of those real dedicated drivers at all. Are you sure you're here to *race?*"

An instinctive defensiveness flashes in Britt's eyes. The girl sees it and changes the subject: "Well, Mr. St. Vincent, you are never going to find a place to stay in town at this late date. The jet-setters who follow the races around the world all year long keep standing reservations here and every place else on the whole international circuit."

THE MIND MASTERS

Britt leans against the fender of his car and folds his arms. "Great," he says. "Just what would *you* suggest, since you seem to be so knowledgeable about all this?"

"I just happen to know of a place where you can *still* get a good room. The food's hearty and home-cooked—and the rent is very reasonable."

"What's the name of it?"

"The Palazzo de Benudo."

"And just where is this 'palace.'"

The girl raises her slender arm and points to a large building about a mile down the road. It sits alone halfway between the castle and Palermo. "Come on, Mr. St. Vincent. I'll see that you get situated there." She walks past Britt, opens the car door and seats herself in the passenger side. She leaves the door open and glances coyly at Britt. He smiles and closes the door. Britt drops heavily into the driver's seat and twists the ignition key. The little engine bursts busily to life. Britt starts to make a U-turn, but suddenly slams on the brakes when another Fiat buzzes angrily past, its tiny tires screeching in protest as the driver forces his car through the turn at high speed.

"Looks like somebody else is getting in a little unofficial practice," Britt comments.

"You'll see more of that during the next few days," remarks his sweet-smelling passenger.

XX

"Ah, Maria! Are we honored with another guest?" The old woman holds open the screen door and Britt enters the huge house with a suitcase in each hand. "Welcome to our home, Signor..."

"St. Vincent... Britt St. Vincent," says Britt. "Uh... is this your *home* Signora? I was told that this was the hotel Palazzo de Benudo."

"But, yes... and I am Signora Benudo, Maria's mother," replies the smiling old woman.

Britt raises a scolding eyebrow at the grinning Maria.

"Please. Come with me," the mother urges, taking Britt by the elbow and leading him up the grand staircase. The stairway had long ago been grander. Now, the gold leaf on the ornate balustrade is not gleaming as it must have been when new. The red carpeting leading up the steps is worn, but not worn out—and it is immaculately clean. The three walk along the hallway, passing closed doors, each of which is framed with a hand-carved scenic jamb. From behind one door comes the faint sound of a phonograph playing a scratchy operatic aria. From behind another, as they pass, Britt catches the excited chatter of an Italian television soap opera.

Noticing Britt's curiosity as she walks along beside him, Maria explains: "Most of our guests are not jet-setters or racing enthusiasts—anything but *that*. Our usual guests are almost all older couples who come here to get away from the hectic pace of Rome. Many of them are originally from Sicily and knew my parents since long before the war. They come back each year to stay here a while, to live in a house like that which some of them once owned themselves in Sicily before it was 'liberated.' It brings back memories for them."

Maria's mother has scurried ahead of Britt and Maria and

THE MIND MASTERS

has opened the room at the end of the balcony overlooking the front of the house.

"No, Mamma," Maria calls down the hall to her mother, "I think the gentleman would like the room on the other side, near the back. Go open the corner room."

"But," her mother protests, "the young man must be a racing driver, and from this front room he can see all the way down to the starting place of the race, and he can watch the other drivers practice."

"Go, Mamma," Maria orders firmly. The old woman shrugs her shoulders, relocks the door, and hurries to open the room in the back corner of the second floor.

"Why did you tell her to do that?" asks Britt. He stops walking, waiting for an answer, but Maria continues toward the room. Britt adds: "I just might *like* to see what my competition is doing during practice."

Maria does not stop or turn around to reply: "But you can see more of Castellum Mortis from this back room."

How could she know? Britt asks. *She doesn't,* he quickly decides after a nanosecond-long evaluation of the facts, *but I'd better be careful.*

"Mamma, our guest has had no lunch," Maria announces upon entering the back room. "Why don't you go down and bring up some bread and cheese and Chianti? I'll finish airing out the room for you."

Her mother leaves, and Maria walks over to the huge, drape-covered window. She flings open the drapes. Bright, late afternoon sunlight explodes through the glass doors and floods the room. Britt stands in the doorway squinting momentarily in the light. Maria now grasps the handles of the French doors to the small porch and opens them.

The view is magnificent, Britt can see from the doorway. The barren cliff top behind the Benudo home stretches away toward a sudden cliff high above the waves. The shoreline far below the cliff top cannot be seen from the balcony, but the quiet hiss of the afternoon surf drifts peacefully into the room. Far away, the horizon of the Mediterranean Sea shimmers in the sunlight. A ship's distant wake carves a glittering V-shaped trail through the golden band of sparkling water that flows from the sagging sun toward the island of Sicily.

"Put your bags on the bed and come here a moment, Mr. St. Vincent."

Britt walks onto the balcony where Maria is standing and looking westward.

XXI

A mile west of the Benudo home, the Castle of Death sits alone on the edge of the high black cliff. Britt can see over the castle walls from his vantage on the balcony. He notes that the building's design makes it appear like a huge misshapen skull, brooding bodiless on the cliff's edge.

"It's certainly an unusual-*looking* place," Britt quietly says.

"Who *really* told you about it, Mr. St. Vincent?"

Britt snaps his head toward Maria and stifles a sudden impulse. "I suppose it might have been someone on the ferry on the way over here. Why is *that* important?"

"It's not, really," replies Maria casually. "It's just that I didn't believe you when you said that someone in Palermo had told you about it. I'll show you how superstitious they are . . ."

Signora Benudo is just entering the room again and carrying a tray heavy with slices of thick, white cheese, a small loaf of round bread, and a bottle of red wine.

"Mamma, Mr. St. Vincent wants to know about Castellum Mortis."

The old woman nearly drops the tray as she sets it on the table. She straightens up and crosses herself quickly with the crucifix she wears on a small chain around her neck. "Oh, Mr. St. Vincent, it is a terrible place! Please remove it from your mind! Excuse me, but I have to bring some food to another guest." The old woman hurries away.

Maria is smiling smugly as she turns to Britt. "And my mother is one of the *least* superstitious people around here. Just look around us . . . our home sits alone in the no-man's land between the castle and the town. There are no other houses between us and the castle on this side, and if you look out the other side of the house, toward Palermo, you'll see that there aren't even any homes between the town and *us*."

Maria sits down at the table and pours herself a glass of

THE MIND MASTERS

Britt's wine. She breaks off a small piece of cheese and nibbles at it. Britt watches her delicate lips as she eats. They look as smooth and creamy and sweet as the soft white cheese. He feels saliva rising in his mouth.

"Sit down and eat," says Maria. "After all, *you're* paying for it."

Britt sits. Maria pours him a glass of wine which he sips while she explains:

"You see, Mr. St. Vincent, my father had a college education—something still very unusual even today in this part of Italy. He was not superstitious even back in the early 1930s when he chose this site for his home. This spot here has the best view on the entire northern coast of Sicily, but no one had ever built here before because of that Castle of Death and its so-called ghost. The villagers would not even work in the construction of this house, although my father offered them excellent wages. He had to import laborers from Malta."

"You don't appear superstitious either," Britt comments. "In fact, you don't seem to fit in around here at *all*. You have no noticeable accent in your English—and your speech sounds very familiar."

Maria smiles. "Would you believe northern California. I'm a junior at Berkeley, majoring in sociology. I come home every summer to help my mother run this place during the racing and tourist season.

"Now, I'll ask you something," she adds. "You sure don't talk like any of the racing drivers I usually see around here every year—where do *you* fit in?"

Britt tilts back his head and downs the glass of wine; then, reaching for the bottle again, he says, "Maybe I'll tell you about myself if you tell me a little more about yourself—first."

"Fair enough," Maria replies. Her smile fades to a frown while Britt waits for her to begin.

"Well, Mr. St. Vincent..."

"Call me 'Britt.'"

"Okay, Britt," she agrees. "Well, I have several sad stories in my twenty-three-year-history, and this setup"—she waves her arm to take in all the Palazzo de Benudo—"is just a minor one. You see, my parents once owned a thousand acres of olive trees that stretched from across the road in front of this house and on down the valley to the very foot of Mount Etna over there." Her sweeping arm stops and is now pointing out the window to the southeast where the black, tapering cone of the deadly volcano is visible.

"The fascists and the Nazis came and expropriated our olive orchards. We thought we would get them back when the Allies landed—but we were *very* wrong. No sooner had the American soldiers swept through than a team of geologists from an American oil consortium appeared and pinpointed a vast natural gas field under our property.

"The oil men threatened to 'expose' my father as a fascist collaborator unless he signed some papers to 'sell' our land to the oil companies."

"And was your father a collaborator?" asks Britt.

Maria's eyes flare angrily at Britt's question: "Of course not!!! No Sicilian that I know of *ever* was. We are proud and independent people—neither the Axis nor the Allied political machines were able to break our independence!

"Ah, well," Maria smiles a weary smile, "what happened to my family was not unique. Across Sicily and all of reconquered Europe the scene was repeated many times . . . the goodwill earned by the blood of the Allied soldiers was turned to bitterness by the packs of wealthy industrial wolves who scavenged behind the brave fighters. My father received nothing for the 'sale' of his property; nothing except a job as a roustabout in the gas fields. He worked long hours for many years and managed to send all his children to school —two of my older brothers are now lawyers in Rome, and the third, Carlos, owns a savings and loan bank in Westmont, Illinois.

"I was the youngest. When I was just finishing grade school over in Collesano, my father broke his leg on a drilling rig. The oil company refused him either a pension or medical benefits. For a while it looked as if he would lose this house."

Maria pauses, remembering the events of those bygone days. "Next to his wife and children," she now continues, "my father loved nothing so much as this house. In order to keep it, he turned it into a hotel and reluctantly sent me to the United States to live with Carlos and attend a private Catholic high school there in Westmont. Each summer, my brother has paid my way home so that I could help Mamma and Papa run the place during the busy summer months."

Britt and Maria sit silent for a lengthy moment while they both think their own thoughts about her story.

Maria is first to speak again: "Time, however, and the urgings of his old friends changed my father's mind...."

Rising emotions choke off Maria's words. She stands and walks out onto the balcony. There, she stares at the looming castle. Britt remains at the table. The wine's warmth is throbbing gently through his veins... but now the drowsy thudding of his pulse increases and he feels that tightness again high between his legs as Maria steps to where the slanting sunlight silhouettes her perfect, naked body through the thin dress she wears.

Maria turns around. Britt cannot see her face clearly because of the sun behind her, but he can hear the trembling in Maria's voice as she goes on with her story: "Three years ago, my father bought a small fishing boat. Mamma and I told him it was foolish because the fishing in these waters has been growing steadily worse because of the pollution from the gas and oil wells." Maria pauses. She inhales deeply, quickly, and exhales. Now she speaks in a steadier tone: "But my father said he had a plan. Britt, if you could see the seaward side of that castle up there you would see that the awful place sits on the edge of a small, round—but very, very deep—bay. The bay was formed from a dead volcanic cone that filled with water which comes in through a narrow slit in the seaward side of the cone. The bay is alive with huge colonies of squid that find the lava-warmed waters to be a perfect breeding place. All the fishermen on Sicily know that the squid are there... but no man will dare fish for them inside the bay. The only man who ever successfully fished that hidden bay was a Roman merchant who built that horrid castle centuries ago—and even *he* died in those black waters... his skeleton is still down there somewhere. And alongside his are the skeletons of many men and ships who have tried—tragically—to take those much-prized squid from the waters of that hole to hell!" A tone of anger has been rising in Maria's voice as she speaks. Now she pauses to regain her composure.

"My father thought he had the answer to fishing the bay. While everyone else said the place was haunted by the ghost of the dead Roman, my father said the reason for the deaths of all the other fishermen was because they were too distracted from their seamanship by fear of the so-called ghost. You see, Britt, the squid appear in greatest numbers near the surface of the deep bay only on nights around the time of the full moon. Of course, this is when the highest tides are running, and the water is surging powerfully and treacherously back and forth through the narrow inlet of the bay. The wind that is pushed by the fast-flowing sea often causes moaning sounds that can be heard even down here at our home; it is easy to understand how superstitious fishermen could be distracted into making fatal errors while struggling against the tide in their small and frail wooden boats in the narrow, rocky inlet.

"My father's plan, however, was to ride with the tide into the bay, do his fishing, and then—rather than try to struggle out against the tide—he would wait until the moon was gone and ride out again with the tide." Maria's voice suddenly cracks. It trembles again as she adds: "He tried his plan only one time . . . and they have never found a trace of him or his little boat."

And silence once again follows Maria's last sentence.

Britt looks at his watch: *6:00* P.M. The hours have passed quickly while he and Maria were talking.

Now the thoughtful quiet of the room is broken by a knock on Britt's door: "Mr. St. Vincent?" comes a voice through the barrier. "Dinner is ready."

XXII

Britt is now sitting alone on the steps of the Benudo back porch just after dinner. The sun disappeared only minutes before dinner ended. Above, the dark blue sky is changing to a somber purple. A lone star already shines steadily in the zone where the deepening purple blends with the still-blue portion of the heavens that are catching final rays from the sun below the horizon. Britt's gaze is focused on the strange castle that is silhouetted black against the deepening purple of the sky . . .

Strannggg!

Britt starts at the sudden sound of the stretching screen door spring.

"What did I tell you about Mamma's lasagna?" asks Maria as she steps out onto the porch.

"I couldn't have expected less spectacular cooking from the mother of such a beautiful daughter," Britt smiles in reply.

Maria stands still for a moment, looking at Britt; her head is tilted slightly and a smile is spreading across her lips. "Why, thank you . . . thank you for Mamma—and for *me*.

"You were staring at the castle again, Britt." Maria stands over him as he sits on the steps, and she too looks toward the brooding building. Britt glances up at her. In the dim light that filters through the screen door, he now sees that she is wearing tight blue hot pants and a loose-fitting blouse. Her legs are smooth and slender. Her full soft thighs perfectly fill the short, tight pants. Maria turns slightly to look at the castle and Britt's eyes wander up the back of her legs to where her thighs' smooth roundness flows out to form her firm, young buttocks. Her eyes suddenly snap down toward Britt.

"You changed clothes," he quickly says.

"Yes, it's always hot in the kitchen when I help Mamma

with the dishes. She doesn't approve of these hot pants, but they're comfortable."

They make me feel warm, Britt thinks to himself.

Maria sits down close to Britt and looks out over the sea. "The moon should be about three quarters full when it rises tonight, Britt," Maria comments.

"I used to be frightened," she goes on, "back during high school days in the States whenever the television had those werewolf movies on the late show. They scared me, but I couldn't help watching them."

"Now *that's* interesting," says Britt with mock indignation. "Here I sit on a warm Mediterranean night with a pretty, young girl and all she can think of is *werewolves*."

Maria laughs delightedly. "Oh, Britt . . ." She pauses, still shaking with laughter, "It's just that our conversation this afternoon about the weird things at the castle—and now the moon—somehow combined to remind me of the horror movies in which the moon turns people into monsters."

"The moon *does* greatly affect people, you know," says Britt seriously, "as do many meteorological events."

Maria looks quizically at Britt. He interprets her glance to mean that she wants to hear more.

"Scientists have known for years," he explains, "that even small changes in barometric pressure affect people—a drop in the barometric pressure, like before a storm, makes people irritable and drowsy. A recent scientific study in Florida even confirmed that crime rates go up during periods of the full moon; and just recently some scientists whom I personally know have come up with an explanation for those ages-old werewolf tales that you just mentioned. It is an explanation that may benefit many unfortunate people who suffer from epilepsy."

Maria's bemused expression has changed. Her eyes communicate a look of disbelief.

"Sorry," says Britt with a shrug of his shoulders, "I didn't mean to get off on *that* kind of thing."

"No! No," responds Maria quickly. "I was just . . . well, just *amazed* to hear such talk coming from a race driver. Usually, all they want to talk about is four-wheel drifts or going to bed . . . what was that you were saying about werewolves?"

"I know a brilliant physiological psychologist back in the States," Britt begins again. "He started working from the clinically proven premise that certain forms of psychoses—

especially paranoia—are caused by *physical* rather than psychological problems."

"You know, Maria, often the paranoid person will complain of hearing voices of people plotting against him. Well, laboratory dissection of brain-stem tissue—especially tissue from the primitive areas of the medulla—of paranoid people has shown that parts of the axions and dendrons of nerve cells in these areas are lacking the fatty insulation—the myelin sheath—that they are supposed to have. So the theory today is that these people may *actually* be hearing hostile voices—their uninsulated brain cells might be telepathically receiving the subconscious hostile thoughts of other people."

"You mean like mind-reading?" asks Maria.

"More or less," Britt replies. "Telepathic projection of thought has been proven so frequently in controlled tests that today most scientists acknowledge that ESP is a real and natural ability. The average person isn't yet aware of or able to accept that fact—but it is a *fact* nonetheless. So, what the poor paranoid person is suffering from, then, is involuntary ESP reception of jumbled 'voices' from other people's minds. Since most people are competitive and subconsciously as hostile as our primordial cavemen ancestors, the voices are interpreted as 'plots' by the paranoid. In fact, if a paranoid person comes under the subconscious influence of a strong brain-wave transmission of another person, the paranoid may exhibit the classic 'split personality' syndrome while under that influence—that is, the paranoid's own personality might be temporarily submerged and the 'incoming' personality become dominant."

Maria listens, fascinated by what Britt has said so far, but she is waiting for him to return to the original topic: "What happened to the werewolves?" she asks impulsively.

"Ah, yes," Britt nods his head. "Have you ever heard of Tourette's Syndrome?"

Maria shakes her head.

"Well, Maria, it's a very rare illness that is characterized by bizarre behavior in which the victim will compulsively shout, grunt—or make snarling animal noises. Tell me, Maria, if you were living back during the Middle Ages and were walking through the dark woods one moonlit night and suddenly were confronted by a man who was making raging animal noises and threatening gestures, would you stop and say, 'Ah! that is a case of Tourette's Syndrome'?—no, you'd probably run like crazy back to town and tell people you just met something that was half-man, half-animal . . . you might throw in the bit about hairy face and clawed fingers just to make the story interesting."

"But why is the *moon* important, Britt?" asks Maria. "You even said on a 'moonlit night' just now . . . does the moon influence Tourette's Syndrome?"

"Apparently it does," Britt states. "It has been discovered by researchers at MIT that the brain has a magnetic field. Other researchers have shown that shifting the brain's magnetic field can alter a person's behavior. If that is so, then perhaps some people with defectively shielded brain nerves —like the paranoid—can be affected by the magnetic field of the moon when it is at its fullness. Perhaps physical brain defects that allow the *moon's* magnetic field to interfere with the *brain's* magnetic field can explain a lot of irrational behavior—and maybe more scientists should start looking into the past again to see if old so-called superstitions have real bases in fact. Remember, the word 'lunatic' comes from the Latin word *'luna'* meaning 'moon.'

"And you know, Maria," Britt quickly adds, "even the anciently feared curse of *possession* may be nothing more than a problem caused by a person with a defectively insulated brain being overpowered by the conscious or subconscious thoughts projected from a dominant brain."

"Jeezzzz," Maria exclaims softly. "All that's so . . . so *fantastic*. It's just so hard to believe the things that science can do today . . . so hard to keep up with the knowledge explosion . . . tell me, Britt . . . do you think that science can explain things like what goes on up *there* . . ." she nods her head in the direction of the Castle of Death. The mammoth building crouches in the distant darkness on the edge of the black cliff. The great dome of the sky is black now but for a final few seconds of dark purple on the distant horizon. This somber, dying light casts eerie shadows across the barren, rut-scarred mile of cliff top that lies between the Benudo home and the hulking castle.

"It *is* a strange place, Britt," adds Maria quietly; she is speaking in a monotonous trancelike tone and staring unblinkingly at the brooding building. "You know, I just now remembered that once when I was a small child my parents wanted to make the room that you're staying in now into my bedroom. I spent two terrifying nights alone in there before pleading to have my room moved back again to the front of the house." Maria's eyes grow glassy: "I can re-

©Lorillard 1973
KENT
WITH THE FAMOUS MICRONITE FILTER
DELUXE LENGTH
Micronite filter.
Mild, smooth taste.
America's quality
cigarette.
Kent.
King Size or Deluxe 100's.
Kings: 16 mg. "tar," 1.0 mg. nicotine; 100's: 19 mg. "tar," 1.2 mg. nicotine;
Menthol: 18 mg. "tar," 1.3 mg. nicotine; av. per cigarette, FTC Report Sept. '73.

Try the crisp, clean taste of Kent Menthol.

The only Menthol with the famous Micronite filter.

Warning: The Surgeon General Has Determined That Cigarette Smoking Is Dangerous to Your Health

THE MIND MASTERS

member—almost *see*—how I lay in my bed those two nights and stared out the window at that place. I could feel that something awful was up there in the blackness . . . watching me . . . waiting . . ."

"Maria!"

"Sounds like Mamma needs someone to put away the dishes," says Maria with a quick smile. She rises to go inside.

Britt holds the door open for her, then he enters the house himself.

He climbs the stairs to his room, taking the steps on the grand staircase two at a time. His footsteps are muffled by the thick carpeting as he hurries along the second-floor walkway toward his room.

Britt's hand is on the doorknob when he suddenly stops. *Something seems strange . . . yes, yessss . . . those closed doors to other rooms that I just passed again . . . the sounds coming from them seem to be the same exact sounds that I heard this afternoon . . . exactly the same . . . and why do those people all have their doors closed on such a warm night?*

XXIII

Britt enters his room and picks up his camera. He walks over to the bed on which he has laid his suitcase and opens one of the bags.

Inside, amid the clothes, lie a dozen foil-wrapped cassettes that resemble rolls of 35mm film. Britt removes a single cassette from the suitcase and carefully loads the film into one of his special cameras. The camera loaded, Britt glances at his watch: 8:30 P.M. *According to the tide charts, the moon should not rise tonight until ten o'clock, so now that gives me an hour and a half during which the atmosphere will be free of the sun and the moon and their electromagnetic energy.*

Britt fingers the unusual camera that he holds in his hand. He walks across the room and switches off the light. For a moment now he waits . . . his eyes quickly adapt to the dark and he walks through the darkened room and out onto the balcony which is shrouded in the gauzy, moonless blackness of the night.

The gloom lies heavily, like smoke blanketing the land and sea. This darkness is so absolute that it seems to swirl as Britt's eyes strain to see. He feels dizzy and reaches out for the balcony railing. Now, as he leans against the cold, stone railing, Britt's brain lets loose of its dependence on its eyes and allows other senses to guide the camera . . . slowly, Britt feels the presence of the castle out there on the cliff top . . . and now he can see it . . . or perhaps he *imagines* that he sees it out there, looming larger than a mountain, blacker than the night.

Britt raises his camera in the direction of the brooding black bulk. . . .

Click!—the small, sharp sound of the camera shutter splits the stillness of the night.

"Hey! What are you doing up there?"

What!?! Where did she come from!?! Britt's Self level of

THE MIND MASTERS [119]

consciousness demands the information from his lower levels of awareness. But they, too, and all his sensors have failed to detect that Maria had again walked out of the house and was standing in the yard just below and to the side of the balcony.

Maria's question was asked in a deceptively friendly tone, but Britt is suspicious of why she seems to be so interested in his activities. "Just taking some pictures, Maria."

"Taking pictures in the *dark?*" retorts Maria. "Listen, if you want to get photos of the place that badly, I'll be glad to take you there any time you say."

"No. But thanks anyway," answers Britt. "I think I might go up there tonight on my own."

"Oh, no, you won't."

Britt stiffens. Maria's reply is interpreted as a warning. Earlier that afternoon Britt had decided that Maria is exactly what she has said she is. Suddenly, however, Britt is not so certain that he has correctly evaluated this distractingly beautiful young woman.

"Why *won't* I?" he asks, leaning casually on the balcony railing and looking down at Maria whom he can barely see in the deep dark of the night.

"Because last winter the government put a live-in guard inside the castle," Maria calls up to him. "And I'm the only one who knows how to get past him."

Jesus! A guard! Britt's mind starts racing: *Webster probably hadn't updated his information on the castle since he ran the computer analysis to select the haunting sites . . . things like that could wreck our research and get us killed . . . if we're going to play this dangerous game seriously, we'd better brush up on our spy-guy tactics!*

"Hey! Mr. Ghost-Hunter!" Maria calls up playfully from the dark, "whatchya thinking on so hard?"

Ghost-hunter!!! Britt's mind lurches. With speed too fast to be measured in increments of time, his mind recalls and reevaluates everything he has learned and observed about Maria that day. The analysis is inconclusive. *I'd better be careful,* he thinks, and says to her: "Oh . . . just thinking about your offer to take me to the castle, pretty lady . . . think I'll take you up on it—and I want to go *now.*"

"*Now?*" asks Maria. There is reluctance in her voice. "But it's *dark* now . . . and the old place is . . . is . . ."

"Is what, Maria," replies Britt, testing her. *"Haunted?"*

Challenged, Maria shoots back her answer: "Okay, then—let's go!"

"Be right down." Britt slings his camera strap over his shoulder and disappears back into the shadows of his room. Switching on the light, he tosses his suitcase on the bed again and removes several more rolls of the special film. He is careful to lock the door of his room as he leaves to go down to meet Maria. . . .

"I didn't see you standing down here," he says as he walks up to Maria in the darkness.

"I guess you *didn't*," she smiles back.

"Are you sure you want to go up to that place?" Britt asks and nods toward the black, menacing hulk of the Castellum Mortis.

Maria's answer is to pivot quickly on her heel and begin walking toward the strange structure. Britt must run several steps to catch up with her—and he nearly stumbles. The cliff top is a black, shadowy, pockmarked desert of cinderlike volcanic ash and stones. Britt is fascinated by the dead, barren landscape. "This reminds me of some of the photos I've seen of the surface of the moon. Old Marcus Piscatorus must have been pretty much in love with that bay up there to want to build such a great mansion on this godforsaken cliff."

Maria agrees, with amusement sounding in her voice: "It was even stranger for him to think that a woman like Aurelia could survive in such surroundings." Maria suddenly stops walking. "By the way," she adds in a suspicious tone, "how do *you* happen to know about Marcus Piscatorus? *I* didn't mention his name."

Britt recognized his slip as soon as it had passed his lips. He hoped that Maria would not notice. But she did.

Britt stops too, and turns toward the girl. His eyes scan the eerie emptiness of the black and barren cliff top around them. At this moment, Britt and Maria are standing midway between the Benudo home and the ill-starred castle. The dense, moonless darkness of the night is swirling around them like a black fog. Britt can vaguely see the strange, silent castle. Its massive bulk has been growing with each step they have taken toward it. Now it already towers above them . . . black . . . silent.

The silence that surrounds the couple is complete. Britt's ears are filled with the sound of his own breath that is flowing in and out of his nostrils. "Maybe," he says after a pause,

"I'll answer your question, Maria, if you will first explain to me how you are going to get us past that guard at the castle."

Maria looks at Britt for several seconds. She seems to be considering something. Abruptly, she pivots and starts walking away again, toward the castle. "We *aren't* going to get past him," she says to Britt who is already walking beside her.

"What do you mean, we *aren't?*" Britt asks cautiously.

"I mean just what I said—we are *not* going to 'get around' him. I'm going to *ask* him to leave."

They crunch several steps farther across the cliff top while Britt considers what she just said.

"Maria," he says gravely, "I have no time for games now."

Maria sighs. She continues walking as she talks: "The guard's name is Ernesto Gullermo. He used to be a servant in my parents' household before the war. He was very old even then—I used to call him my 'grandfather.' I still do. He took special care of me, as if I actually were his granddaughter. Today—I take care of *him*."

"What do you mean?"

"Oh," explains Maria as they near the black bulk of the dreaded castle, "I bring him wine and cheese when we have it to spare . . . and I sit and talk to him when he is lonely. He is very old, you see, Britt, and nearly deaf and blind."

"Some guard."

"Don't make fun of him . . . !"

"No! No," Britt protests, "I don't mean to make fun of him. But I *do* find it hard to see how a frail old man has the job of guarding a castle."

"He didn't particularly *want* it," Maria says and slows her pace. The castle walls, now only yards ahead, loom high above the couple. Like a vapor oozing from the obscuring blackness of the night, Britt feels a strange foreboding.

"Ernesto," Maria says quietly, "accepted the work because he was becoming too old to do even odd jobs, and he did not want to go into Sicily's *other* House of Death—the government-run old folks' home. Anyway, none of the big, brave men of Palermo would take the job. They all feared the ghost of the castle."

"Why," Britt wanted to know, "did the Italian government feel that they needed a guard for this old ruin?"

Britt and Maria stop walking. They are standing directly

in front of the massive wooden gates that open into the courtyard of the mysterious castle.

"I'll answer those questions later," replies Maria in hushed tones.

The thick, high walls beneath which they now stand cut off even the faint starlight. Britt can locate Maria only by the sound of her voice, and he is startled for a split second by the sharp rap of Maria's knuckles on the monstrous wooden gates.

Once more a total silence engulfs the couple.

"I hope he heard me," Maria whispers.

THOCK!

Reacting immediately to the surprising sound of something striking the huge wooden gates, Britt spins round and crouches, ready for anything.

"Take it easy," Maria quickly says. "It's just Ernesto opening up the peep-hole."

No sooner has Maria said that than a tiny window opens in the center of one half of the great gates. A gaunt, craggy face materializes in the opening. The shadow of a large Roman nose dances across the face's fissured flesh.

"Who's there?" the face's voice demands in frail tones.

"It's Maria, Grandfather. I have a friend who wants to see the castle . . . let us in."

WHOCK!

The little window slams shut.

ScreeeeBOCH!

The sound of a heavy, rusty metal bolt being drawn open penetrates through the thick beams of the door.

Grnnnnneee . . .

One side of the massive barrier swings open just wide enough for Britt and Maria to slip in.

Britt is barely through the door when a hot lantern is thrust into his face.

"Put that down, Grandfather!" scolds Maria. "Do you want to burn his face?!"

The old man lowers the small oil lamp and looks sheepishly at Maria.

"I apologize, Maria," he says as contritely as a child. "And to you also," he adds, casting his eyes toward Britt. "It's just that those things are happening again . . . and I've been frightened."

"What *'things,'* Grandfather?" Maria demands gently.

The old man seems not to hear her question. He is staring over Britt's shoulder.

Britt quickly turns around and scans the area in which they stand. The small flame of the lamp provides dim light and Britt can only make out that they are in a broad but shallow and paved courtyard. The tongue of tiny, flickering flame from the lantern cannot reach into the dark corners of the courtyard . . . and as the flame dances, strange shadows seem to leap out and retreat . . . leap out and retreat from every corner.

Maria waits for the old man to reply, but when he does not, she grasps him gently by the arm.

"You wait here, Britt."

Britt watches them in the lamplight as they walk away. His eyes can see now where the two are heading: toward a small shack built flush against the wall and directly alongside the gate. The girl, old man and his lamp are suddenly swallowed by the shack, and Britt is instantly smothered by the dark.

Only faint starlight now reaches into the courtyard. Britt's eyes slowly adjust to it once again. The pavement of the courtyard is tile, chipped and broken and covered with gritty, volcanic soot. Britt squats on his heels and takes a closer look at the tile. He brushes away the gritty dirt. Beneath it, the brilliant colors of the tile are still beautiful even in the dim starlight.

Britt feels a sudden chill *There should be no breeze like that in this enclosed courtyard,* he thinks. Slowly, carefully, he turns his head and looks over his shoulder in the direction of the strange cold that he felt on his back.

There, Britt sees a huge doorway—a doorway that he cannot recall seeing when he entered the gates. The strangely inviting passage leads into the interior of the castle. It seems unexplainably brighter inside the castle . . . a dim blue-white glow appears to be escaping like a vapor from the stone floor of the long hall down which Britt is looking. . . .

GRINCH! The sound of grit being crushed against tile behind him causes Britt to jerk around again.

"Didn't mean to scare you," Maria says, noting Britt's sudden move. "But Grandfather says he will go into the village for some of his medicine while we watch the castle for him."

"Thank you, Maria," the old man says in an age-weakened

voice. "But please be careful . . . remember, it is near *that* time again."

"*You* be careful," Maria cautions. She pats the old man on his hand as he walks out through the open gate. "Take as much time as you like. We will lock up for you when we go and I'll leave the key on our back porch."

Greeeeeeee . . . THOCK!

Maria swings closed the massive gate and pushes the iron bolt into place.

"There!" she says while brushing her hands together to remove the dust and rust which her fingers have gathered from the ancient bolt.

"Does he have an extra light in there?" Britt asks.

"No," replies Maria, "but *he* needs that lamp more than we do. Anyway—look," she adds, pointing behind Britt and toward the yawning doorway into the castle. "See how that white marble of the floors and walls picks up and amplifies tonight's faint starlight . . . even through this gritty volcanic ash that's everywhere. It's bright enough for us to go in there without a light."

Maria walks past Britt and up the steps and into the gaping doorway . . . the black mouth of the castle. Britt follows her. As he goes up the steps, he is fingering his camera.

Now, down the eerie starlit passage they walk, accompanied by the sound of their own gritty, grinding footsteps.

"What's *that?*" Britt whispers suddenly and stops.

Maria, too, pauses and listens.

"I think it's the surf," she says after several tense seconds pass. "As I recall, Britt, at the end of this passage is the ballroom. Like the master bedroom which is right next to it, the ballroom is completely open to a porch—a balcony, actually, that juts out over the edge of the cliff and runs across the entire length of the back of the building."

"Then you've been in here before?"

"Oh, yes, Britt. When we were kids, my brother and I would play hide-and-seek in here during the day. It was just spooky enough during the day to add a special flavor of excitement to a game . . . but we never came *near* the place at night."

"Is that why they put a guard here—too many kids getting to the place?"

"No, Britt. No . . . the children of Palermo—*none* of the people of Palermo, in fact—*ever* bothered this weird old place . . . it was only a few months ago that the guard was added by order of Rome. It was around the time that the ghost began to walk again and that things began to disappear from here."

"Things like what?"

Their footsteps are sending sandy echoes skidding before them down the long, narrow hall. Maria stops again.

They have reached the end of the long hallway and are standing at the entrance to the ballroom. The walls of the mammoth room seem to slowly pulse with the twinkling of the distant stars which are visible in the night sky beyond the balcony. Britt's eyes scan the huge, high-ceilinged room. A few pieces of dusty, ornate furniture of the style popular in Imperial Rome are standing around the walls. On one wall there hangs a huge tapestry.

For a moment, Britt lets his imagination create the scene of that room as it must have appeared when flooded with the light from the flames of a thousand oil lamps and perfumed candles, and filled with a jabbering throng of gowned guests.

"Those"—Maria's word explodes Britt's phantom Romans —"are some of the kinds of things that were disappearing."

She is pointing to the chairs.

"Some of these things," she explains, "apparently have real historical and artistic value. A team of government people from the University of Rome catalogued these furnishings right after the war, and when the Cultural Ministry discovered some of the items were missing during a routine check last winter, they demanded that a guard be stationed here full-time."

"There have been a lot of art thefts around the world lately," Britt agrees. "I can see why they want to protect this. It can certainly conjure up images of days when wealth could buy anything."

"You mean it can't now?" remarks Maria. "Come. I'll show you the master bedroom."

Britt follows her through the length of the huge ballroom and out onto the balcony. Maria walks over to the low wall and looks down into the black void.

"The 'hole to hell,' " she whispers softly while staring down into the bottomless blackness. "That's what the old women of Palermo call that bay down there."

Britt moves up next to Maria and leans his body out slightly, balancing over the dizzy black depths. "How far down is it to the surface of the bay?"

"My father once told me that it is nearly a thousand feet," Maria replies. Her voice becomes quiet and she bends forward, dangerously bracing her body by leaning with her legs against the top edge of the thigh-high wall which divides the boundary between the balcony and the unending blackness.

Britt assumes that Maria is merely trying to better hear the hissing of the surf which far below rolls invisibly onto the black ash beach and disappears down into the porous cinders. Britt, too, is looking down, listening to the eerie sound.

Britt stares for several seconds before he's distracted by a slight movement seen in the corner of his eye. . . .

Maria!" he calls out and suddenly lunges for her falling body—he catches her by the waist just before she completely loses her balance.

"Maria! What's wrong?!"

Britt holds her shoulders gently but firmly as he turns her around to face him.

"Oh, Britt! . . . My God!" Maria speaks weakly, blinking as if awakening from a trance. "I don't know what happened. I just leaned over the railing because I thought I heard someone—something down there in the surf—and the next thing I remember, you are pulling me back."

Britt guides Maria several steps away from the edge of the balcony before he lets loose his hold on her shoulders.

"You gave me a scare," he says. "You must have become dizzy looking into that blackness. There are no points of visual reference down there that your brain could use to compute balance when you quickly leaned your head to look down."

Maria nods in vague agreement while Britt asks: "What was it you thought you heard down there?"

"I don't know . . . really," Maria answers slowly. She is puzzled. "It seemed like someone was calling out . . . the voice—if that's what it was—seemed strained and hoarse." She shakes her head. "Now, isn't that silly?" A tear breaks free from the corner of her eye.

"No," says Britt, remembering her father, "that's not silly at all."

"But of *course* it's silly, Britt," Maria protests. "How could there be a voice coming from down *there?*"

"Maria . . . did it really seem like it was coming from

THE MIND MASTERS [127]

down in the bay?" he inquires. His tone is suddenly serious, demanding.

Maria is puzzled by his change of mood. She somehow senses danger. "Well . . ." she begins as she tries to recall, "it *seemed* like it did. At first I thought it was just part of the hissing of the surf in the cinders and rocks . . . but it seemed to be more than that, too . . . a voice, hoarse like the surf, but speaking words I could not understand."

Britt's whole body flinches slightly and a chill shoots through him. He can feel the hairs on his arms rise up quickly and lie down again as the chill passes.

"Oh, but you're right, Britt," says Maria. She speaks rapidly, trying to rush her thoughts away from what just happened. "I must have just become dizzy from leaning over too far. Come . . . we can get to the master bedchamber by walking down to the far end of this balcony."

Maria turns and begins to disappear into the inky blackness. Britt follows. A few steps farther into the thick gloom and a monstrous black mouth opens wide in the wall to Britt's left side. This is the high, wide entry to the fateful bedchamber of Marcus Piscatorus. It yawns blackly, outlined by the castle's exterior walls that glow dimly in the faint starlight. Britt and Maria stop on the balcony outside the room and strain to see in.

"Lord! Is it ever dark in *there*," whispers Maria.

Britt steps carefully backward on the balcony and removes the lens cover from his camera.

Maria is puzzled: "You're going to take pictures of *that?*" she asks. "An empty room?"

Britt focuses the camera on apparent nothingness.

Click!

"Could you move over to this side now, Maria?" Britt asks, ignoring her question. "I want to get the whole room in this next shot without any bioplasmic interference."

Maria steps to the other side of the room while Britt focuses his next shot.

"Okay," says Maria firmly. "Now let's suppose you tell me who you really are and what you're up to—planning to steal the rest of the stuff in here? There's a bed in the bedchamber here—as you probably know if you're an art thief. It's the original one that Marcus had custom-made in Crete . . . even the wool-stuffed mattress is almost as good as the day that it was brought here. Bet you could get a nice price for *that!*"

Click!

Britt walks past Maria and is swallowed by the darkness in the tragedy-scarred bedchamber.

"Do you believe in ghosts, Maria?" comes his voice from the dark. Britt has positioned himself in the right rear corner of the cavernous, night-blackened bedchamber. "Maria . . . come over here and stand behind me while I get this next exposure."

The girl's footsteps hiss harshly on the grit covering the marble floor.

"Ghosts?" she repeats the question aloud as she steps into the shadows behind Britt. "Is that what you're doing here, Britt?"

Britt focuses his camera for another shot of the room. Without waiting for his reply, Maria tells herself aloud: "Yessss . . . that would explain your behavior and that *feeling* I have . . ."

Click!

"What 'feeling' you have?" Britt inquires while he checks the settings on his special camera.

"Oh . . . I don't know," replies Maria. "Just a *feeling*, I guess . . . You don't look like a race driver, you know," she says, changing the subject. "And the way you explained to me all about the new research into paranoid psychosis. I mean, after all, for all the years I've been coming over here and listening to these high-speed jocks, I know what they sound like—and you don't talk like *that*."

"Ha!" exclaims Britt with genuine amusement.

"But, you *are*, aren't you, Britt?"

"Are *what?*" he asks, looking up from his camera. He folds his arms and looks toward the barely visible outline of the girl. Britt inhales deeply, slowly, and purses his lips.

Maria can dimly see his features in the faint starlight that reflects as a soft, nearly unseen aura emanating from the white marble walls of the room. Britt's face looks hard, like the marble. His words spit out with sudden anger: "I should have been more suspicious of you right from the start this afternoon, appearing as you did out of nowhere on that road . . . then the way you made certain that I didn't get into town to really see if any other rooms were still available in the hotels. And there's the way that you've made yourself indispensable to my gaining access to this castle. It all adds up now!"

THE MIND MASTERS

The expression on Maria's face reflects both her surprise at the anger of Britt's tone and her lack of understanding of what he is saying—but she replies with defensive sarcasm: "Why, Mr. St. Vincent, you make me sound like a reincarnated Mata Hari."

Britt, however, continues on the offensive: "Now you're going to tell me—and tell me *fast*, woman—what group are you working for?"

XXIV

Maria is dumbfounded. "Group? . . . Do you mean *team?* —What *racing team* am I working for?" Her tone of voice is tinged with rising indignation: "Look, friend, if you think one of your racing rivals is paying me to lure you up here with tales of the supernatural in order to prevent you from getting pictures and data about the track for your team's mechanic . . ." Maria stops in mid-sentence: her eyes are waxing wide at something unseen in the blackness behind Britt— and seeing her sudden fright, Britt whirls . . . ready . . .

But Britt sees nothing behind him in the smoky blackness of the inner bedchamber . . . no firm form . . . only a nearly imperceptible aura of starlight like a faintly luminous gas seeping slowly out of the ancient marble slabs.

"NO!!! NO!!!"

Maria's shriek now hangs invisibly in the dense blackness of the bedchamber! Britt spins round again and catches sight of her shadowy form bolting away. Her footsteps sound scratchily on the cinder-strewn floor. *She's running out onto the balcony*, Britt realizes. "MARIA!!" he calls out.

She does not halt, but melts into invisibility in the deep gloom of the night. The sound of her steps fades.

My God! Did she stumble right over the wall of the balcony!?!

Britt's own shoes slip noisily on the volcanic grit as his legs—thighs thrusting mightily—accelerate his body through the bedchamber and onto the night-shrouded balcony.

Sgrittt!

Britt's shoe soles slide—he hits the wall: for a breathless instant Britt's eyes bulge and he stares down into the invisible bay. Shaken, he regains his balance!

Sgrit, sgrit . . .

The faint sound of running footsteps farther down the long, shadowy balcony now registers in Britt's ears. He launches himself in that direction . . . plunging along the balcony, sliding, slipping sideways as he turns the corner into the huge ballroom. Now running blindly, arms out, down the pitch-black hall. *The gate . . . I'll catch her when she stops to open the gates . . .* Britt bursts out of the building's main entry—taking a running leap, hoping to clear the invisible steps, he sails through the night and lands, still running, almost smashing into the gate as he brakes his headlong momentum with his outstretched arms.

Where'd she go!?! Gulping air into his burning lungs, Britt scans the dark courtyard for a sign of Maria. *I thought sure she'd be here at the gate . . . could she have disappeared somewhere back in there? . . . in the ballroom?*

His eyes are useless in the black night, but Britt's ears are hyper-tuned for the slightest sound, his muscles are tense for action. Now there is a soft sound . . . again Britt hears it . . . he listens hard . . . it is reaching his ears in a broken rhythm. *Sobbing! . . . that's her sobbing all right . . . but where is she?* his brain demands to know while already his skull is moving in a slow arc, ears probing the night to locate the direction of the sound. *The shack! She must be in the shack!*

Britt moves carefully toward the vague, dark form of the ramshackle structure that is nestled in the deeper blackness beneath the high castle wall. Cautiously, he pushes inward on the door . . .

Screeeee . . . the rusty hinge protests.

"NO, LENNY! PLEASE, NO!"

"Maria! Maria! It's me, Britt! Take it easy—I'm not going to hurt you."

Britt strikes a match. The tiny flame flickers and reflects like two bright pinpoints in Maria's fright-wide eyes. In the dim yellow glow Britt sees the girl curled up like a terrified child on the narrow bed in the corner of the tiny shack.

Ah! . . . there's another small lantern. Britt steps across the room and grasps the sooty glass shield of the lamp. The glass grates dryly as he lifts it to touch his match to the wick. The flame catches. The glass wind-shield clinks softly when Britt drops it into place again. Now he turns.

The soft, dim light is falling warmly on Maria's smooth cheeks and its glow highlights the silver trail where tears have run. Maria lies there weak and helpless on the rumpled bed. Britt is beside her in a single step, sitting on the bed: "Here . . . stretch out and get hold of yourself." Britt himself notes the tenderness in his voice and he is angry with himself. *Goddam! Her group could be in that courtyard right now and walking toward this shack! Why do I feel so . . . so . . .* Britt's mind struggles to not say the phrase, to not verbalize the way he already feels toward Maria.

Britt slides his arm beneath Maria's naked thighs to move the fear-numbed young woman into a more comfortable position. The touch of her moist, warm flesh against the soft underside of his forearm sexually excites Britt—a tight throb surges back behind his testicles and a hot flash sears through his body.

"Maria . . . who is Lenny? Is he one of the agents you're working with?"

Maria blinks. Personality returns to her fear-blanked eyes: "*Agents?*" Disbelief tinges her tone of voice. "My God! You really *do* think I'm working against you!"

Britt stares unblinking at her big, brown eyes, searching for nonverbal clues to her truthfulness. Water wells up quickly along the bottom of her eyebrows and spills over in the form of two tears that in an instant slide down her cheeks and disappear into the coarse blanket like falling stars into the earth. Maria slowly rolls over on her side and buries her head in the blanket as she curls her body into the fetal position. Her shoulders shudder with gentle sobs.

Britt reaches out and places a hand on her shoulder. . . .

"NO, PLEASE, LENNY—PLEASE . . . I can't take any more!!!"

Britt is startled again by her scream. He grasps her firmly by the shoulder: "Calm *down,* Maria! Take it easy," he says while thinking: *If this is an act, it's a good one.*

"Just take it easy, Maria . . . tell me about this Lenny." Britt firmly but gently turns Maria until she is lying on her back again. "Tell me about him *now.*"

Maria stares sullen and silent at Britt.

He waits.

"He's dead," Maria says flatly. Her blank eyes drift from Britt and point, unfocused, at the sooty ceiling of the rickety shack. "He's been dead for three years."

Britt listens closely, his eyes narrowed in concentration: *Dead three years? . . . don't see any sign in her eyes that she's lying . . . if not, though, then what is she talking about?*

XXV

Maria's eyes remain fixed on the ceiling, they are emotionless, unblinking.

With his right hand Britt gently, firmly takes Maria's face and turns it toward him: "Lenny, Maria . . . how did you meet him?"

She blinks.

"How did he *die?*"

Maria's lips part slightly as if she wants to speak. Britt releases her face.

"He . . . he OD'd on sopors."

Maria inhales unevenly, raggedly.

Britt waits for her to continue.

But the girl lies there, silent. Britt can see in her eyes that she is remembering painful memories which, long-suppressed, are now welling up again. A small spark of sympathy is struck in the darkness of his still-smoldering suspicion: it has been only three weeks earlier that he, too, had endured the surfacing of long-buried, bitter memories. Britt touches his hand to her face and prods Maria with a question: "Did you know Lenny here in Palermo?"

Slowly, Maria speaks: "No . . . no . . ." her words come haltingly, "I . . . I met him at Berkeley . . . I was just a freshman . . . so much younger than today . . . so naïve." Maria looks away from Britt again, but her eyes are more alive now. "He introduced me to the hell of LSD," she says.

"And now you *see* things," Britt states.

Maria glances quickly at Britt, her eyes full of the guilt and shame of a small girl who has been caught shoplifting.

"Are you still using it?" he asks.

Maria shakes her head.

"Then I wouldn't worry too much, Maria. Those LSD nightmares will stop appearing after you've been off the stuff for a couple of years."

"Oh, *Britt!*" the girl sobs despairingly, "it has already been *three* years!" She covers her face with her hands, her shoulders jerk with gentle sobs, and tears stream through her slender fingers.

Britt cannot restrain himself from reaching out and smoothing her long and dark brown hair. "Well, Maria," Britt sighs. He fights a sudden urge to take the girl in his arms and soothe her. "Sometimes the nightmares and visions linger on if the underlying psychological problems associated with the drug use have not been resolved." He pauses. "Have yours been solved?"

Maria's lower lip quivers . . . a tear breaks from her eye and slips slickly off her cheek.

"Want to talk about it, Maria? Is it this Lenny?"

Maria blinks the tears away. Her wet lashes glisten in the warm, flickering lamplight. Stiffening slightly in her effort to control her emotions, Maria hoarsely whispers, "Yes."

Britt waits.

Silent seconds tick away.

Maria is lying quietly. Once again her eyes are aimed at the ceiling, but now they show signs that Maria is consciously guiding her thoughts . . . guiding them back to extract the source of her suffering: "I had won a scholarship to Berkeley to study philosophy," she begins. "It was my first time on my own away from my brother's home in Chicago. Until then, I never realized that I had led such a sheltered life." Maria pauses and shakes her head a tiny bit. "Such a sheltered life," she repeats softly. "I didn't know what had been happening out in the real world beyond my private high school and my private suburban cocoon.

"I met Lenny during the second month of my freshman year at Berkeley. . . ." While Maria is speaking, Britt is looking into her eyes, watching for clues. *No signs of lying . . . she seems to be genuinely remembering . . . her REMs show that she is seeing scenes that could have been real . . . at least they are real to her now . . . have to be careful, though, those psychic opponents of Mero may have re-engineered her mind.*

". . . I was monitoring a junior class in East Indian philosophies," Maria is continuing her sentence, "and Lenny was popular with the girls. He was the leader of a very successful national commune network known as Panta Rei. According to what I was told, the commune preached a modified form of Hindu evangelism. Lenny had been on campus for five years—he was a professional student . . . always switching majors and never quite graduating. During those five years on campus, many students—mostly girls, according to the story my roommate heard—had left school to join the commune either at the huge boardinghouse that served as its headquarters in Sausalito, or had left to disappear to scattered points throughout the U.S. where they could carry on the evangelism or work on the commune's farms and other businesses.

"Lenny wasted no time in striking up a conversation with me. He seemed particularly interested in the fact that my parents lived in Sicily and that I had no relatives or friends closer than Chicago. He urged me to come to the Panta Rei headquarters in Sausalito to spend an evening in meditation with some of the brothers and sisters.

"I resisted him for a long time—much to the consternation of my roommate. She had not been approached by Lenny, but she was anxious to get into the group and she thought that I could help her. Finally I gave in to her urgings ... and to Lenny's."

Maria falls silent again. The pain and hurt in her eyes now give way to a sullen grayness. A blank, abject expression that reflects the bitter, numbing memories that are slowly being resurrected. As she begins to speak again, Maria's words roll out in a slow, unemotional monotone.

"In class one day, I told Lenny I would come to a gathering he was having that weekend—but only if my roommate could also come along. He agreed only reluctantly, and on the next Saturday night, my roommate drove herself and me to Sausalito and the Panta Rei house. I didn't even want to go in the filthy-looking place when I first saw it that night. I didn't get to see too much of the inside, however, because as soon as we arrived, some 'brothers' and 'sisters' escorted us to the top floor and into Lenny's inner sanctum.

"I recognized several other girls from the dorm there that night. Some of the people in the room were smoking grass, but most were just drinking wine. A tape deck was playing the twangy music of an Indian sitar. Lenny smiled strangely when we walked in, and he said something to the effect that 'now the party can *really* begin.' He passed out drinks and turned up the volume on the tape deck. The last thing I remember of that party are the reels on the tape player going round and round...."

Maria's eyes close slowly now ... she shivers ... her lip trembles. Britt soothes her forehead with his fingertips.

"Go on with your story," he gently urges.

Maria's lips are dry. She dabs them quickly with her tongue and swallows before she is able to speak again.

"The . . . the next thing I remember . . ." Maria falters. She squeezes shut her eyes and inhales sharply through clenched teeth as she does indeed remember. ". . . was a sudden, hard coldness between my legs—then inside of me . . . I was groggy and weak and tried to reach down to push away whatever it was . . . but my arms were being held. . . ." Maria's eyes remain closed; she is reliving her horror. "I was being held down on a table . . . above me floated several blurred faces . . . I struggled to raise my head, and looked down to see a bearded face rise from between my legs and nod, smiling at the man and woman who were holding my arms. I was jerked into a sitting position and through my hazy eyes could see that I was naked. My legs were wobbly while I half-walked and was half-carried across to the far end of the room and pushed to sit down on a piece of plywood that lay on the floor. Another naked and dazed girl was already sitting next to me on the board. My eyes and mind struggled to make sense out of what I was seeing —I was able to recognize that I was in what had to be the basement garage of the old building . . . the huge stones of the building's foundation formed the walls of the room. Rusty, sweating pipes were suspended like metal snakes along the ceiling. Another naked girl was being placed on the table that I had been on . . . it was my roommate. The table was like the one my doctor had always used for examining me. While Lenny and a hard-looking woman held my roommate's arms, the hairy 'brother' at the foot of the table yanked her legs apart and up he went into her with his cold tool and a surgical light . . . then he took his tool out and felt in her with his finger, after which he stood up, shook his head and jerked his thumb. They took my roommate out a side door. I never saw her again . . ." Maria's voice trails off.

Britt uses another question to rescue her from sinking back into the emotional morass of the memory she is recalling: "What happened next?"

Maria blinks. Quietly, eyes staring and seeing scenes long passed, she begins to speak. "It was then that I noticed a line of about a half-dozen other dazed, naked young girls— girls from the party. They were in line for the table. Too weak and too woozy to stand, the girls were being held up

THE MIND MASTERS

by members of the commune. All the girls, including me, I realized, had been drugged by the drinks. I was just beginning to feel the drug wear off when they finished examining the next girl and brought her over to the board where I sat. I tried to struggle when they forced me to lie flat on the board between the two girls, but the commune members who had brought over the third girl grabbed my hands and tied my wrists together. They did the same thing to the other girls and then proceeded to lash us prostrate on the board. Four of them then lifted the board on which we lay and carried it into another section of the basement. There, an old, psychedelic-painted Volkswagen van was parked. As they carried us around to the back of the van, I panicked . . . my mind was screaming, but my drugged and bound body could do nothing. Inside the back of the van were three more 'trays' of naked girls, with three girls on each board. My 'tray' was slid in above these trays on special runners that had been built into the sides of the van. I can remember listening to the quiet sounds of the other girls weeping as we all lay there in the half-darkness of the van." Maria pauses. Britt knows she is again hearing the weeping. "Soon, another tray of girls was slid into place just inches above my face. Then the back doors of the van were closed. Seconds later, the front door opened. I turned my head as far as I could force it and saw Lenny and the brawny woman who had held me down on the table climb into the front seats. Lenny started the engine. The van rolled out of the basement and into the rainy night. In the blackness inside the van, I could hear the raindrops on the metal roof and the hiss of the wheels as they rolled on the wet pavement.

"The ride was long and became rough toward the end—I knew that we had turned onto an unpaved road. Then the van stopped and the rear doors were opened. The girls above me were taken out, but it was so dark outside that I could see nothing. My tray was removed next. I could feel the nipples of my breasts contract when they were touched by the cold rain. We were carried into a small cabin, set on the floor, unbound, and pulled roughly to our feet. In the dim light from a single oil lamp, I watched, still stunned by shock, as the other girls were brought in. Our wet, naked bodies glistened in the warm lamplight. There were fifteen of us, all told. Two of the girls I recognized from the dorm, but most of the others didn't even look old enough to be out of high school. They were probably only fourteen or fifteen years old.

"My mind was spinning and I was shivering with cold. Lenny came in and looked at us with a satisfied grin—then he blew out the lamp and left us in the dark. I heard him lock the door. In the pitch blackness, we all slowly huddled together for warmth. I don't know how or when, but eventually I slept.

"The next morning, I was still sleeping when the door burst open and several manlike women and long-haired men rushed in, yelling like animals. They yanked us to our feet and shoved us out the door. Outside, we found ourselves in the middle of what appeared to be the small village square of a pioneer log cabin community. Around us stood a circle of men and women, and even several children. The men and children stood and laughed as the women rushed at us with thin birch branches in their hands and began beating us and calling us sinners. Even the sting of those switches against my naked body wasn't enough to bring into focus in my mind what was happening to me. . . .

"Lenny appeared from nowhere and the women stopped beating us. Some of the girls lay on the ground with welts on every part of their body . . . all of them were crying . . . except me . . . I don't know why . . . I guess I was just still too dazed. The mean woman who had driven out in the van with Lenny glared at me, grabbed a switch from one of the women, and rushed up and slapped the whiplike branch across my naked buttocks. I could feel the pain scorch through me—my knees buckled. She hit me again across the breasts and I must have blacked out. When I regained consciousness, I was back in the cabin again, lying on a rough mat. Someone was cooling the fire in my breasts with a wet cloth. I opened my eyes, and the worried face of a teen-age girl came into focus. She was coarsely dressed in the same homespun cloth that the other women in the square had been wearing. No one else was around. I asked her where I was. She dipped the cloth in a pan of water, wrung it out, and soothed the welts on my breasts with it while she glanced nervously toward the door. Then, rapidly whispering, she explained that I was at one of the commune's farms located in the hills of Napa County. From what more she told me, I learned that Lenny was a white-slaver and that the communes were merely a 'front' for his organization. The girl told me that Lenny brought weekly shipments of girls to the farm and sold them to customers all over the world. He preyed on unsuspecting teen-age runaways who swarmed to San Francisco and other West Coast cities, and on foreign students at colleges who often had no U.S. family to become involved in searches for them. Lenny carefully processed his catches—the virgins whom he was able to gather in the various cities were shipped to the farms where they were used to fill 'orders' from rich customers. The nonvirgins were forced into prostitution in the huge 'homes' that the commune maintained in the cities.

"The youngster told me that the other girls in my group were now being bathed down at a nearby stream prior to being shipped. She told me that most of us were slated for shipment overseas on private corporate jets to Arabian buyers. She thought, however, that I and three other girls were going to fill a special order from some petrochemical executives who had been temporarily transferred to Prudhoe Bay, Alaska, without their wives.

"The girl had just finished telling me that when the cabin door opened and the woman who had beat me stepped in. She shoved the young girl aside and grabbed me by the hair, pulling me to my feet. The woman growled something to me that I didn't understand and pushed me out the door. Outside, all the girls stood naked in a line with tin trays in their hands while a woman with a steaming pot went down the line, ladling a soupy mixture into each tray. Little clutches of commune members stood by watching, and some of the children ran around the naked girls slapping them with the birch switches that the older women had used earlier. Every time one of the girls flinched, all the children would swarm around her and hit her more.

"I told the woman escorting me that I had to go to the toilet. She got angry and pushed me so hard that I fell, sprawled on the ground . . . then she grabbed me by the arm as I rose again and she half-dragged me toward the bathroom. Inside, she sat me down on the rough outhouse-style board and began strapping my wrists to the wall on either side . . . 'Don't want you to ruin your market value, dear,' she said. While she finished tying my wrists to the iron rings on the walls, she added, 'Virgins are getting hard to find these days.'

"Her remark gave me some hope—I knew that at least I could avoid being shipped to sexual slavery in Alaska if I could somehow manage to break my . . . my 'seal' of virginity and thereby make myself unacceptable to the waiting customer in Anchorage. I asked the woman if her precautions meant that she would be wiping my ass, too. She glared at my question, but didn't answer. So I knew that she would have to do just *that*. I tilted back my head and laughed at her—I taunted her, saying that that little piece of skin up inside of me was my ticket to easy living with a big-shot in Alaska, while she was nothing but an asswipe!

"She became enraged, grabbed my pubic hair and began pulling it out a pinch at a time—I held in my screams and taunted her further, hissing in her ear that she was just a bad case whom I would soon leave behind, and that she could do nothing to ruin my virginity. With that, she ripped off the thick, black leather belt she wore around her waist and began forcing it up inside of me . . ." Maria's voice stumbles and Britt sees her shiver as the memory is acted again in her mind's eye: ". . . when . . . when at last I saw . . . at last I saw the blood on the woman's hand," Maria struggles to continue, "I screamed as loud as I could! Two other women came running in and kicked my tormentor in the ribs to get her away from me—then . . . then I fainted." Maria abruptly stops speaking.

XXVI

There is perspiration on Maria's forehead and several strands of her long, dark hair are matted down by the moisture. Now she inhales deeply and with a slight tremor: "When I revived, I knew that I was once more strapped to a tray in the back of the van . . . the van was driving fast. Soon, the van stopped and the back doors opened. Lenny and another commune member dragged me out of the van and up to the first floor of the Sausalito headquarters. They threw me, naked, in a small room that had no windows and nothing in it except for a dirty mattress on the bare wooden floor and a bare bulb hanging from the ceiling. Lenny forced me to eat another sugar cube containing LSD. He left me then and I drifted into a dream world of weird, distorted shapes and colors . . . the walls of the little room appeared to expand and contract with my breathing . . . the cracked, brown boards of the dirty floor suddenly slithered like snakes, and the torn, old mattress seemed alive and trying to roll itself around me and smother me. But those drug-induced dreams suddenly became a real, live nightmare when I saw the door of the room open again—I knew that the door was being thrown open quickly, but everything was happening in slow motion in my mind. A big, bald, fat man, drunk, came stumbling toward me . . . I was standing on the edge of the mattress and he collided with me, falling on top of me on the stained old pad. I tried to struggle, but he was far too big and strong for me . . ." Without thinking as she is speaking now, Maria brushes the back of her hand across her mouth as if she can wipe away the memory of the drunk's lips on hers that night. "The stubble of his beard burned against my chin as his saliva-slick mouth engulfed mine and his tongue forced itself into my mouth . . . I could feel him wrap one strong arm around me and hold both of mine pinned to my sides . . . I could feel his other hand forcing itself down between our bodies as he lay heavy on top of me . . . he spread my legs with his knees and I could feel his fist between my thighs, in my groin . . . then I could feel the hot, hard pulsing of his penis as he guided it into me with his hand—and when he removed his hand and thrust himself deep and hard into me, I felt that I would choke and vomit . . . I can vaguely remember just . . . just drifting away . . ." Maria's voice trails off now in the same manner that her mind must have drifted away from the reality of what was happening to her on that night years ago. For several seconds she remains silent.

Britt waits.

Quietly, Maria begins to speak: "When my mind returned to where my body was, the man was gone . . . but, it only seemed a moment passed before I heard the door of my room open again. I turned. There, another derelict was shuffling toward me, grinning a gap-toothed grin through wine-stained lips."

Maria has been staring vacantly into space while she recalls the psychological shocks which have sustained the LSD hallucinations so long. But she turns now to Britt and looks sorrowfully into his eyes. For several long, warm seconds their eyes remain locked in a communion of understanding. But Maria's story is not complete and her subconscious continues dredging up the last of the painful memory while she looks at Britt. A glassy stare now descends again like a film over her eyes. "For the next three days, Lenny's pimps sent into me a steady stream of cheap ten-dollar tricks—old men, cripples, kids and anyone else who couldn't afford a real professional prostitute. They must have come in about one every thirty minutes. I passed out many times and was unconscious when some of them had me. . . .

"Finally, they stopped coming in. I was so sore and sick that I wanted to die. Soon Lenny walked in my room. He was smiling like a snake and sat down next to me as I lay on the urine and semen-spotted mattress. He ran his long, sharp fingernail down the middle of my chest and on down between my legs. Then he pulled an envelope from his shirt pocket and showed me about a dozen pictures of myself with various men who had had me during the past days. He forced me to eat another sugar cube and when my mind began to drift, he spoke to me in a sweet, quiet voice and told me that I could return to school if I promised to come back to the commune every weekend and work as a prostitute. He told me that dozens of other girls in the dorm—even married

THE MIND MASTERS

women from prominent San Francisco families—worked for him part-time, unknown to their friends and families.

"I thought about those pictures and what they would do to my family if they ever saw them . . . I had to tell him 'yes.' He demanded proof of my submission and he told me to get on my knees and put my forehead on the mattress. I did. I heard the zipper on his pants, then felt the stab of fire in the raw flesh between my legs. Then he left.

"I slept for a while. But Lenny came back. He said he had a favor to ask. Several of his regular girls were out at the Napa farm and he was giving another party upstairs and needed some house girls to help put the sopors in the drinks of the girls he was going to kidnap that night. I had little choice . . .

"Most of the girls that night were really young—mostly runaways who thought that they were going to have a good time. I imagine that today most of them are either slaves in Arabia or Africa or South America . . . slaves, that is, if their purchasers didn't just kill and bury them when they grew tired of them."

Maria pauses a second now.

"At least Lenny never got to enjoy the profit of their sales," she adds.

Britt remains cautious. He has heard stories similar to Maria's. The format is a familiar one in former counter-culture centers such as Haight, the Village, and Denver. *Her story is an easy one to fabricate, Britt reminds himself. Yet . . . damn! I can't help feeling that she's telling the truth! Damn!*

"What happened to Lenny?" Britt asks.

Maria appears more in control of her emotions at this moment than she has been since she began. She inhales deeply, without a tremor: "I killed him," she says flatly.

Britt waits again for her to explain.

"They were processing the girls down in the basement that night after the 'party,' " Maria continues. "Lenny and I were alone in his room. He told me to fix him a cup of coffee while he went to the bathroom.

"I fixed him . . . yes," Maria says, nearly whispering, "I fixed him . . . I took a handful of capsules from the candy dish. I opened them and dumped the foul powders into the coffee. Lenny returned and drank down the coffee quickly. Almost immediately, he grasped his stomach . . . Oh, *God*, forgive me!" cries Maria suddenly. She turns her head away. Sobs again wrack her body.

Britt hesitates, his hand held in mid-air above her shaking shoulder—unsure even at this second whether he can believe her . . . but, slowly, his hand descends . . . he touches her gently. "Get hold of yourself, pretty lady . . . take it easy on yourself . . . c'mon, tell the rest of it . . . things will seem better when you've got it all out."

Maria responds to Britt's soothing touch. She allows him to turn her once more toward him . . . the sobs subside: "Oh, Britt, I can still see him . . . even now . . . his eyes began bulging . . . he sagged to his knees unable to even gasp for breath because the drugs had already paralyzed the lung and chest muscles that he needed . . . oh, God! I can still hear his head hitting the floor—a million times since that night I've heard that sound and remembered that horror: the slamming of a door . . . a heavy footstep . . . all remind me of the sound of his head hitting the floor."

"What happened next?" prods Britt, pushing her mind away from the sound that is echoing through it.

"I . . . I was glad . . . *glad* that he was dead . . . I went through the pockets of his corpse and took the pictures and the negatives he had of me. Then I left.

"I went back to the campus . . . because of my shame and the fear of what I had done, I told no one of what really happened. The police only routinely investigated the disappearance of my roommate, overloaded as they were with looking for runaways." Maria rolls her body toward Britt and looks in his eyes: "Oh, Britt," she whimpers as big tears begin to flow from her eyes. Her slender arms slowly reach up, almost pleading. Her sparkling, wet eyes close, squeezing out crystal tears. Britt opens his mouth slightly and he gradually, tenderly lowers his lips toward the warmth of hers . . . moist . . . open . . . waiting.

XXVII

Foamy whitecaps boil from blue-green waves which dance, glistening everywhere across the wide, windswept sea channel.

This lively water is the Strait of Messina, the broad swath of Mediterranean Sea that separates Italy's "toe" from the wooden, rotting Sicilian dock on which Britt stands at this moment.

A warm, strong sea breeze is blowing across the choppy water and pushing endless legions of small waves to slap and pop against the decaying timbers of the dock.

Britt stands on the very edge of that long dock. He savors the dry spring wind while he peers intently into the Strait . . . waiting. His hands are jammed into the back pockets of his faded Levi's. The sea breeze feels both warm against his face and cool as it moves through his armpits. The sun's rays are hot and Britt is vaguely aware of a tingling sensation on his chest where the wind stirs blond hairs that grow above his low-necked body shirt.

On these cloudless, clear Sicilian summer afternoons, the sky is as blue as the sea. It is hard to tell one from the other. They blend together and there is no distinct horizon. Sometimes a distant boat will seem to be sailing in the sky. Britt is looking on such a sunlit scene right now; far down past the mouth of the broad Strait a tiny fishing vessel returning from the deep Mediterranean seems to be returning from the heavens, sailing down a gleaming blue sea of sky.

"Nice day, Maria," Britt says and turns to the young woman who is standing close beside him. Maria is shielding her eyes with both her hands, and she, too, is watching intently for something to appear out in the blue waters of the Strait. Her long brown hair tosses softly in the breeze. Her suntanned arms gleam moist and golden in the sunlight. She is wearing faded bell-bottom bluejeans and a tattered, oversized green sweatshirt with the word "Berkeley" barely visible across the front. The sleeves of the shirt have been ripped off at the shoulder seams and her slender arms only half-fill the arm opening. Inside the shaded warmth of the shirt, Britt can see her soft, braless breast trembling imperceptibly with each gentle throb of her heart. Britt's fingers ache with the urge to touch that smooth, warm flesh.

Maria senses that Britt is looking. And she likes it, because although she answers "Yes" to his comment about the weather, she maintains her revealing pose until Britt turns his gaze once more to the sparkling sea. Only then does she sit down on one of the large, low timbers that line the dock's edge.

Maria absently pulls a six-inch splinter from the old rotting wood, tosses it into the dancing water beside the dock, and remarks as it bobs away: "Your friend should be docking in about thirty minutes. I think I saw the ferry just leaving Reggio Calabria."

"Where?" Britt asks, surprised and anxious to see.

"Follow the line of the dock straight toward the little cluster of white houses on the hillside over on the mainland. Then look on the sea right below them."

Britt does as she directs and discovers a black dot near the point where the sea line meets the land. A small, white cloud suddenly appears above the dot—and just as quickly disappears. Seconds later, the low-pitched belch of a ship's horn drifts faintly to the dock.

"You've got good eyes, Maria," Britt says with a grin as he turns around to look at her. He stares at her briefly again, thinking: *You've got good EVERYTHING.* Suddenly the wind gusts hard—Britt nearly loses his balance when the old dock shifts and creaks. "Whew! That wind is blowing stronger . . . and hotter!" Britt steadies himself and glances up at the cobalt blue sky.

Through an amused smile, Maria says, "It's the Sirocco. It blows up from the Libyan desert, across the Mediterranean and into southern Europe."

"Kind of like the Santa Anas—the desert winds of California," replies Britt.

"Oh, yes," agrees Maria, "very much like those winds. In fact, the Sirocco occurs with the phases of the moon, just like California's hot winds, and, too, the Sirocco's hellish blowing is thought to have strange, evil influences on people. More than once, the presence of the Sirocco has been a factor that has won acquittals for defendants in murder cases in this area and all through southern Europe."

THE MIND MASTERS

Britt thinks about that for a moment.

"No," he slowly says, "it's not the *wind* . . . it's the *moon*. I believe it's the moon that influences people. Remember what we talked about the day we met?"

Maria nearly laughs. "Werewolves," she smiles.

"And lunacy," Britt smiles back. Living now emersed in their special regard for each other, he, too, finds amusement in recalling the topic of their first talk together. "The dictionary defines lunacy as 'intermittent insanity, formerly supposed to change in intensity with the phases of the moon.'"

"So?" says Maria with a twinkle in her eye. By now she is well aware of her lover's tendency to want to share his broad experience and vast intellectual store of knowledge; if at times Britt seems pedantic, Maria ignores her impulse to tell him so. She listens, and, most often, she soon finds herself interested and intellectually stimulated by what Britt shares with her.

Britt grins and nods at her response; he, too, is aware of his urge to share his knowledge and information—to the extent of sounding overbearing.

"Well," he begins, "I'll make it short—recent studies have shown that what dictionaries—and most of the scientific world in general—have long dismissed as an archaic *belief* is actual *fact*. The effect on behavior of lunar cycles is a phenomenon which has been accurately and consistently described by observers for more than twenty centuries. It is *fact*, not folklore."

Britt thoughtfully watches the waves lap at the dock for several seconds. Then he turns again to Maria: "Computers are even now trying to discover what constitutes the precise basis of lunar influences on the human body and psyche. We know that bizarre and violent crimes are more likely to occur during phases of the moon. Perhaps the lunar factor is a physiological influence. Remember—the moon's electromagnetic gravitational pull lifts even the mighty seas . . . and the human body is ninety-eight percent salt water, like the oceans. Suppose, for instance, that the moon changes human behavior by changing the distribution or concentration of water in the body—or that its electromagnetic gravity waves interfere with the electromagnetic fields of human brains."

Maria looks at Britt with pretended smugness. "I know one physiological fact that the moon does definitely influence."

"What's that?" Britt asks, knowing that he must.

"You mean *you* don't know, Mr. Scientist?" Maria teases.

Britt smiles and cocks his head.

"Why every twelve-year-old girl knows the answer to *that*, Britt. The female menstrual cycle has always been based on twenty-eight to thirty-day cycles that coincide with phases of the moon."

Britt can only shake his head and grin broadly. Maria flicks her eyebrows playfully and turns her attention again out to the ferry on the Strait.

Of course, she's absolutely right! Britt admits to himself. *All the careful pursuing of scientific literature that Webster has done at Mero in order to program his computers to find correlations between human cycles and lunar cycles—and he overlooks one of the most obvious . . . score another one for women's lib and their point that women have a lot to contribute. . . .*

Britt's Self level of consciousness drifts into reverie. He looks a while longer at Maria. *She certainly is not the typical young Sicilian woman.* Britt glances shoreward down the dock toward the plain young women who are walking along the waterfront street. They are shopping at sea-front stalls to buy squid, octopus, and less unusual fish to put on the family dinner table.

Sicily! Still the troublesome stepchild of Rome. The island's clannish families continue to this day to successfully frustrate attempts by the central Italian government in Rome to make the proud islanders pay all their taxes and obey all the laws —laws which the Sicilians feel intrude into what have traditionally been family matters. Bloody family feuding remains common in sunny Sicily. Local police shrug their shoulders, see and hear nothing. The central government maintains small garrisons of federal troops around the island to keep what order they can when interfamily warfare flares.

Perhaps because Rome feels the cost of troop garrisons kept on the island is already more than what it should be spending, the government disburses very little federal aid to the people of Sicily. The island is physically poor, and the poorness is evident everywhere. Britt notices that even the women shopping along the waterfront appear older than they probably are. Their clothes are rough and plain. Britt mentally undresses some of the girls as they pass and decides that, although their clothes do not match the fineness and the

THE MIND MASTERS

color of the women of Rome, the Sicilian women possess a taut, proud beauty all their own.

Weathered wooden warehouses and fish stores line this street at the end of the dock. Rising on the hills behind these shabby stores is the ancient city of Messina. The city gives the appearance of having simply been flung across the hills. It is a jumble of crumbling, multistory buildings separated from each other only by narrow, meandering cobblestone passages that serve as streets. Two tiny Fiat 850 sedans can barely squeeze past each other side by side in these serpentine alleys. Britt watches now the activity as, with one hand on the steering wheel and the other hand holding down the horn button, Sicilian drivers are rattling along at breakneck speeds, scattering crowds of people, dodging carts, donkeys and dogs, and somehow managing to pass oncoming cars.

Sicily is a rugged, mountainous island. Millions of years ago the land had heaved itself from the depths of the ocean with a planet-shaking blast of volcanic hell-fire. Of all the volcanic mountains on the island, one dominates: the feared Mount Etna. Blasts and lava from Etna's two-mile-high peak have frightened and buried countless numbers of people for thousands of years. The ancient Greeks had sought to explain Etna's sky-blackening fury in terms of their gods. Typhon, the hundred-headed fire-breathing giant, creator of dangerous typhoon winds, was believed to have made war upon the gods. He was struck down by a thunderbolt from Zeus and buried in hell under Mount Etna. When the earth shakes and the red, molten rock boils forth, Greeks still believe it is Typhon trying to escape his fiery grave.

Sicily's rugged, rocky terrain and hilly, volcano-pocked face make farming difficult. Many Sicilians instead herd sure-footed sheep which are able to feed on the sparse grass that grows out of rocky clefts or in an occasional boulder-strewn field. Many Sicilians, too, are fishermen. But the principal product of Sicily was and remains *olives*. The gnarled olive trees, like the gnarled Sicilians themselves, dig in and hold onto the poor, thin soil, and, patiently, they bear their fruit.

. . . and Maria, Britt thinks, *how very much she is like the patient Sicilian olive trees . . . victim of a hard and unyielding world . . . yet rooted into life . . . not just hanging on, but living . . .*

Like gentle leaves, the days since they met have fallen from the calendar. Britt has become convinced that Maria is all she says she is. Britt's coded communications with Mero headquarters have substantiated Maria's story about her life in America and the existence of the Panta Rei communc. Mero's external operatives have tipped the Los Angeles *Times* about the commune activities, and authorities across the nation have conducted raids on the commune's scattered buildings and farms.

Britt himself has deeply penetrated Maria's emotional barriers. He has seen the wounds bleeding in her psyche and has helped start the healing process. Together, he and Maria have shared nights of true communion of Selfs.

And Britt has shared with her part of his own secret life. Although, for her safety, Britt has not revealed to Maria the full story of the international intrigue that is threatening the world, he has explained to her his purpose in Palermo. He truthfully told her that he is a parapsychologist and that he is in Palermo to communicate with the ghost of the Castle of Death. His racing identity, he explained, is merely to prevent his work from either being hampered by too much publicity or from being halted by reactionary officials.

Maria is enthusiastic about Britt's real work. She had surprised Britt when she told him of her own interest in psychic phenomena and the life that death brings. She confided something that she had never told her religiously conservative family for fear of being disowned: early in 1971, while vacationing on the U.S. East Coast, she—along with 2,000 other rock music fans—had participated in a psychic experiment with the Grateful Dead rock group. The experiment was conducted by Stanley Krippner of the Maimonides Hospital Dream Laboratory. Its purpose was to discover if extrasensory messages could more easily be transmitted when the person or persons sending the message had a particular receiver in mind—whether or not they had ever met the receiver or even knew who he or she was. Maria said that two subjects were put to sleep, one in the Dream Laboratory and one at his private home. Forty miles away at the Grateful Dead rock concert, the audience was shown a slide of an art print and told to try to communicate the image of that slide to the subject who was sleeping at the Dream Laboratory. Nothing was said about the control subject who was asleep at home. The experiment was repeated each night of the six-night concert, with a different print shown each night. When the six nights of experimentation were complete, it was found that the experimental subject who slept in the lab, and toward whom the 2,000 rock fans had directed their thoughts, had dreams that closely corresponded to what the audience was beaming toward him on four of the six nights. The control subject had only one dream that somewhat resembled the pictures which the audience was beaming out.

Now, as Britt stands waiting for his team to complete the final leg of their journey that will bring them all face to face with man's greatest mystery, he recalls Maria's story of the simple experiment with the rock group. *The Grateful Dead,* he thinks. *How appropriate.*

XXVIII

The ferry is drifting very slowly toward the dock. Its captain has cut the engines, and the only sounds as the huge vessel approaches are the soft whistling of the wind through the boat's open lower deck and the sharp slap of the waves beneath its broad bow.

"Hang on!" Maria cries. She grabs for a rope that hangs from a rusted iron ring on a wooden piling. Britt is reaching for another piling when the mammoth vessel wedges irresistibly against the dock—the old wooden platform sways nearly a foot out of line and Britt falls to one knee just as the air is shattered by the blast of the ship's horn.

"Jesus," Britt softly exclaims. He slowly, unsteadily stands, holding out his arms for balance as the dock rocks back to its original position.

"Why, that was a very good docking," says Maria. She is grinning broadly and walking to Britt's side. "The captain could get into trouble with the Mafia-controlled construction union here in Messina if he keeps up that kind of good work."

Britt reaches down and pulls a splinter from his pant leg. He looks up at Maria with a question reflecting on his face.

"You see," she explains, "this is a *federal government* dock, and there is not much new construction here in Messina."

Britt tries to grasp the relation of these facts. His puzzled expression delights Maria.

"So," she continues, "periodically the captain knocks the dock a bit out of line. Messina's Mafia safety inspector storms down here and declares the dock unsafe. Then, according to federal law, the government in Rome *must* send funds to rebuild the dock—public safety, you know." She winks. "It is one of Sicily's ways of getting her fair share of the federal taxes."

"Hey, Britt!"

Britt and Maria turn quickly toward the ferry. A young

man is leaning over the railing of the lower deck which is several yards above the dock.

"That's Greg, there, waving," Britt points out to Maria. "The tall skinny one with the light blond crew-cut hair is Karl . . . and the short one with the oversized head and pointed chin is Dr. Hollender."

Maria giggles happily. "I bet they'd be real flattered to hear how you picked out their best features to point them out to me."

"C'mon," says Britt, walking forward toward the ferry. The main open deck of the huge boat is twelve feet above the dock, and as Maria and Britt watch, a wide gangplank suddenly juts out from the deck like a stiff tongue. The "tongue" dips down as if tasting the air and slowly stretches down toward where Britt and Maria stand. Greg, Krimmel, and Hollender step back from the railing where they were standing and disappear from view.

Now, like some strange animal cautiously sniffing the wind before stepping ashore from a fantasy ark, the low snout of one of the Porsche 917/10Ts appears at the top of the gangplank.

Slowly, at first, the sleek machine begins to glide forward. Greg's head is visible through the windshield as Karl and Hal give the Porsche one final push and turn and disappear again into the shadow of the cavernous lower deck.

The car picks up speed suddenly as the front wheels leave the level deck and start down the steep gangplank.

Maria gasps softly as the now fast-moving machine nears the bottom of the gangplank—it seems impossible for Greg to make the right-angle turn at the bottom and Maria is certain the car will crash off the opposite edge of the dock, which is only yards away.

Greg jerks the steering wheel. The machine responds instantly, seeming to turn a perfect right-angle away from the sea. The long snout glides quickly down the few feet of dock toward Britt and Maria and is nearly on Britt's toes before he hears the dry rasp of caliper pads grabbing hard on the disks. The car stops instantly.

Greg unwinds himself from the low cockpit and stands smiling in front of Maria.

"Maria," says Britt with mock flourish, "I'd like you to meet the soon-to-be-famous world driving champ, Greg Leland."

Taking his cue from Britt, Greg makes an exaggerated

gesture of kissing Maria's hand. Britt feels a strange twinge when Maria smiles at Greg.

Suddenly this scene is shattered by explosions echoing from up on the boat's deck, and the monstrous flat face of the team's diesel transporter truck appears at the top of the gangplank.

Britt and Greg push the first Porsche on down the remainder of the dock and up onto the cobblestone street as Krimmel in the driver's seat begins to ease the huge transporter out the opening in the boat's deck. He clears the top of the deck opening with only inches to spare. The gangplank creaks and sags as the heavy truck, its air-brakes hissing angrily, inches down the nearly-too-narrow incline. The turn at the bottom is almost too close for the long transporter. Holding the steering wheel to full left lock, and listening to directions Hollender is calling from his side of the cab, Krimmel eases the massive vehicle through the tight turn.

Now, the truck lumbers along the unsteady old dock, climbs up onto the street and stops there, its diesel engine idling with a heavy breathing sound like that which East Indian work elephants make when they pause after moving a giant log.

Britt and Greg clamber up the truck's steel flanks at the rear, and from its empty top deck they slide out two narrow metal runways to where the beams are just balancing. The two men hop down off the sides of the truck, run to the back of the vehicle, and gently ease the ends of the beams down until one end of each rests on the ground. Next, they push the Porsche around behind the truck and line up the car's wheels with the steel planks. A winch cable is now unwound and connected to the front of the car. Britt slowly pulls down on a handle which protrudes from the truck's steel side—the cable begins to rewind, pulling the Porsche slowly up the runways and onto the top of the transporter truck.

Greg wipes the perspiration from his forehead with his wrist. "I wish that ferry's first deck had been a little higher, Britt. We could have left your car on top during the trip over and saved ourselves *this* job."

Just ahead of the open section where the cars are carried, the transporter truck has a large steel storage compartment, itself about as large as a small van truck. Ahead of this compartment is a four-door crew cab. Krimmel is driving;

THE MIND MASTERS

Hollender sits in the front by the right-side door. Greg and Britt climb into the rear seat with Maria between them.

As they drive away from the dock, Britt looks at Hollender and nods his head back toward the compartment, while asking, "Can you get the film developer out as soon as we get to the garage in Palermo?"

Hollender nods that he can, but also he gives Britt a stern, questioning look, his eyes shifting toward Maria.

"It's all right, John," Britt says in response to the glance, "I'll explain on the way."

Greg only half-listens to Britt's background information as the mammoth transporter lumbers along. Greg is observing the road. In order to drive to the garage area which lies along either side of the race's starting point in Palermo, Krimmel must first head the huge truck along the narrow waterfront street and out of Messina in the opposite direction because there are no streets in the western portion of the city that are wide enough for the big transporter.

Dock street cobblestones soon give way to the weathered asphalt of the government-maintained highway which circles the entire island. The road is a Sicilian panic of cars and carts, people and animals.

"This is what you will be racing on," Krimmel announces over his shoulder to Greg as he steers the truck over the rough "highway." Greg leans forward and looks out the windshield toward the road that stretches out before them. It is not a "highway" in the American sense of the word. The Messina chamber of commerce brochure optimistically describes it as a two-lane highway. But there are no lane markings to support the chamber's claim to that width. In fact, there are no centerlines or curbs. The huge transporter requires so much room that there is very little road left for the tiny Fiats which come buzzing toward the behemoth truck, their lights flashing, horns bleating, and the driver's arm stuck out the window making obscene gestures. Always at the last moment, the little cars give way and drop one wheel into the gravel roadside as they speed by.

"Karl," asks Britt after such a driver's duel has just been acted out again, "did you see who you just 'chickened out' *that* time?"

"Sergio Alverici," replies Krimmel, unemotionally. Alverici had been the winner of the Targa for the last two consecutive years. He is favored again this year in his new Ferarri 312P. But today Alverici—like every other driver wanting to practice or to learn the course—must drive a rented Fiat amid the traffic clutter. Tomorrow is official practice day.

The town of Palermo can now be seen ahead. The garage complex parallels the road at the point where it emerges from Palermo. From there, the road runs straight for nearly a mile up the slight rise which leads directly past the front of the Benudo home. The road then turns gradually toward the sea and is parallel to the cliff edge until it nears the Castellum Mortis. At that point, the road veers sharply to the right and begins a treacherous, twisting ascent up the rugged face of Mount Etna. On the inside of that first turn is the slight depression through which the villagers have worn their shortcut to avoid that feared castle. That depression widens and lengthens as it stretches inland until it becomes the broad, deep valley which separates the towering volcanic mountain of Etna from the ancient town of Palermo.

Like blood gushing from many wounds, rust-red springs rich in volcanic iron oxides spill from cracks and crevasses in the brooding mountain's body. The streams feed the quick river that runs through the center of the valley floor.

The water of both the streams and the river is warm, heated by the fire that seethes deep beneath Etna's black, crusty skin. Vapors rising from the warm water fill the valley with an eternal fog that shrouds the treetops far below the plateau on which Palermo sits. At night, the fog often fills the valley so densely that a stranger might think it a level moor and try to walk across the misty plain toward Etna's distant walls.

Fifteen garages stand in two rows that flank both sides of the road at the western edge of Palermo. The garages are constructed into what from the back looks like a single common wall. Each garage is large enough to accommodate one team of up to three cars and to sleep six men on barracks-style bunks. The low, flat roof that covers the line of garages is considered the best vantage from which to watch the race, because from it one can see the start on the street below and then turn around to focus field glasses across the wide valley on the dangerous section of the road that climbs, twisting up, then drops dizzily down the angry steaming face of Mount Etna.

Sound of unmuffled Fiats driven by men practicing on Etna's danger-filled flanks is already drifting faintly across

THE MIND MASTERS

the valley and into the garage area as Britt and his team unload their Porsche racers off the transporter.

The garages and their accommodations are just as Maria had described them: only for men with oil in their veins. Krimmel has seen the garages before and stayed in them many times; Greg is so excited about his first international race that he would even sleep in the cars.

Only Hollender seems momentarily perturbed about the quarters. But his attention and enthusiasm are quickly captured by the sight of the well-equipped workbench area that stretches along the entire wall of the garage. He tosses his suitcase on the topmost and cleanest bunk.

In most of the other garages, doors are open and mechanics are preparing to tune the engines of their cars while the drivers are out practicing in the rented Fiats.

But the door on Britt's team's garage slowly closes again as soon as the cars are pushed inside.

The neon light inside the closed garage is cold and dull in comparison to the bright Sicilian sunlight that is suddenly shut out. This artificial light makes the room, and those in it, appear to be pale, blinking creatures from another world. Greg and Krimmel begin to unsnap the body panels of the cars. But Maria is watching Hollender as he assembles his portable darkroom on the workbench. Britt hands him the rolls of special film which Britt has exposed in the castle on the previous several evenings that he and Maria have spent visiting the castle.

"I'm going to turn out the lights, now," Hollender announces over his shoulder to Greg and Krimmel. The two men stop their work. Hollender opens a can of special developer that is labeled as racing oil. Quickly, he flicks off the light switch, plunging the room into darkness.

A few moments later, the lights flash on again. Krimmel returns to his task of removing the last body panel from Greg's car, and Greg lifts open the garage door again.

Bright sunlight gushes into the room. Its glare casts skeleton shadows of the bare cars across the floor.

Maria notices that the shadows stop at Britt's feet. Britt notices too. He looks at her and smiles. "Superstitious?"

Maria does not answer. She walks out of the garage and sits down on a sun-warmed stone near the roadside.

Britt watches intently as Hollender hangs up the strips of negatives to dry.

"Can we get going on *this* now, John," Greg asks Hollender impatiently.

The little man with the too-large head slides off his workbench stool and walks toward the clutter of electronic equipment that Krimmel has unloaded from the transporter's huge storage compartment. Hollender selects a box about the size of a portable stereo phonograph. While he connects its wires to the engine in Greg's car, Britt pulls down the dried negatives, places them on the back-lit viewing screen, and studies them with a magnifying glass.

Quiet moments pass.

"John! Look at this! In the last frame on this roll here! It's the last roll I took of the castle's bedroom balcony!" calls Britt.

Britt hands the magnifying glass to Hollender. The man stoops over to study the frame to which Britt is pointing. He straightens again slowly and hands the glass to Krimmel. Then Hollender says: "This is *it!* This is what we've been hoping for. Thirty minutes ago, when we entered this garage, Britt, I looked around and asked myself what I was doing in a place like this. But, now, here I am looking at what must be the world's first picture of a human spirit! Why, any scientist in the world would give almost anything to be here participating in this."

Krimmel leans low over the workbench. He is studying the negatives closely. "I can see the moon just barely rising over the balcony's low wall in this frame," he points out. "Are you positive that this glow which could be the spirit is not actually produced by moonlight reflecting from one of the lens elements?"

Britt's excitement suddenly drains away when confronted with Krimmel's sound, logical question.

Hollender takes the negative strip in his hand. "No. No, Karl," he dissents. "Look here." He uses a sharp pencil to point to seven faint pentagon-shaped outlines in the lower middle of the frame. "You see, there *are* some refractions here from the moonlight. But they are just where we would expect them—in line with and between the aperture of the lens and the light source. No, this white blur on these frames is definitely *not* reflection or refraction. Furthermore, since this whiteness does not appear in any of the other exposures on this roll that were made immediately before and after it, I would also rule out the possibility that the glow is the result of a light leak in the camera or film cartridge. No,

I am *convinced* that this is exactly what we had predicted and what we have been hoping to see."

"Okay, John," says Britt, "you've done your part for now." He turns to Krimmel. "Now—tonight we need *your* special skills." Britt looks quickly at Greg who is leaning over, peering into the engine compartment of his Porsche. "While we've gone to the castle tonight, Greg, you can get the engines in shape for tomorrow's practice runs."

Greg stands and looks at Britt with a pained expression on his face. Britt knows that Dr. Webster's son agreed to his father's plan only because it would enable him to drive the international circuits. Britt has resolved to leave Greg to his racing as much as possible. Greg closes the Porsche's body panels and leans against the car while the others pick up their equipment and leave the garage.

Early this morning, Britt had parked his tiny Fiat 850 outside the garage and he and Maria had then ridden the local bus over to Messina to meet the ferry. Now, Britt, Maria, Hollender, and Krimmel all squeeze into the little car. Britt guns the tiny engine and buzzes away in a cloud of oily blue exhaust smoke, dry dust, and bouncing gravel. Once on the pavement, however, the tiny car is incapable of such dramatic display and Britt contents himself with merely accelerating the machine as fast as it will go in each gear before he upshifts to the next.

Maria looks at him disapprovingly.

Britt glances at her, smiles, then laughs. "You know," he says with mock seriousness, "that I must make everyone in town think that we're just a typical group of racers going to join the madness of this unofficial kind of practice!"

Britt flicks the wheel—the Fiat heels over onto two wheels and roars off the paved road again and into the dirt courtyard of Palazzo de Benudo. The car skids to a dusty stop in front of the steps of the house.

Britt, Hollender, and Krimmel get out and go up to Britt's room. Maria goes to the kitchen for two bottles of wine and several glasses.

A few minutes later, when she pushes open Britt's door with her shoulder and swings into the room, she sees the three men huddled on chairs around the table. They look up quickly in surprise.

Britt has drawn a diagram of as much of the castle's floor plan as he can recall and the men are studying it. Each man takes a glass of wine which Maria has poured. The wine served, Maria leans on Britt's shoulder and plays with his ear while he speaks to Hollender and Krimmel.

"You can see here how at least this much of the first floor looks—and I really don't think we will have to search any further than that for our spirit. Tonight, however, when we all go in there, Karl, we employ your special talent to conduct a psychic scan of all the rooms. Maria, you will get the guard away from the castle——"

Hollender interrupts: "It may take Karl a couple of hours to investigate all those other rooms in a thorough manner. And if you want me to be able to get the really precise readings tonight which I need, then I might need an additional hour or so beyond even that. Can Maria keep the guard away for that long?"

Maria is amused. "There will be no problem," she says, "Ernesto always stays away at least until the moon sets. He sits in the back room of the tavern with his old cronies, drinks wine and plays cards. They do not tell the carabinieri on him—after all, it is only the federal government in Rome paying him for guarding the castle. In any case, he will be particularly pleased to leave tonight—last night was a nearly full moon; tonight it will be more full, and on the night after the race has ended, there will be a full moon. Ernesto will not return to the castle either tonight or tomorrow night because of the full moon. He is too afraid of the strange things which he claims occur especially on those nights. No one—not even his closest friends—knows that on these nights, soon after dark, but before the moon begins to rise, Ernesto creeps down to our house. Mamma gives him a room and a bottle of wine. Before dawn, Mamma wakes him, gives him breakfast to sober him, and points him back to the castle."

"Okay then," says Britt to Hollender and Krimmel, "we'll all stay here in this room until dark. Then Maria and I will go to the castle. You can watch from the balcony here in the dark. When you see the guard appear here at the back door, you come on up to the castle. Now, let's go over this layout." Britt smooths the rough-drawn plan with his hand and points with his pencil

"This is the bedroom. Approximately *here* is where I was standing when I got the shot that showed the spirit."

Hollender takes the negatives from his pocket and holds them up to the light. "Let's see," he says as he studies the frame carefully. He glances down at Britt's rough sketch of the floor plan, looks at it for several seconds, then points his finger to a spot near the railing of the patio. "Here, Britt—this is where we should begin to focus for an initial triangulation reading."

Krimmel has wandered away from the table and is standing now on the porch, arms folded. He stares blankly at the castle. The side of the strange building which faces Britt's room is already being swallowed by darkness as the sun slowly slips beyond the distant horizon. Krimmel lowers his eyes —the lengthening black shadow of the castle is slithering across the rutted open ground of the cliff top. The shadow is reaching out toward the Benudo home, sliding slowly, silently over the scorched black volcanic ash, coming irresistibly closer with every tick of the clock.

XXIX

"Britt?" whisperes Maria from out of the nearly total darkness. She and Britt are inside the castle gate and waiting for Hollender and Krimmel to arrive.

Britt walks away from the gate and across the narrow courtyard; there, he sits on the castle's steps. The moonless night is so intensely black that Britt could feel the darkness like thick, inky smoke brushing his arms and face when he walked across the small courtyard.

"Britt, where are you?!" Maria's voice trembles slightly as she speaks

"I'm over here on the steps, pretty lady. Watch yourself . . ." He holds out his hands to her as she materializes from the gloom, unsteadily groping, her arms outstretched. She sits down and huddles close by his side, leaning against his shoulder.

Britt suddenly stiffens. Maria grabs his arm tightly: "Britt! What is it?!"

A small noise has broken the stillness; it had not been loud, but sounded sharp, strained—like a distant, muffled cry. Suddenly the castle gate opens and two shadows move into the courtyard.

"Over here!" Britt calls in a hoarse whisper. "Close the gate behind you—and lock it."

The rusty hinges creak slowly again as Hollender closes the gate. Now, a dim purple glow seeps across the courtyard, providing just enough light so that everyone can see each other.

"Are you positive no one outside of here can see that light?" Britt asks.

"Not unless they're an owl," replies Hollender. He hands one of the tiny flashlights to Britt and one to Krimmel "It's my own invention. It produces light near the ultraviolet end of the spectrum. It's enough to see a few yards with, but it can hardly be noticed by anyone more than ten feet away."

THE MIND MASTERS [163]

Britt turns to Maria. "Stay close to me now as we head for the bedchamber."

Their cautious footsteps echo faintly in the huge main room. Centuries of grit and dust on the marble floor rasp beneath the soles of their shoes. Britt and Maria lead the way.

"Hold it, Britt!!" Hollender suddenly whispers.

Maria and Britt stop and turn. Behind them, Krimmel stands motionless—rigid. His eyes are squeezed so tightly shut that his face, bathed in the dim, violet glow, is weirdly distorted.

Suddenly, quickly, Krimmel relaxes. He gulps a quick, deep breath and says, "Yes, there *is* someone in this place."

Puzzled, Maria looks at Britt: "Didn't you already *know* —or *think* you knew—that the ghost of Marcus is here?"

"We knew that some*thing* was here," Britt explains as the little group resumes its gritty walk to the bedchamber. "Now . . . we can be fairly certain that some*one* is here. You see, Maria, some things that can be mistaken for psychic phenomena are actually caused by nonliving objects or conditions. Karl's particular gift, however, permits him to distinguish for us between what is alive and what is a nonliving phenomenon. His ability is one vestigial part of the ability of mental telepathy which all humans had at one time. For some reason—probably a reason locked in his genetic makeup —Karl was given back just *part* of that primordial human telepathic ability. He can sense when a phenomenon is a manifestation of an actual, living consciousness—a person. Without him, Hal and I could waste a lot of our time trying to set up our equipment to communicate with some phenomenon that might actually be caused by anything from nuclear radiation to sunspots." Britt stops walking. They have reached the bedchamber.

Britt turns to Krimmel. "Does it feel stronger in this room?"

"Yes . . . stronger . . . much stronger than in the main hall," the man replies

"Okay." Britt reaches into his pocket and pulls out a scanning device that looks like a photographic light meter. "Holl and I will stay here, Karl, and try to triangulate in on the strongest point in this room in order to get a wavelength reading on it. Karl, I want you to walk through the castle— up and down every corridor, in every room and closet on both floors. See if you can sense any other places where we might try to get wavelength readings and location fixes."

Dimly outlined in the eerie purple glow from his tiny light, Karl disappears into the inner hallway of the huge, night-shrouded building.

"Maria," cautions Britt, "make certain that you stay near us—but try to stay behind us and out of the range of our energy scanners."

Maria looks apologetically at Britt: "I don't mean to be a bother, Britt," she says while stepping aside. "And you have taken time to tell me in general terms about Mero Institute and your work for them . . . but could you also explain to me now what that thing is that you have in your hand."

"No trouble at all, Maria," Britt replies. He thinks a moment, then says: "If you could see across the bedchamber through this darkness, you would notice that Dr. Hollender has this same type of device in his hand. The devices are disguised as photographic light meters, like the kind people use for taking exposure readings to set their cameras by.

"Well, these gizmos here work on the same principle as camera meters. But where regular photographic light meters are sensitive to electromagnetic waves in the visible part of the spectrum—that is, to the electromagnetic waves that men call 'light'—our little special devices here are sensitive to energy waves in the extreme lower and *invisible* reaches of the electromagnetic spectrum, like invisible light such as ultraviolet and infrared energy—but far, far lower in wavelength. These meters here read electromagnetic energy in the same super-strong low wavelength to which the Mero film that I use in my camera is sensitive. That film is based on the same principle as common infrared film—only Mero's technology is more advanced.

"Hollender will stand over there on the other side of the room and move his device back and forth until he locates the direction from him of the highest reading on the dial. I'll do the same from this side of the room. That will give us two straight lines from two different directions that both point toward the strongest source of energy. So then we just walk along the straight lines that are indicated by our scanners—and the spot where we meet—that's the location of our energy source. It's a process that military and law enforcement groups have used for decades to locate illegal or enemy radio transmissions. It's called 'triangulation.' "

Britt turns from Maria and calls softly to Hollender on the other side of the dark bedchamber: "Ready, John?"

"Ready," replies the invisible scientist.

THE MIND MASTERS

For several moments, both men slowly move their scanners back and forth.

"I'm not getting anything," says Britt.

Hollender looks in the direction of Britt's voice: "Isn't your indicator needle moving at *all?*"

"Well, yes. But only very slightly . . . too small to get a reliable, steady reading."

"So is mine, Britt," replies Hollender. "Let's wait and see if Karl comes back with any more likely locations to investigate."

Hollender walks out of the dark bedchamber onto the fate-damned balcony. He leans over the low railing and looks down into the blackness of the bay. The waves far below the balcony are hissing against the porous black rocks, the water itself is unseen deep in the dead volcanic cone. "That hole could go all the way to hell, for all you can see of the bottom from here," comments Hollender.

"Did you find anything?" Britt asks. Maria is startled both at Britt's sudden question and the manner in which Krimmel now materializes beside her.

"Nein," the German mechanic replies. "In fact, the feeling became weaker the farther I went from this room. But I can strangely feel it here. I am certain this room is the best location."

The thin silver edge of the rising moon appears now far out over the sea-battered walls of the bay. Cold moonlight slowly seeps into the bedchamber. The sea shrugs and, like an obedient monstrous being, begins lifting itself up, higher and higher toward its silver master in the sky.

The rising tide surges irresistibly, compressing moaning water and air through the narrow opening of the bay below the castle. The dim light of the partially visible moon sets the ancient white marble building aglow with a faint eerie aura. Yet the bedchamber's growing luminescence contrasts with the stubborn darkness that will not leave the water-filled crater below. The blackness there refuses to yield even one glimpse of the surface of the cursed bay.

Maria shivers with a sudden chill. She walks from the cavernous bedchamber out onto the balcony. Again she stares as if hypnotized, down, down toward the sound of the surging waters.

Britt walks over and gently places his hand on her shoulder. "There's a ten o'clock meeting for all mechanics tonight, Maria. The officials will brief all team mechanics on the rules for use of the garage and fuel facilities during practice tomorrow. If Karl and Dr. Hollender aren't there for that meeting, it could jeopardize our entire effort. So now, we have to be . . ."

"Britt!" Hollender calls out quickly, excitedly. "I'm getting a much stronger reading now."

Maria and Krimmel move to the back of the bedchamber, out of range of interfering with the scanners. Hollender and Britt take up their positions again on opposite sides of the room.

"Yes . . . I've got a reading, too," Britt says.

The two men move their scanners slowly back and forth again until each instrument is registering the strongest measurement. Watching the readings on their meters, the two men now begin walking slowly, deliberately. They are gradually approaching each other but are moving out of the bedchamber . . . now Britt and Hollender stop. They are face to face near the balcony railing. They look down at the floor directly beneath . . . and they step back and aim their scanners down at the marble slab on which they had met.

The needles of the instruments quiver violently near the top of the scales.

"This is it," Hollender says fervently. He slowly kneels down. As if in a daze, Hollender extends his hand. His fingertips gently brush bits of black volcanic ash off the white marble slab. Dim light from the rising moon is now shining on the slab, giving it a peculiar glow.

Karl walks over, followed by Maria who is both frightened and strangely fascinated. The glow of the rising moon provides enough light for everyone to clearly see the outline of the stone. It appears to be about eighteen inches wide and three feet long. Judging from the thickness of a broken slab several feet away, Britt estimates the mysterious stone to be six inches thick and weigh nearly two hundred pounds.

"If this is really it," says Hollender, "chances are, since it's not integrally joined to any other stones, we could ship the entire thing back to Mero Institute. Then we could study it under laboratory conditions!"

Maria's flesh crawls with a chill. Britt, too, finds the thought instantly repulsive: "John, if this is the stone we're looking for, then it contains a human *soul*—a human *being*. We can try to communicate with it to test our theories and devices . . . and we can try to help to free it . . . but bring it back to the lab?" Britt shakes his head:

"A human soul for *lab* study?"

"I didn't mean it *that* way," says Hollender. "I just never thought about it really as a . . . a *person*."

"Never mind," says Britt quickly. "You're the one with the filters on your scanner, John—can you narrow down the wavelength reading enough so you can set the tuner on our communicator for my attempt at contacting the spirit?"

Still kneeling, Hollender aims his scanner at the stone and for several moments makes adjustments to the device. The others stand over him, watching.

"I don't know what the trouble is," he finally says. He stands, shaking his head. "I can narrow the wavelength range down quite a bit with the filters, but there is still some kind of interference that I can't identify."

Britt looks at him. "Can't identify?"

"That's right. I've never encountered it before. Or, at least, we haven't been expecting anything like this within the context of the theories we have developed at Mero." Hollender thinks a moment and tugs at his ear. Finally, he offers an opinion: "I'd say there is some element missing from our theories. You'd better code this information and wire it back to the Institute right away. Here are the readings." Hal hands Britt a scrap of paper on which he has written the readings from his scanner.

Meanwhile, Maria slowly kneels down. Hesitantly, she reaches out to touch the marble slab.

"It feels like a tombstone," she whispers.

Britt glances at Hollender. "Does this interference mean that we won't be able to tune the communicator and complete our experiment?"

"No, not at all," Hollender replies. "Contact will be more difficult because I won't be able to precisely preset the tuner on the communicator before you attempt to use it. I can set it for automatic fine-tuning within the range recorded by my scanner, but when you attempt to make contact by yourself, you will probably have to do some dial twisting, like with the fine tuner on a television set. I frankly don't know what your chances are of finding the precise wavelength—these are unbelievably broad bands."

"Britt! Look here!" Maria, still kneeling, is looking up from the stone—her eyes are wide and frightened.

All three men kneel down quickly to see what she is pointing to on the slab.

"Look at this," she says, outlining a faint, dark area on the stone with her long fingernail. "This dark pattern doesn't appear on any other stone in this area. All the rest are pure white."

"I wonder what it is," Hollender says quietly.

Krimmel places his bony digit finger on the large darkened area within the outline traced by Maria. He looks over at Britt: "It seems to be a bloodstain."

Maria gasps. She quickly stands up. Britt and Hollender rise quite slowly. They stand in silence, looking at the slab beneath their feet.

Now, everyone stands around the bloodstained slab ... all are silent ... thoughtful.

"Well," says Britt, breaking the silence, "it's time that we leave."

Quickly, they retrace their path through the dark castle.

Britt locks the heavy gates behind the group as they leave the courtyard and walk out onto the barren, moon-washed cliff top. They walk only a few paces away from the towering castle walls when Krimmel suddenly stops and stands rigidly still. "I feel someone watching us."

"Oh!" cries Maria and grabs Britt's arm. "Who was *that!*"

The three men snap their eyes toward the corner of the castle wall to which Maria is pointing.

The increasing moonlight is casting ethereal shadows which appear to pulsate in the blackness of the night.

"Did you see something?" asks Britt. He holds Maria tightly, trying to calm her trembling.

"There *was* someone there," she says. "He ran around the corner of the wall when we stopped."

Krimmel dashes to the spot which is only a few yards away. He stops abruptly and stares, body tense. Slowly, he relaxes. He turns now and walks quickly back to the group: "There is no one there now that I could see. There seems to be no place for anyone to hide, either. The castle wall runs right to the edge of the cliff."

"I'm *sure* I saw someone, Britt! I'm *sure!*"

"Okay ... okay, Maria. But maybe you just *thought* you did," Britt says gently. He looks at Krimmel.

The tall German is staring directly into Britt's eyes. "I felt someone watching us," the man says flatly. Krimmel pivots quickly and resumes walking back toward the Benudo courtyard where Britt had parked the car. . . .

Britt drives slowly back into Palermo. The illuminated clock face which hangs over the starting line that is freshly

THE MIND MASTERS

painted on the black road reads 9:55. The garages are completely deserted. The drivers, their followers and fans have either left for the nightlife of Messina or are at Palermo's only tavern—the Fighting Cock. All the mechanics have also left the garages for the race rules briefing that is scheduled for 10 P.M. in the town hall.

Britt stops the car in front of his own team's dark, deserted garage.

"It looks like Greg has gone already," he says. "I'll drop you two off at the hall," he adds, turning to Krimmel and Hollender. Britt reaches to turn on the ignition again, but Krimmel grabs his arm:

"Not *everyone* is gone, Britt."

All their eyes followed Karl's gaze across the dark street. There, deep in the shadow of a decaying wooden warehouse, a red dot glows . . . curling cigarette smoke rises silvery in the dim moonlight.

"Can you make out who it is?" asks Britt.

Krimmel peers hard into the darkness. "Ah, yes," he says slowly after several intent seconds. "I remember him from today as we were unloading the cars. He is with the French Matra team in the garage stall next to ours."

"Is he a mechanic?" asks Britt.

"I am not certain," Karl replies. The shadow suddenly moves and tosses the cigarette to the sidewalk. The night-shrouded figure grinds out the butt with his foot, then glides swiftly down the street and disappears into the darkness.

"He was certainly trying hard to look casual after we spotted him," Maria comments.

"Karl," says Britt, directing another question at the experienced mechanic, "why do you say you are not certain about him being a mechanic?"

"Well," Krimmel replies, "all the while we were unloading our cars this afternoon, that man was leaning over the Matra racer with a spark plug wrench in his hand. He was watching us. Yet, when he noticed me looking at him, he put the wrench on the engine and began to tighten the cam cover with it."

"That's not unusual," laughs Britt, "I've already tightened cylinder heads with a tire wrench!"

"You would not do that as a mechanic on the Matra team," Karl points out. "That team is sponsored by the French government and its operation is very professional. They began seriously competing in international races only a few seasons ago, and today they are already a top competitor—to do that requires the utmost professional care and skill. Yet this man's hands were not even hard—like mine!" Krimmel holds up his hands, fingers spread. The skin is thick and leathery from repeated exposure to gasoline and oil; the scarred knuckles are permanently black from years of stain. "That man's hands were like Maria's," Krimmel states.

"He could be a new man," suggests Britt.

Krimmel scoffs. "Ha! A top team does not come to a major race for championship points and bring an inexperienced mechanic. I say he is with that team for other reasons than taking care of the cars."

Britt rubs his fingertips across his lips, thinking. "Okay, look," he says seconds later, "you two have to get to that rules meeting." He twists the ignition key and guns the engine.

Maria is quiet while she and Britt ride home.

"What are you thinking about?" Britt asks her as he turns the car into the courtyard of her home. He switches off the engine and they sit in silence for a moment.

The clock ticks sleepily on the dashboard.

Maria looks up at the moon. The silver orb will reach its zenith in about an hour and a half—near midnight, then it will begin to drop until it is out of sight over the horizon . . . the moon, the cold, dead ghost of the heavens chasing the life-giving sun in a race it can never win.

"It feels good to have you here, Britt," Maria sighs. "So much has happened during the last few days . . . my mind is spinning."

"You're tired," Britt breathes the words softly into her hair. "Why don't you go in and go to bed."

"No, I really am not very tired," she says softly. "I just feel good being with you. Let's talk some more about your work; I was so out of it that night in the shack when we shared our secrets that I don't know if I clearly got all of what you told me."

"Well, I'll tell you what, pretty lady . . . there's still some wine left in my room in that bottle you brought us this afternoon. Let's go up and have a glass. I have some reports and observations to write about the occurrences of these past few days—and tonight. I have to encode it all in a telegram report to send to Mero. We can talk while I do the report— you might be able to help me remember some details of the events I have to report on."

THE MIND MASTERS

The couple enter the sleeping house and they go up to Britt's room. Maria pours them each a glass of wine.

Britt opens his briefcase on the table. He sits down while Maria walks away and flings open the French doors to the balcony.

Maria stands in the doorway, her hair catching the moonglow. She looks for some moments toward the Castle of Death. Now she glances at Britt. He is at this moment sitting and staring at her, his pen stuck in the corner of his mouth.

Maria waves her hand in front of his eyes.

Britt blinks: "Sorry, Maria, I was thinking."

"I hope that's what you were doing," she says with a little laugh.

"I'm convinced," Britt goes on, "that some factor is definitely missing from Webster's otherwise accurate theory for contacting the Beyond. Some factor . . . and I can *almost* put my finger on what it is—*almost*."

Maria walks over and sits down behind Britt on the edge of the bed. She lies languidly back on the bed and slowly stretches out her arms straight above her head. Britt glances up from his report; he can see her breasts outlined by the tight-stretched blouse. The blouse has pulled up from her shorts, exposing her soft, tan belly above where her short hot pants end. The lower half of Maria's shapely legs hang off the end of the bed and their weight stretches her blue pants taut so that a crease is formed in each side of the shorts—a single crease running from each hip, down and in, the two lines forming a "V" that meets between her soft, moist thighs.

High and deep in Britt's crotch that tightness flashes again. He feels an erection beginning to firm. Pushing away from the table, Britt moves smoothly, quickly to the bed and eases his hungry body down next to the girl.

Maria's eyes are closed.

"Hey, sleepyhead," Britt softly whispers. "Wake up."

Maria slowly opens her eyes. They glisten with sleep. Britt leans over and kisses her soft, sweet lips. He kisses them gently, longingly, and while their lips press and rub so moistly, Britt raises his free arm. He reaches across Maria's waiting body and places his hand on the bed. As his tongue probes forcefully, hungrily into Maria's warm mouth, Britt slowly moves his body on top of Maria's. Their breasts are pressed together beneath Britt's weight and he can feel her nipples erect and firm against his own. Maria's arms, outstretched above her head, are limp with desire, and Britt overlaps her delicate wrists with his free hand, pinning them against the bed. Maria opens her mouth more and sucks in hard—Britt's tongue flashes deeper, insistently into her. He suddenly lets his body rest on his groin, pressing hard against hers. Quickly, he lets loose Maria's wrists, lifts himself, reaches down and unzips his pants to free his hard, straining penis. Maria puts one arm around his neck and with the other reaches down and takes his passion-aching organ in her hot soft hand. Britt's body slowly sags down full on her again and he slowly rolls his chest back and forth over her breasts. Maria lets go of his penis and puts both her hands under Britt's shirt, grabbing at his skin. Her hips begin to move—first with a sudden, spasmodic jerk, and now in a strong, slow, steady rhythm.

Britt's mouth opens wide over Maria's open mouth, his tongue is devouring all her sweet taste while she moans from down deep in her throat and writhes beneath Britt's strong body. Maria's pelvis jerks convulsively once . . . and now again . . . instantly, Britt is kneeling up, both hands on her breasts, kneading them—he opens her blouse with a finger flick . . . her breasts beneath are red from his rubbing and her nipples stand erect, full and dark and brown. Britt slides quickly down between Maria's legs while his hands slide down from her breasts and catch the top of her shorts, peeling them and her panties off in a single, swift motion. In another instant Britt is standing, dropping his own pants, lifting Maria's legs as he kneels quickly on the floor and places one of her legs over each of his shoulders. Britt's hands slip under her hot, moist buttocks and he can smell the perfumed powder in her pubic hair as he places his mouth on her vaginal lips— lips even softer, moister than her mouth. Now his tongue darts in and out of her, in and out, massaging her everywhere it can reach as Britt devours the salty sweetness of Maria's hidden lips. Those lips quickly swell large and hot and slick and sweet as Britt sucks them into his mouth and presses them with his tongue . . . so warm and smooth and salty-sweet they taste. A sudden moan escapes from Maria's mouth and Britt can feel her fingertips reaching down, her nails grabbing at his shoulders, trying to pull him up from his knees—and in an eyeblink he lunges up, stretching his naked body full on top of hers with his hard, hot, aching penis sliding fast and slick and deep into Maria as her legs lift and wrap around his waist. Britt leans quickly forward with all of his weight and breaks the hold of Maria's legs—they yield, folding at the knee, up and under Britt's chest, so that Maria's knees are now almost at her shoulders. Britt slides his hands under Maria's soft back, his arms enclosing her legs, holding them folded beneath him. Now Britt begins to move faster—faster, punctuating his rhythm with deep, long-held thrusts. Maria is moaning more, more wildly—almost crying. She reaches above her head where her frantic hands grab the bedspread and pull it down over her face . . . she presses a corner of the spread into her mouth to muffle her screams. Britt grasps a pillow and places it next to Maria's smooth, naked hips and without taking himself from inside her, he turns her over so that her sweat-glistening, soft belly now rolls on top of the pillow and raises her rubbed-red buttocks at an angle in the air. Britt kneels across Maria's legs and tightly squeezes a soft, smooth buttock in each hand as he slowly moves his hard, hot penis in and out of her . . . in and out . . . Maria buries her face deeper in the wadded bedspread as Britt begins to pump faster now—faster and faster, harder and harder, faster and faster, harder and harder until he is now gasping for breath, his lungs burning, head bursting at the same moment that Maria screams loudly into the bedspread and her muscles tense and strain and strain more until suddenly she screams and stiffens and goes limp at the same instant that Britt feels that ecstasy of rapid, hard contractions between his legs and in his throbbing penis.

Several blissful seconds later Britt is lying quietly on top of Maria. Her soft, moist back is sticky against his chest, her buttocks so soft beneath the weight of his belly. Now Maria's body twitches and she moans long and low with pleasure. Britt can feel her vaginal lips contract around his softening penis . . . again her body twitches and she moans . . . seconds later, a longer, gentler tightening grips him.

Peaceful moments are ticking past . . . slowly Britt rolls off Maria. He lies on his back quietly for a moment before reaching over, gently taking hold of Maria's shoulder and rolling her over next to him. Eyes closed, Maria snuggles her head into the crook of Britt's shoulder as he puts his arm around her. She lies against Britt warm and moist. Her smooth, warm thigh rests across his penis . . .

XXX

WWWWWWWHRAM! . . . WWHRAM! WHRAM! WHRAM! Maria presses her hands over her ears at the instant Greg starts the engine of his powerful Porsche racer.

All up and down the row of garages, similar staccato blasts are shattering the morning air as the teams ready their cars for this first—and only—day of official practice before tomorrow's race. A flapping, fragmented cloud of frightened pigeons rises over Palermo's square and dogs and children who had been born after last year's race begin to yelp in fear.

The first car to leave the pits shoots past Maria—a bright orange blur snarling up the road until it disappears around the curve. Now another and another car blasts out of the pits, trailing streams of smoke and waves of noise which buffet Maria.

The back body panel cover of Greg's rear-engined car is open. Hollender is making final adjustments to the fuel injectors. Satisfied with his tuning, he lowers the blue aluminum panel, snaps it secure, and soundly slaps his hand on Greg's helmeted head as Greg sits impatiently in the car's cockpit.

While Maria watches in fascination, Greg pulls his skin-thin racing gloves tight around his fingers. And now, holding the small, thick steering wheel in his left hand, Greg reaches down for the stubby shift lever and shoves it forward. He glances quickly over his shoulder—Hollender signals a thumbs-up—the engine revs, and the car suddenly catapults away like an arrow released from a bow.

Maria can feel the impact of the hot engine exhaust blast pummel her like concussion waves from a series of rapid explosions.

Near the crest of the road, just where it turns right before the dreaded Castle of Death, Greg's sky-blue car seems to melt into the light blue horizon.

"Oh!" Maria exclaims, "did he go off the turn?!!"

All the cars have roared away and the pits have become

suddenly quiet. Maria's exclamation is heard by the mechanics across the road. They turn and laugh.

Britt walks over to Maria, takes her wrists in his hands, and removes her hands from her ears. She blushes, realizing how loudly she must have asked the question.

"No," Britt says smiling, "he made the turn easily. Let's go up on the garage roof and see if we can see him going along the mountain section." Each garage has a ladder that leads to a trap door exit to the roof. Britt grabs Krimmel's binoculars from the workbench as he and Maria start up the ladder.

The snarling sounds of dozens of race cars echo faintly across the wide, deep misty valley. "If I close my eyes," Maria says to Britt who stands looking through the glasses, "I can imagine that I'm in a meadow and listening to the buzz of bees gathering honey from white and golden flowers."

"I think you'll find," says Britt, handing her the field glasses, "that from here, even with these, the cars don't look much bigger than bees!"

Maria puts the glasses to her eyes and peers across the valley at the distant and black flank of deadly Mount Etna.

At first she sees nothing but the mountain, but a sudden reflection of sunlight on a windshield quickly shows her where the road is cut into Etna's face.

The cars are moving across the massive volcano's face like ants scurrying up a sand pile.

Maria has never before had an opportunity to see her island of Sicily from this vantage point on the garages. Now, aided by the glasses, her eyes trace the 44.7-mile section of road. Snaking through the twisty heights of Etna and the adjoining Madonie Mountains, the course circles the huge valley and then turns back, descending dizzily from the high-speed heights toward Collesano and then back to Palermo. The race tomorrow will be eleven laps long—491.7 miles—over this, the most treacherous road course in the world: the Little Madonie Circuit.

While the speeding cars are still charging up the dangerous switchback curves that scar brooding Etna's black face, Maria's binocular-boosted eyes are speeding ahead of them and along the road, past where it clings tightly to the sheer cliffs at the far end of the valley, and now to where it dips dizzily to streak briefly across a sandy beach before climbing again up a twisty rock-lined route through green pastureland grazed by small flocks of sheep.

A cloud of dust in the corner of her field of vision brings

Maria's eyes back quickly to the beach stretch. There, the sea wind is eternally blowing in hard gusts, whipping sand across the road. The combination there of speeding cars, blasts of wind, and sand-slick roads has sent many $50,000 racing machines into flips and flames.

"It looks like someone has gone off the road on the beach," says Britt as he squints toward the tiny dust cloud. "That's where the wings on our Porsche 917's give us an advantage by breaking up the turbulence and helping us pull an extra two hundred rpms."

Maria has already turned her eyes away from the spot . . . she is thinking that it could have been Greg . . . or Britt.

Through the glasses, Maria now sees distant sheep, which have been grazing near the road, suddenly scatter as a red streak shoots up along the pavement that knifes between the green grass fields. After passing this pastureland section, the cars cannot be seen again from the garage area until they have raced through the streets of Collesano and most of Palermo.

Maria can mentally picture the activity in Collesano at this very moment, for she watched the race there many times as a child.

She can remember as a little girl, sitting with her friends on the limbs of trees that hang out over the road. Small boys then—and now—tried to spit on the racing machines as they blurred past beneath the branches. And, to prove their manhood to their watching girlfriends, older boys in shorts and open shirts dash across the streets in front of the hurtling machines. In her mind's vivid eye, Maria can see the crowds today—the young married men with too much wine in their bellies gathered on the street corners to yell and wave their arms as the cars snarl past them, close enough to touch. Deaf old women pushing carts of flowers try to cross the streets, only to be restrained in the nick of time by the comic carabinieri who wave their arms and shout a great deal so the town's people notice their dress white uniforms which the chief of police lets his officers wear only on special occasions.

The commotion on the town's sidewalk contrasts with the sight of old men sitting, peacefully smoking pipes in upper-story windows of ancient three- and four-story homes that crowd in on the extremely narrow streets. Occasionally, reverberations from the blasting engines loosen a slab of plaster from the outer walls of an old building and the fragments crash to sidewalk in a dusty clump.

THE MIND MASTERS

Sicilians are stubborn people, and when it comes to relinquishing their roads to a group of rich, foreign racers, they often chose *not* to yield—especially in the rugged hill country where there are few carabinieri.

Even today while Britt and Maria watch—but cannot see because of the distance—former world driving champion Paul Virchek smashes his McLaren racer and his pride when he rounds a blind turn at the start of the climb in Caltavuturo and collides with a donkey-drawn cart loaded with sweet melons. The braying donkey disappears down the road with its arm-waving owner in panicky pursuit, leaving behind a steaming salad of brightly colored fiberglass and splintered wagon boards, wooden wheels and mag-mounted tires, all mixed together in a pile of cracked melons. As the laughing crowd watches, one of the melons begins to move ... the melon wears racing stripes ... and a sunvisor. By the time Virchek walks back to the pits, he is surrounded by a cloud of swarming flies that have been attracted by the sticky sweetness on his helmet and coveralls.

"Maria!" She jumps, startled from her concentration of looking through the glasses. Britt takes her by the arm. "It's time to get ready for my practice run."

Britt's car, too, soon roars away and disappears around the corner, heading for the section of road that passes the Castellum Mortis. Britt has purposely delayed his practice. Nearly all the other cars have now finished their first practice runs and are silent once more, sitting in the pits. The drivers are explaining to their mechanics about the conditions of the road and the way their car is accelerating, stopping, or cornering. The mechanics will translate the driver's impressions into different tires, harder brake pads, and a myriad of fine adjustments to the engine and suspension of each machine. While the mechanics work, the drivers sit together on spare tires or under trees and complain to one another how badly their cars are running.

At this moment, Greg is sitting on a sunny stone wall with a group of drivers across the street from the garages where Krimmel and Hollender are working on his car.

Slowly, everyone realizes that Britt has been gone too long on his first lap. Whispers are exchanged. All the drivers normally keep mental lap times on their competitors, but now they begin to glance nervously toward the garage where Maria stands watching Krimmel and Hollender.

Maria notices the other drivers looking. She, too, knows

that Britt is overdue on his first lap around the treacherous circuit. She is worried to the point of being almost ready to ask Krimmel about Britt's lateness—but at this instant, before she acts, an uneven, rumbling sound causes everyone to look back down the street toward Palermo's town square.

Britt's car is lurching slowly up the street, its engine running badly.

Britt swings the sick machine in toward the garage and brakes. As soon as the wheels stop rolling, Krimmel is unsnapping the engine cover of the car. Britt climbs out and Maria runs over to him.

"What's wrong? Are you all right?" she asks breathlessly.

"Oh, I'm okay, Maria," Britt replies angrily and loudly. "But this goddam car isn't!" The words spit out of his mouth. He kicks the machine's tire and storms away into the garage where he flops down on a bunk. He lies there leaning on an elbow, one leg stretched out, his foot resting on the floor.

Maria stands speechless for a moment by the car. She has never seen Britt so angry. She walks over to him.

"Can't it be fixed? Are you out of the race?"

Britt quickly turns his face away from her.

"Shh, Maria," he says as she opens her mouth to speak again. "It's all a *fake*."

Britt is whispering. He glances around to see if any of the other drivers are looking. None are.

"Somehow, we have to get all that equipment"—Britt points to an array of devices on the workbench—"into the castle for tonight. And by 'we,' I mean *you* and *I*, Maria."

"Is that the communicator?" she asks.

Britt nods. "Yes, that's it. John has laid out a diagram according to which I have to arrange the sensors in order to produce the best reception and transmission. I have to set it up that way tonight and then run the system through a series of check-outs. If everything is okay tonight, I'll attempt to make contact then. But the purpose of having a 'dry run' tonight is like the purpose of this practice for tomorrow's race—if anything needs further adjustment on the communicator, we'll have time to do it before tomorrow night, which is the night on which our records show the haunting phenomenon seems to occur most frequently.

"If the equipment does not check out properly tonight in the sensor arrangement that John has laid out, we will be able to come back here and—based on my observations of the problem—John will try to come up with another arrangement that might work."

"Do you really think you can make contact tonight?" asks Maria.

"That's hard to say," Britt replies as he stands up. "The phenomenon is usually manifest on the nights of a full moon. Tonight is the night *before* the full moon."

Krimmel is beckoning Britt over to his car again.

Britt gets up and steps toward the machine. But he stops and turns to Maria. "If I don't come back from this practice lap for a while, don't worry."

He turns again before she can ask him what he means.

The engine's roar once more now shatters the stillness of the pit area . . . and Britt is gone—up the hill, now into the turn by the Castellum Mortis. At that turn, although Britt has already disappeared from view, everyone in the pits can hear his engine sputter again and die. Britt coasts silently out of sight around the turn.

Hollender hurriedly loads a number of devices from the workbench onto the equipment section of the transporter. To the onlooking drivers and mechanics, Hollender appears to be loading electronic engine analyzing equipment with which to determine what is wrong with Britt's engine. Hollender climbs aboard the truck and drives out after Britt.

Now, moments later, the sound of Britt's engine roaring to life again breaks the sleepy quiet that settled over the drivers while they sat in the warm sun. Almost in unison, the drivers all rise again . . . some stretch . . . but all begin to walk, each toward his own car. The drivers inspect what the mechanics have done. They settle into the cramped cockpits—and now the air is again filled with powerful engines igniting to life.

Britt is smiling to himself as he drives swiftly through the sharp switchback curves. *It feels good to be driving,* he thinks. *How I DO enjoy the feel of a fine machine.*

Although Britt is driving quickly, he is not driving at racing speed. He feels strange. At this moment he is becoming unusually apprehensive. He reaches the spot where the road begins to grow more narrow and climbs higher up Mount Etna's forbidding face. Turns twist sharply around sudden outcroppings of black volcanic lava. Blasting exhausts from the morning practice session have loosened clumps of volcanic ash which have fallen to the road and have been ground into a fine, slick grit by the wheels of the cars. Britt feels his car sliding sideways on this grit each time he pours on the power in a sharp turn.

What a time to be freezing up, he angrily admonishes himself. *Here I am, in Sicily to investigate a haunting . . . even to try to make contact with a spirit . . . yet high on this mountain I'm suddenly being overtaken by a strange fear . . . a fear of WHAT, I wonder . . . a fear of crashing off the cliff? . . . a fear of dying? . . .*

As he drives on, Britt's thoughts are also troubled by the nagging knowledge of that important factor that appears to be missing from Webster's theory about earth-trapped spirits. Britt feels apprehensive, too, when he recalls the mysterious nonmechanic of the Matra team. . . .

Suddenly—there's movement in Britt's rearview mirror.

Britt quickly glances into the vibrating reflective silver surface and sees a black machine rushing at him from behind, its long, low snout is skimming along the black road surface, its flat, wide radiator open like the mouth of a strange species of vengeful shark.

The Matra is overtaking Britt's Porsche at a tremendous rate of speed. Now it is only yards behind and closing in fast—too fast to stop! Britt steps on the gas hard just as the shark-snout darts forward and nudges his Porsche, nearly lifting the machine's rear wheels. Britt's racer suddenly skids, but he recovers control with a skilled twist of the steering wheel. The snarling black Matra is now so close that in his rearview mirror Britt can see the leather-covered lumps of the driver's knuckles on the machine's steering wheel. The mysterious pilot's helmet reflects the afternoon sun with blinding intensity . . . yet in the shadow of his pursuer's helmet visor, Britt can only see black goggle lenses staring out like the artificial eyes of some diabolical robot.

The two machines roar on, hurtling recklessly up the dangerous heights of Etna . . . running so close together, the shrieking machines seem linked by an invisible bond. Bellowing and then screaming, in and out . . . on the left side of the narrow road, Britt is crowded by the sheer, black, razor-sharp cindery shoulder of Etna, by cliffs that soar into the clouds . . . and on his nearby right, the road's ragged edge ends in space beyond which and far below on the valley floor the river appears to be a thin silver ribbon that is glistening through the mists—a pretty sight were not Death on Britt's heels.

That idiot! shouts Britt's mind.

At this moment, Britt is driving as fast and hard as he can—his back and shoulders are tight and tired from the constant twisting of the heavy steering. But Britt knows that he cannot let up or slip for even an instant or the menacing Matra will hit him from behind and send both cars crashing like flaming comets into the mists of the deep valley.

Meanwhile, in Palermo, some of the other drivers have not yet begun their afternoon practice session. Some are sitting in their cars ready to roar out . . . others have their helmets in their hands but they all pause . . . silent . . . listening as the distant sound of the racing machines drifts into the pit area from across the valley.

Mechanics pause . . . drivers let their helmets sink slowly to their sides. Every one of them knows that the road on Etna's face is slick and dangerous from the morning's practice. Very dangerous. Very deadly.

Krimmel and several other mechanics immediately grab their binoculars and dash up the stairs to the garage roof. Even viewed through powerful lenses, Britt's car and that of his attacker are seen only as indistinguishable dots speeding along the massive mountain's thrusting heights.

Suddenly a giant red and orange flower blossoms against the blackness of the volcano . . . and in another instant the deadly flower is gone!

. . . And now . . . like faraway thunder, the muffled rumble of the blast drifts in from across the broad, misty valley.

XXXI

Britt lifts up the dry branches of the bush. In the darkness of the night the crackle of the leaves sounds loud enough to hear in Palermo, whose lights twinkle in the distance two miles down the road.

"Here, Maria," he whispers, "if you can hold these branches up now, I'll be able to pull the equipment out."

From beneath the clump of bushes, Britt drags the canvas bundle that he and Hollender had hidden there earlier in the afternoon. Maria and Britt kneel next to the bundle while he carefully unwraps it to check the equipment inside.

"I'm certain no one noticed you drop this here this afternoon," says Maria. "I know that *I* certainly didn't! I just assumed when Hollender came back to the pits after you had restarted your engine up here that he still had this equipment inside the truck."

"Yep. I think we got away with it," Britt says with a tone of satisfaction in his voice. He looks down the road toward the flickering lights coming from the garage area in Palermo.

"All the mechanics down there are working on their cars tonight to have them ready for the race tomorrow," Britt explains. "It would have been too suspicious to have John load all this equipment into his truck at this time of night and drive out here with it. He and Karl both have to appear to be working on the cars tonight."

"Where's Greg?" asks Maria.

"He and most of the other drivers are at a driver's meeting tonight where the race officials are briefing the teams on the ground rules for tomorrow's race."

"Won't they miss you?"

"No," Britt replies, "the mechanics in the garages will think I'm at the meeting, and the drivers at the meeting will think that because of my car problems today I'm still in the garage."

THE MIND MASTERS [183]

Maria shivers with a sudden chill as she recalls the events that occurred this day on Mount Etna: "Oh, Britt, that was so terrible. When I saw that flash of flame out there on Etna, I thought it was your car that had gone off the cliff and exploded."

Britt pauses from unwrapping the equipment. He looks at Maria who is barely visible in the moonless darkness: "I heard that they still haven't found out who that driver was in the Matra. Everyone in the pit area apparently went rushing to the crash site behind the emergency vehicles, and no one noticed that the Matra crew just packed up and disappeared."

"Was he really trying to kill you, Britt?"

"It looks that way to us, Maria."

Maria and Britt work silently, wrapping the delicate sensors for carrying into the castle. While they work, both Maria and Britt each think their own thoughts about the attempt on Britt's life. Maria, who still does not know the extent of the conspiracy which Mero Institute is combating, is searching her mind for conventional explanations: "Do you think," she now suggests to Britt, "that just possibly someone did see you hiding this equipment here today—just possibly, you know."

Britt pauses and looks at her as she continues. "Smuggling is still big and serious business here in Sicily, Britt. Our island has so many conveniently hidden coves and bays left behind by Etna's 'little children' volcanoes, that Sicily is kind of the smuggling capital of the Mediterranean. Goods can be off-loaded here and hidden until they can be transported to Italy, France, and Spain. Maybe some hidden smuggler saw you and thought you were muscling in on his operation."

"Yeah, maybe," Britt answers casually—but he is thinking more than "maybe." The smuggling explanation is very possible. *But what kind of smuggling operation would have the resources and sophistication to try to attempt murder with a $50,000 thoroughbred racing machine?*

Britt has fashioned a sling out of the canvas equipment cover. He carefully places the equipment into the sling. Now he stands and swings the bundle over his shoulder.

"Good. I can carry all the equipment in this rig. But you, Maria, are going to have to open those gates for me with Ernesto's key."

The couple begin to cautiously walk across the open ground between the road and the castle which looms massive in the still and moonless blackness. The moon will not appear in the sky for another half-hour and at this moment the night is so black that Britt's eyes ache from the strain of trying to pick a course over the rutted, barren cliff top.

Maria flinches in surprise as Britt's voice breaks the silence.

"I can't really answer your questions about the smugglers, Maria. All I know for sure is that we chose that curve as the place to unload the equipment both because it is close to the castle and because we knew that no one would be walking or watching in that area because of the fear of the castle. No . . . I'm *certain* that no one saw us."

"Then who's been watching us? Who tried to kill you? And *why?*" asks Maria. "No one even knows why you're really on the island—do they?"

I should have told her the WHOLE story of who Mero is battling with . . . now I may have to before this is over . . . she must be warned . . . "Let's talk about that later, Maria—here's the gate."

Maria had given Ernesto his bottle of wine when he had appeared at her back door shortly after dark this evening. She had asked him immediately for the key to the castle gate, but at first he had refused to give it to her. The old man told her that he was afraid for her, and pleaded with her not to go. But Maria persisted, and Ernesto gave her the key before he went to his room where he would stay until the period of manifestations had passed for another month.

Maria turns the key in the rusty lock and pushes hard to open the tall and ancient gates. She is afraid. Before entering into the courtyard, Britt makes one last scan of the barren stretch of ground which they have just traversed.

He suddenly squints and peers hard into the blackness behind them between the castle gates where he now stands and the deserted road.

Breathlessly, Maria hisses, "What do you *see!?* What is it?" She holds tightly onto Britt's free arm.

"You're trembling, Maria," says Britt gently. "It was nothing. I just thought I saw some kind of shadow pass in front of the lights twinkling up from the garages down in Palermo. It was nothing, I suppose, but my eyes reacting to the strain of trying to see in this awful darkness. Don't worry, Maria, there's really nothing to fear once we get in and lock these gates behind us."

"Are you sure?" asks Maria hopefully.

Britt gives her the answer she wants to hear: "Of course

I'm sure. Now, let's get to work." But he knows that he is not certain.

The heavy wooden gates close with a soft, dull thud. With his shoulder, Britt pushes the massive iron bolt into place, and Maria locks it with the key.

Once again their footsteps hiss down the dark, dusty corridors of the castle. Through the great hall they go and out onto the narrow, precarious balcony. Now the yawning black mouth of the bedchamber looms on their left. "Here we are," says Britt. He locates again the bloodstained slab and kneels down next to it. Even while Britt busies himself with assembling the equipment on the balcony outside the inky blackness of the eerie bedchamber, deep in his subconscious a howl of hate is building and waiting . . . waiting for something to release it.

Maria stands beside Britt watching him arrange the sensors around the bloodstained slab. She is standing with her back to the cold, pitch-dark interior of the bedchamber. Maria tries to concentrate on what Britt is doing in order to keep her own mind from returning to think about the evil presence which she imagines is again, even at this very moment, watching them from the cavernous blackness of the huge room behind her.

Maria's eyes and ears, her very flesh seems hypersensitized by the dread that pulses in her head. From within the black and unexplored recesses of the castle interior, Maria's overly sensitive ears seem to be hearing sounds . . . strange sounds she has never heard before.

Maria knows that she must distract her mind away from such unfounded fear. "Britt, do you think you can explain to me how this equipment works—and can you do it in a way I'll *understand?*"

Britt is tightening a wiring connection on the communicator. Now he finishes, looks up at Maria and smiles a smile she can feel but barely see in the dark that washes round them. "Sure can," he says.

"These sensors," he begins and points at the parts, "are similar to the electrodes that hospitals use on their electroencephalographs and electrocardiographs. *If* human spiritual energy is what we think it is . . . and *if* there *is* a human soul ensnared in the magnetic field of this stone, and *if* it does manifest itself on one of these nights of a full or nearly full moon—then these electrodes I've placed on the slab will pick up the spirit's energy emanations and transmit them to this device over here." Britt points to a piece of equipment which resembles a small reel-to-reel tape recorder.

"This," he explains, "records the energy impulses on magnetic tape. At the same time, however, the impulses also go into this device"—he nods toward a small, upright box which looks like an oscilloscope of the type which mechanics use for tuning car engines; in the device's center are two small green screens that resemble the round picture tube of early television sets. The surface on each of the screens is covered with a gridwork of lines. Britt flicks on a switch from the battery power-pack and the screens begin to glow like two green eyes. He touches another switch and a thin white line appears across each screen.

"The energy waves of the spirit will make the line of *this* screen"—Britt points to the screen on the right side—"move up and down in a specific pattern. Now," he says, looking directly at Maria, "the reason we had to come here last night with Dr. Hollender was so that he could use his energy meter to get a general idea of just what kind of pattern of line—that is, what kind of *wavelength*—we might expect to be emitted by this spirit. Even with the unsteady wavelength reading he obtained last night, Hollender was able to adjust this tuner here"—Britt lays his hand on a small shoebox-sized device which is connected to the oscilloscope—"to operate within that relatively narrow wavelength range. You see, this main tuner is like the channel selector on a television set—each human spirit has its own energy wavelength channel, according to Mero Institute's theory, just like each television station has its own wavelength. With the reading we obtained last night, Hollender set this main tuner to the kind of broad wavelength band for this spirit. So Hollender got us on the right 'channel' and set the fine tuner as well as he could to help us bring in the channel— the spirit, that is—as clearly as possible. The unsteadiness of the reading last night was caused by some interference which made Hollender's calculations uncertain, however, that's why we're doing this test tonight. If Hollender was too far off, we will still have time to go back to the garage and have him reestimate the wavelength. And we will be able to come back tomorrow night after the race and try again." Britt glances at his watch—in the dark, he can see only the green glowing dots of the numbers and hands: "Let's get on with this explanation. When the communication pattern emanating from the spirit appears on this screen on the right side,

THE MIND MASTERS

I will recite this phrase"—Britt shows Maria a piece of paper on which is printed a sentence of nonsense syllables.

"These syllables," he explains, "were designed by the main computer at Mero Institute to duplicate in one short phrase all the basic sounds that make up normal conversation. I will recite the syllables into this rig," he goes on and removes from the canvas sling a headset resembling the one telephone operators use. "The pattern of *my* speech will appear on the screen on the *left*. When it does, I will begin to make adjustments with the fine tuner until my speech pattern on the left-side screen matches the pattern on the right-hand screen.

"When they match, the spirit and I should be on the same wavelength—we should be able to communicate verbally!"

Maria forces herself to believe what Britt has just said, although she does not entirely understand it. "Britt . . . even if your machines do what you hope they will—how will the spirit make the *sounds,* and how will he *hear* you? He has no mouth, no ears."

"It's basic physics, Maria," replies Britt. "Speech is really nothing more than sound waves generated by compressed air which is pumped from the lungs and over the vocal cords to make the cords vibrate in specific patterns. A child's learning to talk involves nothing more than his mind—that is, his conscious Self—learning to understand the different patterns of air pressure which strike his ears, and then learning to duplicate these sounds by controlling certain muscles of his own lips, throat, tongue, and so on.

"Now, just think about that," Britt continues, "and remember how after you learned to speak in *words,* even your innermost thoughts were suddenly *verbal*. You cannot think without words once you learn to use them. Look at the trouble children have in school when the teacher starts teaching them to read 'silently' without moving their lips—at first, it's hard for them to do because their lips and tongue keep wanting to form the words that their minds are thinking. That is because the energy impulses from their young, untrained minds spill over and activate the tongue and lip muscles until the kids learn to control or modulate their brain energy correctly. Some people never learn to completely control that mind energy and they spend their entire lives moving their lips while they read.

"Even after the body dies, Maria, when the mind tries to communicate, the *source energy* it formerly produced to activate the body's speech muscles is *still* produced—the energy patterns of verbal communication continue to emanate from the spirit when it attempts to communicate. Now, then, what our equipment simply does is to tune in on that energy emanating from the spirit and then translate it both into a pattern of light on this screen so we can match it, and also into a pattern of electrical impulses that produce speech sounds in the earphones of my headset, just like electricity produces a voice from your telephone. The process is merely reversed for my transmission to the spirit. The result is that we—or anyone using this equipment—can talk to a spirit . . . one no longer has to have a special gift."

Maria shakes her head slowly. She already possesses some understanding of how radios and televisions work, and what Britt says makes sense. Still, she has an important question: "Why can't the spirit just communicate with you by telepathy—reading *your* mind to find out what *you* want to say, and then beaming thoughts into your head when it wants to say something?"

"Oh, it *can*," answers Britt as he turns his attention again toward the communicator. "The only problem with telepathy is that unless I am completely undistracted and receptive—which usually occurs only when a person is deeply asleep or in some sort of trance—or unless I am well practiced in the art of concentration . . . unless one or more of these conditions exist, the ghost will receive from my mind only a jumbled barrage of thoughts and feelings flying out from all levels of my conscious and subconscious. The spirit would not be able to make any sense out of the jumble, nor would it be able to insert into my stream of consciousness any words which I could readily recognize as having come from a *spirit* rather than from some other of the myriad of stimuli to which my mind is reacting at every moment."

Britt glances toward the distant horizon. There, quietly, like a silver cyclops eye, a nearly full moon is rising out of the sleeping black sea. The white marble of the castle begins to glow with a soft whiteness as the silver beams grow brighter. Britt checks the connections to the communicator powerpack and then switches on all the pieces of equipment. The reels of tape begin turning slowly. He puts on the headphones and waits. The white line holds steady across the green righthand screen.

Maria crouches behind Britt, her fear subdued at this moment by her fascination. She, too, closely watches that white line... waiting.

For several long minutes, she and Britt remain motionless... silent.

But the moon... the moon is heaving itself higher and higher into the black sky, and casting on the balcony long, sharp shadows of Britt's equipment and the balcony railing. These shadows are shrinking very slowly toward the railing as the moon rises higher in the night sky.

Maria stares hypnotically at the bloodstained stone around which and on which Britt has arranged the electrode sensors. As the shadow of the railing slips away from its ancient, stained surface, the white stone slab becomes washed with cold, silver moonlight.

Suddenly Britt whispers, "There it is!"

The line of the right-hand screen has begun to quiver. Slowly and slightly at first, but now faster and wider and taller!

In a moment, the line steadies into a strong wave pattern. Britt carefully turns the dial of the communicator's fine tuning device. While doing so, he also recites into the headset microphone the carefully structured syllable sentence that Adam has designed.

As Britt speaks, he continues twisting the tuning dial until the line for his voice on the left-side screen is moving in a pattern that nearly duplicates the pattern on the right screen. *Hollender has pre-set the tuner very accurately,* Britt thinks and at this same instant his hands freeze on the tuning dial: "I think I hear something!"

He pauses and listens intently: "WORDS!" he croaks in an excited whisper.

Impulsively, Maria puts her head close to Britt's so that her ear is nearly touching the headset that Britt wears.

"I think I hear something, too," whispers Maria in a tone of quiet amazement.

Britt begins once more to slowly, carefully twist the fine-tuning dial... searching for the precise wavelength and utmost clarity possible.

Maria stands stooped over, her hands on her knees. She is staring at the marble floor and at her own body's moon-cast shadow... this shadow slowly moves as the minutes pass on and the huge moon lifts itself higher into the heavens. For more long minutes, Maria alternately watches either her moving shadow or Britt while he adjusts the dials with infinite patience. Slowly, too, as the tense minutes are passing, the shadow of the main castle itself begins to inch out onto the balcony where the historic contact is taking place . . . slowly the brooding building's blackness creeps closer as the moon moves up above it . . . the shadow slowly slides up to Britt where he kneels, concentrating on his work. Maria watches as the castle's creeping shadow now swallows Britt and begins to crawl up her own leg . . . Maria can feel the darkness like a cold hand touching her skin. Ever so slowly the shadow inches onto a corner of the blood-stained stone.

"Damn it!" Britt hisses. "The signal suddenly seems to be fading, and I haven't yet been able to match up the patterns precisely enough to get through. I wonder what's wrong? I was sure I heard a voice . . . only it sounded so far away I couldn't be positive."

"But you did get something!" says Maria excitedly. "I put my ear up next to your headphones and think I heard it too . . . *something* . . . someone far away calling out in words that sounded vaguely Italian . . . and saying something over and over." She shivers.

Britt looks up at her. "Then you heard it too? There was a lot of static and something like a voice from a record that was being played at too slow a speed."

Britt glances skyward. The moon was overhead just a moment ago but is now out of sight beyond the high peak of the castle. The balcony, the bedchamber are again completely dark.

"Yes," says Britt, reflecting on what has just occurred, "there was a *lot* of magnetic interference that we didn't expect. I wonder where it came from?"

"*Now* what will you do?" asks Maria as Britt begins switching off the equipment.

"Well," he replies, "we'll leave the equipment here for tonight. Tomorrow night after the race is the night of the totally full moon—and the night on which the phenomenon occurs most frequently, according to our charts. Maybe tomorrow night the signals will be stronger and clearer."

"Do you think that Hollender can adjust the tuner better tomorrow morning?"

Britt is removing the tape reel from the recorder. "He'll try, Maria. Tonight's manifestation is all recorded on this tape. Tomorrow morning we will take the tape to Hollender so he can duplicate the signal on his screens at the garage. After studying it, he should be able to tell me how he thinks

I should handle the tuner when we return here tomorrow night."

Britt stands quickly. "For now, though, let's get out of here—I have to be wide awake tomorrow morning so that I can at least put on a decent show of trying to race."

Maria locks the massive gates behind them as they leave the Castle of Death. Across the desolate mile of craggy cliff top, the windows of the Benudo house glow warmly in the night.

Maria turns to Britt as they walk along in the mysterious moonlight and she asks: "Do you think anyone will be suspicious when you drop out of the race tomorrow and then don't show up at the post-race celebration tomorrow night?"

"No," Britt explains, "I've already established today that I'm having trouble with my car. Karl has rigged a cable which runs from the cockpit of my car back to the distributor. All I have to do is pull on the cable and my engine begins to misfire and run rough, like it did today. I'll just come sputtering into the pits and get out of the car in 'disgust' again."

Britt's feet crunch for several steps more along the blackened earth before he adds:

"Once the carousing sets in late tomorrow after the race, no one will notice that a bad-tempered nonfinisher has slipped away to sulk."

XXXII

Race day dawns a rerun of the weather back in '71—sunny, dry, and very hot. That was the year the Tipo 33/3-liter Alfa Romeos finally broke the string of Porsche's Targa victories that had begun in 1966. Although the Porsches have regained the Targa crown in recent races, the Alfa drivers with their new twelve-cylinder 33TT prototypes are hopeful today of another win. Their machines, painted in Italy's international racing color—blood red, were lustily cheered during yesterday's practice by throngs of fiesta-minded Sicilians.

The Targa Florio race is an important excuse for a holiday in the hard-working Sicilian fishing and herding villages. On race day each year, fishing nets are left unattended, animals unfed, crops unharvested. Sausage-eating, Marsala-drinking Sicilian families line up along the Little Madonie circuit that winds around the countryside. Donkeys, cattle, and old farmers in dusty black farm clothes drift toward the villages and vantage points along the course of the race—everywhere but at the corner near the Castellum Mortis. Families with overstuffed picnic baskets lie in the sun wherever a rocky pasture overlooks the road.

Amid the excitement and noise in the racing pits, Britt is almost able to forget for a moment about the coming night's work.

It is 7:45 A.M. Now, all the cars are ordered to the starting line.

In two parallel rows, thirty menacing machines soon sit snarling on the road. Their flaming reds, hot orange colors, gleaming silvers, blues and whites add to the carnival feel of this race day.

The waiting cars crouch tensely. They snarl like nervous circus cats waiting for their trainer to begin the act. Brilliant morning sunlight is flashing sharply off mirrors and windshields. At precisely 8 A.M.—this punctuality is unusual

THE MIND MASTERS

for Sicily—the mayor of Palermo walks to the front of the line of impatient cars. The short, rotund mayor is grandly dressed in a tailed tuxedo and a broad red satin sash across his chest. In his left hand he holds a large gold pocketwatch. He lifts his arm slowly skyward. His hand holds a gun.

Many of the spectators, surprised that the unpredictable Targa is actually starting on time, have been caught out of position—now they surge toward the roadside as the mayor's thumb cocks the hammer of the gun.

Maria glances nervously from the cars to the gun.

A sudden silence smothers the crowd.

As the spectators' chattering quiets, the rumbling of the anxious racing engines grows in volume until it is pounding through Maria's head in rhythm with her pounding heart!

BLAM!!!

The explosion seems to blot out the rumble. The air suddenly fills with billowing blue clouds of acrid smoke from burning rubber and bellowing exhausts.

They are off and racing! Earth-shaking blasts from wide-open racing engines shake leaves from trees and launch frightened pigeons wheeling into the air. Maria screams happily in unison with the crowd, although the roar of the mighty machines is so tremendously loud in the narrow street that she sees only many mouths moving and countless arms waving everywhere.

Greg qualified yesterday in tenth position, based on his practice lap times. He is the fastest of the drivers who are not factory-sponsored. Everyone is talking about his remarkable lap times, and he is sure to be a popular figure in the wild celebration tonight which traditionally takes place after each race.

For many Sicilians looking on at this moment of the start, the race will not go fast enough. The celebration *after* is the thing!

Britt has started in the second to the last row because yesterday he turned in no official practice lap times on account of his feigned mechanical problems. The only cars behind Britt are two last-minute entries. But Britt, too, is excited at this moment as he accelerates away amid the charging pack of thoroughbred machines. Britt knows that many of the cars ahead of him are there only because they have turned in *some* lap times. Britt knows he can easily pass them—and he knows also that he must *not*. Improving his position too much and too fast would only earn him unwanted attention. People would seek him out after the race to congratulate him. No, Britt knows he must drop out of the race in a very unspectacular manner so that he can drift away from Palermo without attracting attention.

The sounds of the start are echoing in the now-empty street. Those fans who have access to the garages are running for the ladders to the rooftop.

Krimmel, professional mechanic that he is, does not go to the roof; he will wait in the pits to be instantly available to Greg if he has to pull in with problems.

Maria, however, turns and dashes toward the ladder. She pauses at the workbench to grab Krimmel's field glasses—but there she notices Hollender quietly sitting at the bench. The tape reels are turning slowly on his duplicate communicator. He is concentrating on the strange patterns that are moving across the little green screens. And he is shaking his head.

Maria's fingers slowly unwind from the binoculars. Her hand moves away, leaving the glasses on the workbench.

"Can you tell me how that tuner works, John?" Maria asks impulsively, trying to occupy her mind with thoughts that would wipe away other thoughts and feelings that at this moment are surging again into her mind. *Tonight*, she thinks, trembling inside, *tonight there may be more than just a voice*.

Hollender looks up at Maria. He seems mildly surprised by her question, but his expression now changes to a pleased smile.

"Why, yes, Maria," he says as he switches off the tape-drive motors, "I think I can . . . in fact, I'd be *delighted* to try."

Hollender turns himself around sideways on his stool and beckons to Maria: "You'd better sit down over there on the bunk."

"I've got nothing but time today," Maria replies pleasantly. She does not mind how long she may listen, as long as Hollender diverts her thoughts until Britt drops out of the race. "Britt explained some of this to me at the castle," says Maria. "But I'd like to know the basic principle behind the communicator."

"Well, Maria," Hollender begins, "I don't know quite where to start . . . has Britt told you anything about my background?"

Maria shakes her head.

"Okay," says the scientist, "I'll start there then. I have a

PhD in quantum mechanics, earned it studying under Dr. Allan Minther. He was famous for his pioneer work in transistors, masers, and lasers. Dr. Minther was an expert on the pure forms of energy that are found at extremes of both ends of the electromagnetic energy spectrum. Minther specialized in the high-frequency end of the spectrum—the end that includes advanced lasers. After my college days I concentrated my own work on the low-frequency end of the spectrum and worked with advanced masers.

"I was not a model student under Minther and I never saw him again after graduation. But I did follow his career. Dr. Minther's work got a lot of headlines, of course, Maria. News media were—and still are—fond of reporting anything to do with lasers, which the media always describe as being the 'Buck Rogers ray guns' of the future. Well, Dr. Minther's work provided the media with all the far-out stories they could want. Taking up where the telephone companies left off with transmitting voice messages over laser beams, Minther developed electric motors that could be activated by laser beams."

Maria's eyes light up with sudden recognition: "I think I remember now, Dr. Hollender. Some years ago I saw a television newscast which showed a man flying a model airplane he had built. It had an electric motor and he was keeping it aloft by aiming a laser energy beam at it."

"That's right, Maria . . . that was Dr. Minther, all right. His development of that occurred just around the time that Britt was finishing his doctoral work. Minther's laser-powered engines seemed to have great promise for improving all forms of transportation by making them noiseless and pollution-free. For a few days, the newspapers were full of articles about how electric aircraft and cars were suddenly possible because the need for them to carry heavy batteries had suddenly been eliminated."

Hollender pauses and frowns. "Even the military was excited, Maria. They had visions of troop support and observation aircraft that would be able to hover indefinitely over battle positions since they would not be limited by on-board fuel supplies, but would get their energy from behind-the-lines laser beams that were aimed toward them. Dr. John F. Laster, Jr., director of defense research and engineering for the U.S. Defense Department, labeled the field of high-energy lasers as 'one of the potentially revolutionary areas' of new technology; and Lieutenant General William Frantan,

Jr., army chief of research and development, estimated that laser weapons would be available in a minimum of six to ten years."

Maria interrupts: "Did anything really come of all the talk?" she asks.

"Oh, yes, Maria," Hollender answers. "One result was that Dr. Minther was practically *forced* to participate in a secret government research program," Hollender says, then pauses.

"He was never heard from again," he adds.

"Most of the military research, too," Hollender continues, "remains a secret. But some quasi-military journals like *Aviation Week* magazine, have reported about details on laser weapons programs which range from surface defense involving land and shipboard laser systems, to offensive laser weapons on fighter-interceptor aircraft."

Hollender pauses and smiles: "Even hand-held ray guns," he adds, "are science *fact* today in government labs.

"But," adds Hollender quickly, "it was a *civilian* agency— the Federal Aviation Agency—that first tried to put a high-frequency ray system into public use as a weapon. Back in 1969, the FAA called on Dr. H. L. Teighard to head their task force for 'Operation Zeke.' The FAA was looking for a secret weapon that could be used on airliners to combat the epidemic of Cuba-bound hijackers they had at that time.

"Dr. Teighard's group developed ray guns that were mounted near the cockpit door and which could be activated by the pilot when the hijacker came within range."

"Were they ever *used?*" asks Maria. She is greatly fascinated by Hollender's revelations of current technology of which she and most other people do not know.

"Yes," Hollender replies, "they were used . . . but only for tests. The FAA decided that it would be too big a risk using such a death ray. Imagine, Maria—if one of a group of hijackers aboard a plane saw one of their group get mysteriously zapped, they might panic and destroy the plane, killing everybody. Anyway, soon after the FAA dropped its program, that hijacking mess occurred at the Munich Olympic games. Critics of the FAA claimed that if the secret program had been continued, the Arabs could have been stunned aboard the helicopters before they had a chance to kill the eleven Israeli athletes. The critics claimed that the portable ray guns might have even been used in the Olympic Village before the kidnapping ever got as far as it did."

Maria is shaking her head in wonder: "It's all so *fantastic!*

It's hard for me to believe that what you're telling me is documented reality."

Hollender grins wryly. "Oh, it's all real, Maria. But let me get on with this explanation of the tuner here. While everyone else in the science game was so fascinated by the Buck Rogers world of high-energy rays, I spent my time on what I like to call my 'Diet Smith Tactic.'"

"'Diet Smith'?" repeats Maria with an expression of puzzled amusement.

"Chester Gould," smiles Hollender as he answers, "has for many years had a character in his Dick Tracy comic strip—a guy named Diet Smith. Smith has learned to control magnetism, and Gould keeps putting in little plugs which proclaim to readers that whoever learns to master magnetism will be a master of the world.

"Well, Maria, I feel the same way about *gravity*. Whoever learns to control gravity will control the universe and all the life in it!

"You see, Maria, gravity is the strongest, most irresistible energy that man knows of. Gravity reaches into the farthest corners of the physical universe . . . and *beyond*. Gravity controls the movement, development, and growth of everything from a one-celled ameba to the mightiest of stars and all the galaxies.

"Yet gravity energy is of such a low electromagnetic frequency that it is only within the last few years that man has been able to detect his first gravity wave.

"Now, my own pet theory has long been that the source energy of everything—of all that we call 'creation'—will be found at the very *bottom* of the electromagnetic energy frequency spectrum. Absolute zero wave frequency is impossible, because energy cannot exist without *some* movement, that is, some wavelength and frequency. You see, at zero frequency, energy would be . . . well . . . nothing. The first increment, however, over on the existence side of nothingness, would have to be just the *most powerful force of all forces!* This frequency would be so immeasurably slow that we might say that it is *unchanging* and *infinite*—like religion's traditional concept of the Divine Power.

"Now, don't get me wrong, Maria," adds Hollender quickly. "No one in my field—and least of all Mero Institute—is seeking to explain God or the human essence in completely physical terms. No, the human spirit is like a beam of light, in that the spirit, too, is *dual* in nature. A human spirit is composed of both *energy* and *intellect*. What we are trying to do here is to contact the intellect by tuning in on the life-energy frequency range within which the spirit exists after death of the body. In no way are we attempting to unravel the mystery of even human—let alone divine—*intellect*."

Hollender pauses. He picks up a tiny screwdriver and thoughtfully rolls it between the thumb and forefinger of his right hand. "The intellect of man," he begins slowly, looking at the screwdriver as he rolls it back and forth, back and forth, "is something which I don't believe science can dissect. It is an inseparable component, with electromagnetic energy, of the entity we call a soul. Our communicator attempts to contact the intellect by tuning in on its energy. To understand the communicator's basis principle, you have to know only one thing about electromagnetic energy, and that is its dual nature, like the dual nature of man's soul.

"Because of its dual nature, electromagnetic energy can only be explained by two separate and distinct theories—Wave Theory and Quantum Theory. These two theories are alike in only one respect: in both, electromagnetic energy has an *associated frequency*.

"It is the Wave Theory which reveals the electric and magnetic character of this energy, and which shows that it is transmitted through space as electromagnetic transverse waves. Now, Maria, I'm sure that you learned even way back in high school about electromagnetic spectrum. The slow, long waves at the bottom end of the spectrum include invisible waves such as gravity and radio waves. The shorter, faster waves in the middle of the spectrum include visible light and all the colors. From there, the spectrum moves into the very fast, very short waves of invisible light energy, and finally into things like gamma rays." Hollender arches his eyebrows to signify a silent question to Maria.

She nods in reply: she is understanding his explanation.

"Okay," continues Hollender. "Now remember that Mero is concentrating its search for spirit energy at the lowest end—the longest, strongest wavelength end of the energy spectrum. What we needed was a way to detect those super-strong, super-low waves." Hollender feigns a smug, triumphant smile and says: "And *I* have found what we think is the way to do it."

"How?" is all Maria asks.

But even that brief question is unnecessary; the scientist is eager to continue: "With a special maser I developed,

THE MIND MASTERS

Maria," he says. "You see, a maser is an extremely sensitive amplifier of *low* frequency electromagnetic waves. Masers are used by astrophysicists and by the armed forces to do such things as detect the very weak radar echoes from planets, ballistic missiles and interplanetary spacecraft.

"Masers make practical use of the strange phenomenon of stimulated emission which was discovered by Albert Einstein way back in 1917. The maser represents the application of quantum mechanics to electronics. Quantum mechanics views all material things as absorbing and emitting electromagnetic waves in packages of energy that are called *photons* or *quantums*. Each time any material absorbs or emits electromagnetic energy, there is a change in the energy level in the material. When an electron in some material drops from a higher to a lower energy level, it *emits* a photon. We call that a *quantum jump* down. Conversely, when some electron *absorbs* a photon, it takes a quantum jump *up*.

"These energy levels exist at *precise* distances apart, which means that absorption or emission takes place at certain *specific frequencies*. Different materials have different ranges of energy levels for their electrons. This, in turn, makes them absorb and emit energy at *characteristic* frequencies." Hollender stops suddenly: "I can see that you're having a little trouble following me, Maria—let me simplify what I just said. This thing of 'characteristic emission frequency,' which I just finished explaining, and can be understood by an example—for instance: what is the color of rusty iron?"

"Oh . . . a kind of dull red," replies Maria.

"That's right," says Hollender. "Dull red . . . that's the *characteristic frequency* at which rusty iron emits energy in the optical electromagnetic energy range which we call 'visible light.'

"Now, Maria, normally a material emits and absorbs photons all the time and stays in a state of balance. Between any two energy levels in balance, there is a steady flow and interchange of electrons—this is *spontaneous* radiation.

"What Einstein demonstrated was that man could disturb the natural balance of things and make any material emit *more* photons than it absorbs! Something almost mystic happens when we do this—the material produces a strange brightening, just the opposite of a shadow! Scientists call it a *negative shadow* or *stimulated emission*—and there lies the point of my thinking, Maria, that led me to develop this maser communicator for Mero Institute. You see, one day it suddenly came to me that the glowing 'ghost' that is often reported at hauntings is in reality a *negative shadow* caused by the human energy trapped in some surrounding material and upsetting the material's natural balance, causing it to emit visible radiation.

"Now, see, we know the normal emission frequency for most materials, such as the marble in that slab up on the castle's balcony. We use our maser to filter out and amplify the emissions that are *not* normal. The 'added on' frequency we get that way should be that of the spirit we want to contact. We then tune in on this excess energy—and we communicate!"

Hollender is smiling triumphantly when he finishes. The look, however, soon fades from his eyes and is replaced with an expression of concern as he adds: "I know that it all sounds so logical, Maria . . . but it is *anything* but simple. It has never been done before, and the heart of our communicator is a new type of variable magnetic tuning coil which didn't exist until we designed and fabricated it at Mero Institute—then, too, there are a *lot* of factors that remain unknown in this area."

"I realize that," says Maria soberly. "Britt has warned me that your group is not even certain about the destructive tendencies toward living humans that a disembodied spirit might possess."

Hollender slowly nods his head: "Yes, that's true," is all he says further. Now, he turns back toward the communicator . . . a second passes and he is once again absorbed in his work, oblivious of Maria. She turns and walks toward the garage door.

Outside the garage, the race is continuing. Today's race is full of the comedy and tragedy that is the long tradition of the Targa Florio.

On the first lap, Sergio Alverici almost loses his life as his brutal Ferarri speeds along Etna's deadly cliff road. Alverici's Ferarri 312P is blasting through the cliff section approaching Caltavuturo—suddenly he is blinded by gooey gobs of guano falling from a flock of startled buzzards which had roosted overnight in the crags above the road. The car swerves to the left and grinds to a spectacular but safe halt against the sharp cinders of the mountainside . . . had the machine swerved to the right, Alverici would have sailed into space just as America's only world champion driver,

Phil Hill, once did at the Targa—Hill was lucky in a comic manner: his car landed upright, like a nesting bird, in a treetop that reached just below the level of the road. Less lucky, Alverici suffers two broken legs.

The race is droning on and the wine bottles are draining . . . peasant picnickers in the pastures now begin tossing empty Marsala bottles at any car that is not painted Italian red.

The village crowds, too, are growing more and more emotional. As handsome Alfa driver Marcello Ardente careens through the narrow streets of Collesano in his new 33TT, a young female admirer of his, watching from her bedroom balcony, tosses a garland of flowers down to him as his racer passes below her—he gallantly grabs for the flowers, but loses control of his car! The machine hits the curb and smashes through the window of Varianno's fish market.

Reports reaching the pits tell that handsome Marcello is unhurt and that the admiring young woman is taking him up to her bedroom to treat his bruises—and to repair his ego with an ancient remedy.

vvVVRAAaammm!—vvVVRAaammvram!—one by one by one the leading cars blast at this very moment past the pits.

Maria has walked out to the garage door to watch the colorful machines flash past again. On this lap, Greg is running in fifth position ahead of the Ferarri factory entry; Britt is now in twentieth place, an improvement of only several places from his starting position. Already, the race cars are strung out so that silent lulls of many minutes, like the slack troughs of great waves, come between the noisy passing of each cluster of cars. These lulls are becoming longer as the rugged course takes its toll. And the crowds are becoming drunker and more bored with the race. Even the gray-bearded old wine drinkers in the *Chiosco dello Sport* in Campofelice no longer turn around from their places at the bar when a racer roars by at 140 mph just a foot away from the grimy window of the *taverna*.

Maria, too, has ceased paying close attention to the race. At this moment, she continues leaning against the old wooden frame of the garage door . . . but her eyes are barely registering the orange and yellow blurs that hurtle across their field of vision—yet . . . Maria is *listening*. Her ears are tuned for that special sound, like the ears of a young mother tuned to hear the cry of her infant above the clamor of a noisy playground. Maria's ears are waiting ...

Suddenly—she hears it!

v-v-vraa ... vraaa ... v-v-vraaa ... vraaa ...

Britt's car now appears at the far end of the street. The engine is misfiring badly and the machine is lurching toward where Maria stands. Relief and excitement flash warmly through Maria's body. For Britt the race against the odds and deadly Etna is over. But ahead—tonight—lurks an even more uncertain adventure.

Britt's car has barely stopped rolling but Krimmel is already removing the rear body panel over the engine compartment. Wrench in hand, the German quickly leans over the red-hot metal heart of the machine. Hollender, too, has run from the dark recesses of the garage and now stands on the other side of the car watching Krimmel.

Now several seconds pass ... more cars blast past the pits and disappear up the road. The attention Britt's arrival attracted moments earlier is already fading, and the fans have mostly turned back either to watching the still-running cars or to drinking wine and necking, or to laughing and arguing.

Britt's charade, however, is acted out in full detail. Krimmel stands up, looks over at Britt and shakes his head in disgust while gesturing toward the Porsche's engine. Britt, still sitting in the cramped cockpit, now places his hands on the door panel and pushes himself erect. He sits on the back cowl of the car and rips open the leather strap that holds on his helmet. He drops the helmet on the seat of the machine, swings his feet over the side, and jumps lightly out of the car.

Maria comes to him now with a half-full bottle of Marsala. She hands it to him and he drinks deeply. And while he drinks, Maria is unzipping the front of his sweat-stained driving suit. When it is open to his waist, Maria sensously slides her hand around Britt's glistening, naked ribs and her lips nibble playfully at his throat.

Britt swings the bottle down and places his own lips— still wet with wine—over Maria's waiting mouth. He kisses her quickly, passionately.

"Let's get out of here, woman!" he says with cavalier flair. "Racing is madness, a pastime for fools! There are better places to be," he says and grabs a cheek of Maria's rump with his free hand.

Maria squeals with delight.

A few bleary-eyed spectators see the action and nod knowingly to one another while Britt and Maria now saunter arm in arm out of the pits and disappear into the crowd.

XXXIII

The Benudo home is deserted at this moment when Britt and Maria arrive. Maria's mother and all the guests have joined with nearly everyone else on Sicily in heading for Palermo and the other towns where huge fiestas will follow today's race.

Maria leads the way up the grand staircase. Britt follows several steps below; his eyes are focused on Maria's delicious legs and the outline of her naked body which can be seen through the short, thin cotton dress she wears. Britt can feel his penis hanging heavy as he walks up the stairs.

Together, they open the door to Britt's room and are greeted by stuffy air. The late afternoon sun is beaming brightly, hotly, in through the glass doors to the balcony. Britt pushes the hall door shut behind them and Maria walks toward the double balcony doors, swiftly pulling them open. The cool sea breeze from the Mediterranean floods in like an invisible wave.

Britt stands in the room, looks at Maria's body sharply silhouetted by the blazing afternoon sun. His heart gives a surge as his eyes scan the curves of her body. He quickly unzips the rest of his driving suit and lets it fall to the floor—Maria turns around at the sound of the zipper.

"Well," she says with a broad smile on her face. "What are *we* going to do!?!"

"*I'm* going to take a shower," Britt replies facetiously.

"Ha!" scoffs Maria. "Like *that?*" she adds, nodding her head at Britt's taut, erect penis. It stands stiff, large, and engorged, throbbing with each beat of his heart.

"Yes," he answers. "Care to join me?"

And she does. . . .

Afterward . . . Maria lies naked, relaxing on the cool sheets of Britt's bed. Britt, too, is naked and sitting at the table, one foot up on the chair and his chin resting on the knee of that folded leg. His penis hangs loose and satisfied, its head on the cool wood of the chair feels good. On the table are many pieces of paper—notes Britt has made after each evening's visit to the castle. Britt is studying his notes again searching for a clue to the mystery of contacting the ghost of Castellum Mortis . . . a clue to the feeling of foreboding that is tightening around Britt's skull like a steel band.

"That felt good," says Maria. She is looking at the high ceiling and holding her breasts cupped softly in her hands.

Britt looks over at her. *God! What a perfect body!* he thinks. But he only answers a simple "yes" before turning back to his notes.

"Well," says Maria, "if we're going to spend the rest of the afternoon here, I think I'll take advantage of that sun out on the balcony."

Britt now watches her stand and walk naked into the bathroom . . . her firm thighs and smooth round rump move delicately. She returns with a large towel over her shoulder and walks out onto the balcony where she spreads the towel on the cement floor and lies down on her back. Maria's tan body gleams golden in the sun. "I can see the cars through the balcony railing, Britt . . . and I thought I just saw Greg's Porsche go through that turn up by the castle."

"Well," Britt humorously replies, "you can bet he didn't see *you* . . . or you'd have seen him go off the cliff instead of around the curve!"

Maria turns to Britt and smiles happily. Now, she turns her face straight up and closes her eyes.

Britt watches her firm, full breasts jiggle a moment from the movement of her head. Gradually they stop. Only Maria's soft, flat belly now moves in and out with her breathing. And even that movement becomes slower and steadier as Britt looks on.

Well . . . she's asleep. Britt turns again to the notes that are scattered across the table top. *It's got to be here somewhere . . . I know it's important . . . perhaps it's the final key . . . but what IS it? What am I looking for?*

The hours now pass slowly while Britt's mind replays and replays each visit to the castle. . . .

The sun is casting long shadows at this moment as Maria's eyes flutter open again. "Brrr!" she says and sits up. Britt turns his head toward her and smiles.

"Why did you let me sleep so long!" scolds Maria. "It's

chilly now that the sun is going down!" She stands quickly and wraps the towel around her bare body. "Britt . . . listen . . ."

Britt listens.

There is no sound. No sound but the quiet hiss of distant surf.

"The race must be over, Britt."

Britt glances at his watch which is lying amid the papers on the table. "Yes," he nods, "it must have just ended. I don't think it has been long since I heard the cars last go around."

Britt stands and picks up the towel he had thrown over the back of his chair. He is wrapping the towel around his hips as he walks over onto the balcony. He stops close beside Maria and looks over toward the curve by the castle. "They should be coming by on the victory lap soon," he says.

Side by side, their warm, young thighs touching, Britt and Maria wait. The cars that finished today's race will soon pass. They will drive this final victory lap around the course in single file, both to indicate the order in which they had completed the race and to show straggling spectators that the race is ended and the fiestas will soon begin.

The slow rumble of powerful engines now precedes the cars up the road.

First to pass through the distant curve is a red Alfa 33TT. In his right hand, the driver holds a checkered flag that snaps smartly in the breeze.

Of the thirty machines which had started the race, only eleven have finished the brutal contest. The runners-up pass one by one after the winner.

"Well, that's good," says Britt as he watches a low blue machine disappear around the turn near Castellum Mortis. "Greg seems to have finished in sixth place. That should make him popular at all the partying tonight. No one will even miss sulking ol' St. Vincent."

Britt turns his head and looks across the valley. In the pale, fading sunlight, he and Maria can see many small groups of people, all moving in the direction of Palermo. The tiny groups, like small streams, join together at intersections and pathways to become wider streams, rivers of humanity moving through the gathering dusk.

Britt and Maria stand silent on the balcony. At this moment they are watching the sun sink . . . and the castle's shadow reach out for them.

The twilight now is dimming into a purple glow, and, like the last drop of water in a basin which trickles toward the drain, the final few spectators are straggling in from the countryside and descending toward the growing sounds of celebration which echo up from Palermo.

"I'd better get dressed," says Maria quietly. She pecks a kiss on Britt's cheek and goes into the room.

Britt leans against the cement railing of the balcony. The cement is warm against his leg and the warmth feels good. There is a sea chill in the air now that the sun has set.

The first stars are already twinkling quietly in the darkening sky.

A mile down the road, Britt now sees the fiesta lights of Palermo duplicate the twinkle of the stars and toss skyward ever-growing sounds of laughter and music.

But a mile up the now invisible road, the massive blackness of the Castle of Death sits solidly on the cliff top and remains surrounded by sullen silence.

Maria goes downstairs to the kitchen to prepare a meal for herself and Britt while he dresses.

Minutes tick quietly away.

Maria returns with sandwiches and wine. She places a glass and plate in front of Britt and sits down. They eat in silence.

Britt is studying his notes again and again, trying to find that clue which he knows is there. Occasionally, Britt looks up at Maria and smiles apologetically for his preoccupation with the notes. She smiles and nods, for she knows the importance of his finding that missing factor. Without it, they might not make contact on this final night—worse: there is a chance they both might be walking into unpredicted danger.

Maria now cleans the table and takes the dishes downstairs to the kitchen.

More minutes pass into unrecoverable eternity. . . .

Now, again, Maria is sitting on Britt's bed, reading. Suddenly he slams his pencil on the table.

With understanding, Maria looks at him. Britt's elbows are folded on the papers that lie scattered across the table. He seems to be listening to the happy sounds drifting up from the village.

"I can't find it," Britt says at last and turns toward Maria. "Remember—you don't have to go with me tonight."

Maria glances at her watch. "The moon will be rising soon. Shouldn't we be leaving now?"

XXXIV

At this moment, the castle's bulk is cutting off all sounds from Palermo. Maria and Britt are kneeling next to the bloodstained slab on the balcony. They can hear only the hissing of the unseen surf in the bay far below.

Britt is concerned as he checks his equipment. "Hollender couldn't figure out this interference pattern," he remarks while he recalibrates the fine tuner.

Maria is kneeling beside Britt and watching him work.

"He could only suggest a slight adjustment along this same wavelength," he says, "and to have a try at using this filter." Britt takes a tiny circuit board from his shirt pocket and with masking tape secures it to the top of the tuner. Now, cutting a piece of wire from a roll in the sling, he begins to connect the filter circuitry to the tuner. While he is working, Britt explains the filter device to Maria: "One of our astrophysics men at Mero Institute helped design and develop the radio telescopes with which the first quasars were discovered . . ." Britt pauses when he notices the expression on Maria's face, although her features are barely visible in the enveloping darkness of the night.

Maria is looking at Britt with eyebrows lifted as an apologetic indication that she doesn't know what he is talking about.

Britt smiles at her expression and proceeds to clarify things as he turns back to wiring the filter: "Quasars, Maria, are 'objects' in deep space—millions and trillions of light-years from our solar system. No one has yet *seen* a quasar—in fact, some may not be visible even if we were standing right next to them. We only know of their existence because of the energy waves they transmit." He pauses and looks into Maria's barely visible eyes. "That energy is so great that it is almost beyond human comprehension."

"If quasars are *invisible*," asks Maria, "how can scientists see them with a telescope?"

Britt smiles again.

"A radio telescope, Maria, is not like the kind of telescope that you have in mind. A radio 'telescope' has no lenses, it is simply a huge antenna which receives energy waves from space. The bigger the antenna, the more precisely it can focus on—that is, tune in on—deep-space energy sources."

"Why do scientists study these quasars, Britt?" Maria is asking questions to prevent her mind from thinking about the sudden dread she feels at this instant—a feeling like an icy draft blowing over her soul.

"Well, Maria . . . all matter . . . all life," Britt explains as he works, "seems to be some form of *energy*. Einstein's theory of relativity states that everything—rocks, trees, birds, boats, people—is made of energy. Solid objects are energy that is structured into specific *patterns* . . . into specific *atomic structures*, such as the atom structure of wood or iron—or flesh. Every*thing's*, every*one's* atomic structure is merely energy magnetically or gravitationally bound together so tightly that the energy is compressed into solid matter that we know as atomic particles."

"That sounds fantastic!" says Maria. "Is Einstein's theory correct?"

Britt pauses a moment in wiring the filter into the fine tuner. He cocks an eyebrow and casts a glance at Maria whose form is hovering in the darkness: "Ask the people of Hiroshima and Nagasaki what happens when man *splits* an atom—when man interrupts and destroys the mutual electromagnetic attraction of the atom's protons and neurons so that the solid atom can change back to pure energy."

"Oh," Maria says softly. She now understands how right Einstein had been.

"Well," Britt continues, "getting back to quasars . . . the unbelievable energy they produce seems to go beyond what can even be explained by Einstein's theory. Learning how and why their energy is produced will give us greater insight into understanding the energy laws that are the basis for everything. *That's* why men study quasars.

"Now—this particular type of filter circuit," Britt says, pointing to the device that he is wiring, "was developed by the Mero lab for use on those radio telescopes. The filters help remove interfering energy waves from other stars and planets—'tune out,' so to speak, their energy emissions so that the radio telescopes can better tune in on the distant quasar emissions. Neither Hollender nor I know exactly what

THE MIND MASTERS

is causing the interference which our communicator is picking up here in the castle, but Hollender feels that this circuitry *might* be able to filter it out. Each one of these printed circuits on the filter board can filter out a different range of interfering waves. By connecting them to our tuner either singly or in groups, I can produce hundreds of different combinations of wave filters—if we're lucky during tonight's manifestation, I might hit on the right combination. It's a long shot, but it's our only chance."

Now Britt falls silent. He concentrates on attaching the last of the tiny wires of the filter onto the communicator. Maria stands up.

Suddenly Maria grabs his shoulder.

"What is it, Maria?"

"Oh," she sighs, indicating a release of tension. Her eyes are turned, peering behind her into the huge, dark bedchamber. Her grip relaxes on Britt's shoulder. "Sorry to have grabbed you like that, Britt . . . I can see now that it is only my shadow forming inside on the back wall of the bedchamber. For a second, I thought I saw someone standing there."

Britt, still kneeling by the communicator, glances back into the room. Now, he turns to look out over the low wall of the balcony. There, far out on the sea's horizon, the full moon is quietly rising; the first light from its silvery surface is causing a faint glow in the bedchamber and is casting Maria's shadow faintly on the wall.

Britt turns his attention back to the communicator. He flicks on the power to the units.

The huge moon now is rising higher, growing larger. As Maria watches the smiling face that appears on the skull-like satellite, its silent, silver glow appears to her to be throbbing like a huge, cold heart.

Maria is leaning against the low railing of the balcony and gazing hypnotically at the grinning ghost-white face formed by the dead lunar craters—a strange dizziness grows again in her head as she stares skyward. Now she leans forward over the railing, trying to keep her balance. A numbness permeates her mind. Without any concern for the danger, Maria leans out farther over the nothingness below her, but the hissing surf, invisible in the darkness far below, now seems suddenly so loud, so close . . . and Maria knows that all she need do is reach her hand down a little more . . . a little more . . . to feel the cool bubbles on her fingers . . .

"Maria!"

Britt catches her by her arm and steadies her.

"Maria? Maria, are you all right?"

"Oh!" Maria is startled. She feels weak, unsteady.

"Yes, Britt . . . I'm okay . . . just a little dizzy, I guess . . . must be the strain of the day."

"My God, Maria. That's the second time you've scared the hell out of me on this balcony! You were just about to tumble over that railing!

"Here." Britt takes Maria by the arm and leads her back away from the railing and into the shadowy bedchamber.

"Now *stand* there . . . and stay away from that railing."

Britt kneels down again and places the earphones on his head. His back is turned from Maria. Britt glances at the dials and sets the tapes in motion with a flick of a switch. Now he again leans over the bloodstained stone, re-positions the electrodes and—*listens*.

Maria is feeling more unsteady while she watches Britt.

The minutes are passing. The moon is rising steadily higher; the shadows of Britt and his equipment and the balcony railing slowly slide toward the sea.

At this moment, the moonlight once again touches the ancient bloodstained slab.

"There he is again!" whispers Britt excitedly.

The white line on his communicator's right-hand screen has begun to surge again, its pattern moves rapidly at first, but now it settles down to the same pattern as the night before. Britt is concentrating intently on the tuner. Over and over, he repeats the lab-designed syllable phrase into his microphone while he carefully turns the tuning dials, trying vainly to duplicate the spirit's pattern, a pattern that suddenly grows stronger than last night! All shadow is gone from the marble slab now—and the communicator pattern grows even stronger—more rapid, more insistent!

Maria glances first at the dancing line on the green glowing screen . . . now she looks down again at the moonlit white slab . . . back and forth . . . back and forth . . . faster and faster . . . her eyes are moving so rapidly that the moonglow on the slab begins pulsing in rhythm with the line on the screen . . . pulsing, pulsing . . . faster, faster . . . the hissing of the surf begins to sound like someone whispering . . . Maria's flesh turns suddenly cold—so cold her body seems frozen, too cold to move. Her fingers ache and her arms become like leaden limbs. She tries to reach out her hand

for Britt, who is still kneeling with his back toward her . . .
but she cannot breath, cannot force her frozen jaws to open
and call out. Maria feels herself suffocating inside her own
body . . . the whole world around her is pulsing . . . rapidly
moving in and out to the frantic rhythm of her pounding,
straining heart . . . her frenzied, suffocating mind now sees
—imagines!?!—that a figure cloaked in blackness is materializing from the dark depths of the bedchamber . . . Maria's
mind screams in deafening silence, unable to open her body's
terror-frozen jaws . . . she aches everywhere with the cold!

But now . . . now, everything is becoming quiet inside her
head . . . the blackness, cold, like seawater, now swirls
around her . . . she sinks into it . . . forever.

XXXV

"Krimmel! Krimmel!" Hollender is shouting over the commotion rising from the drunken, happy mob of revelers who are surging around him in the crowded town square of Palermo. "What is it, Karl?"

Hollender's question is unanswered, however, before the irresistible tide of merrymakers sweeps him and Greg away in a jostling, joking flood of wine-soaked humanity. But Krimmel stands firm, the bodies of the boisterous flood parting around him like river waters yielding to a stolid bridge foundation. The German's craggy features are frozen granite-hard ... those of the crowd around Krimmel who are sober enough to notice him see a man who seems to be in that crowded square in body only ... his mind reaching out to another place ... another reality.

But now, Krimmel begins to walk ... slowly at first, like a hunting eagle locating its prey ... now faster! He moves with long, deliberate strides. The sardine-packed crowd melts away before him and closes in again behind as he passes. Krimmel's blue eyes glint—they are rigid and fixed on some point beyond the noisy square, something beyond the deserted north streets of the town ... something invisible in the blackness far out on the cliffs.

Out of the noisy, bright-lit square Krimmel moves ... onto the dark, deserted street that knifes northeast through the town ... now he is running stiffly past the eerily quiet garages and the dead and silent machines. Krimmel is running like a machine himself, his large limbs picking up momentum like a locomotive, his footsteps pounding with muffled impact on the still-hot, soft tar surface of the dark and empty road.

Now he passes the night-hidden hulk of the Benudo home ... his steps crunch on the volcanic surface of the barren cliff top ... now the black bulk of the massive castle looms in the faint light of the rising moon.

THE MIND MASTERS

The castle's high, thick wooden gates are ajar, but Krimmel senses that something is waiting for him—so, without a break in his running stride, the uncanny German dives through the narrow opening . . . in an eyeblink he shoulder-rolls on the cindery courtyard and is on his feet again just as the huge beams of the gate explode almost noiselessly outward, the heavy wood smashed into a shower of spear-like splinters. A body tumbles out of the black mouth of the castle and rolls limply down the steps.

Now, even before that body stops rolling, Krimmel launches himself toward the entry. The body, arms outstretched, lies face up and sprawled across the steps. Krimmel stops and looks down: in the darkness of the castle shadow, a small scar on the skull faintly shows, glistening, silver flesh in the growing moonlight.

. . . creeeee . . .

Even before this small sound is made by the hinges of the door on Ernesto's shack, Krimmel is turning around—prepared for this second cyborg. The wily German had paused there purposely on those steps to draw the cyborg from his hiding place, and now Krimmel has timed his move to the last nanosecond . . . Krimmel is barely turned away from the cold corpse when the other's eyes flash from the blackness and Krimmel feels the heavy pressure of the psychokinetic blast bulge narrowly by his own head—the death-giving engery wave barrels into the archway of the castle entry and explodes the huge stones, sending pieces flying in all directions. The entire structure of the castle shudders like a giant boxer who has received a crashing body blow. And a large marble block falls out of the top of the archway, striking the steps with an earthshaking thud at the same instant that the second cyborg's life-drained body hits hard on the courtyard tiles.

And now again the goliath castle trembles . . . a split shoots across the entire front of the building, leaving a jagged trail like a black lightning bolt in the once-solid stones.

Krimmel now leaps into the mouth of the dying castle of death. His special senses are telling him that there are no more cyborgs in the courtyard—but that more are inside the building. *Must find Britt and Maria . . . must warn them,* thinks Krimmel as he runs down the long, dark, dusty hallway . . . around him Krimmel hears the death cries of the stones in this black heart of the building . . . they are grinding, twisting . . .

XXXVI

My God! What's wrong with me? Britt asks himself as he walks back toward the balcony from where he has just placed Maria in the bedchamber. *OH SHIT!!! What a feeling is coming over me! I . . . I could just KILL somebody!!!* Now Britt's fingers stretch out stiffly . . . then curl tautly closed like claws. He kneels down on the balcony next to his communicator. His muscles are aching, tense and twisting. His conscious mind is drowning in an internal flood of raging passion, of hate—of a *tremendous* hate that is surging with electric energy throughout his body.

Suddenly, through this cloud of passion, Britt feels a tightness in his chest, a shortness of breath! He tries to inhale, but his lungs and chest will not respond! It is as if the muscles of his ribs have suddenly become paralyzed. His ribs will not expand . . . no air can he draw in through his flaring nostrils.

I'm suffocating!!!

Panic roars like wildfire through Britt's brain! But even as the panic rises, it is replaced by another, more powerful emotion—the searing hate again roars like galactic fire through Britt's body and makes his eyeballs feel like red-hot coals in his skull. Ignited by this consuming passion, Britt's body surges against the strange, strong power which, like a giant, invisible hand, is holding his heart at a standstill: "aaaAAAAAHHH!"—the air, cool air floods into Britt's lungs. His chest expands against the monstrous grip around it—his surging hate breaks the hold like an angry Hercules breaking imprisoning chains . . . instinctively, Britt whirls around!

MARIA! He now sees her body lying motionless on the floor of the dark bedchamber. Around her prostrate form, a faint aura is glowing slightly brighter than the pale moonlight. In the same manner that these beams descend from the moon, the aura around Maria's body is flowing from a source that remains hidden in the deep shadow of the bedchamber.

Britt's eyes immediately trace the beams back toward two small points of light that are burning there in the blackness of the inner chamber. And now again with ancient, reawakening instincts, Britt senses the danger . . . now again the hate flares wildly and his eyeballs burn with the awful energy that is being released from the depths of his primordial subconscious. *Hate! hate! hate!* throbs through his brain! The mindless emotion is lifting long-unused mental gates deep within Britt's being . . . lifting the gates—unblocking a wide channel that is surging with the tidal energy of the galaxies: energy that at this moment is already flooding irresistibly, overpoweringly into Britt's being, boiling into and filling every corner of his body, his soul—and now the ancient timeless energy leaps out of Britt's eyes and stabs instinctively toward the points of light in the bedchamber!

But the target dodges! Britt's beams roll past it like thunder and strike the unseen inner wall of the dark room!

The castle trembles as if moved by a mighty earthquake! But now the aura also fades around Maria's body . . . the points of light in the darkness become eyesockets simmering with sinister evil.

Britt inhales deeply, recharging his lungs and his soul with power—*power!* power hammers through his body!

And now, like the devil emerging from the black hole of hell, Britt's psychic opponent steps out of the room's deep shadows and into the dim moonlight—now the enemy's eyes flash bright red!

Britt and the castle both reel from the blast that narrowly misses its mark as Britt ducks!

Mortar dust sifts down in soft streams from the castle's ceiling. Staggered but uninjured, Britt's own energy builds in a flash and explodes from his eyes! The other man seems surprised and he stumbles . . . the fiery red heat in his eyes dims for an instant—but in an instant again he hurls back a blast of his own!

But he has unleased it too soon! The agent's power had not recycled completely: the psychokinetic shockwave bursts mighty slabs outward from the walls of the castle and hurls part of the balcony's stone railing into the abyss of the bay— but Britt himself shrugs it off as his own strength, like a Fury of ancient mythology, swirls through his soul, shielding him and drawing to infinite limits on the limitless power of the galaxies. Britt's head throbs, *throbs* and *throbs* and thuds with painful impact inside his skull—and at this instant his eyeballs bulge within their sockets as they hurl this crushing hate toward the target of Britt's primitive passion.

The impact hurls the enemy back and simultaneously shoves huge stones aside from the inner wall of the bedchamber. The wall collapses thunderously into dusty rubble.

Britt advances a step now, but is distracted for an instant by the form of poor Maria lying on the floor. The raging hate in Britt's soul falters during that instant—and that instant is all the stunned agent needs to recover!

Fists clenched, the man scrambles to one knee and hurls a ponderous blast at Britt—and Britt, as if slammed by a fast-moving wave, falls back! Yet even as Britt falls, the shock fans the flames of the hate to rage again within his soul. He angrily rolls like a tackled athlete and ends up his fall facing his opponent.

Now both men hurl simultaneous psychic bolts which crash together like jousting knights and send concussive waves of energy ricocheting into the ceiling and walls of the castle! Cracks and fissures dart through the weakening structure! Debris and dust fill the air!

Britt's whole being is tingling with cosmic energy now funneling faster and faster into the waiting well of his soul. In a flash, he spins to his feet and hurls another impulse at his opponent. The man staggers under the impact.

Again and again and again Britt surges with power and sends out his blasts! The enemy agent retreats unsteadily backward under the rain of invisible blows . . . backward, stumbling over the rubble of the inner wall . . . and the castle itself like a monstrous creature in agony is staggering, trembling under the repeated pelting of Britt's power.

Britt's energy is recycling instantaneously now, leaving not a nanosecond of respite for his opponent to recharge his own power. And now that man falls—now he struggles to lift his head toward Britt. But Britt is a glowing dynamo hurling out a merciless, unstoppable barrage of energy in waves and surges that rival the cosmic power of a super-nova star!

The red-glowing light dims in the enemy agent's eyesockets . . . now, it goes out completely—and there, where only moments earlier the hell-fire had burned . . . there are only the eyes of a terrified, mortal man.

At this incredible instant, Britt's Self exerts an ill-timed at-

THE MIND MASTERS

tempt to control, morally hesitant about killing a man! And this instant is all the enemy requires—his eyes again disappear, transmuted once more into fire-filled glass like orbs! But before this man's primitive mind can attack, Britt's primordial subconscious again rips control from Britt's civilized Self and boils out a broad blast of death-dealing hate!

Like waves on a restless sea, the huge marble slabs of the bedchamber floor roll! The bones of the enemy agent's body shatter under the impact of Britt's bolt!—from a collapsing chest, blood belches out thickly through the agent's open mouth!

The man's body is dead, crushed and drained of its life power, its soul blasted into the farthest reaches of the universe by the near-infinite power that even now continues surging from the stars and into Britt. Britt's Self is at this instant struggling to keep from being eternally submerged by the in-pouring flood of primitive energy which, like a runaway dynamo, is supercharging Britt's Id, keeping *it* in control . . . Britt's head buzzes with electric energy . . . his Self struggles harder and harder, straining to lift out of the sucking whirlpool of in-flooding energy. *My God!!! My God!!! Can I not shut off these floodgates!!! Will I never again control my own Being!?!* Britt's Self now calls upon all the energy it can command and struggles to rise to the surface of the swirling currents of energy, but Britt's vengeful subconscious is exulting in its freedom and power!

The dynamo buzzing in Britt's brain grows louder and louder—the power building and building and Britt feeling himself growing godlike, larger than the earth which in his mind's expanding eye is rapidly shrinking, shrinking to a tiny, insignificant ball. . . .

"Britt!"

Like lightning, Britt whirls around toward the source of his name—a thunderbolt flashes from his eyes!!!

But Krimmel, aided by his own psychic insight, flattens himself on the floor—the impulse from Britt's out-of-control power rumbles thunderously over Krimmel's head, pressing him hard against the floor as it bulges past and crashes into the bedchamber wall. The wall bursts outward, its mammoth marble stones fly off into the night and down into the gaping black mouth of the bay. The huge castle convulses in death throes and giant stones fall from its ceiling!

"Look out, Britt!!!"

XXXVII

"Oooohhh..." moans Britt through the pain.

"Here, sit up slowly," says Karl. "You will be all right. The stone only clipped the back of your head."

Britt's skull stabs with pain as he sits up slowly. He is sitting amid the rubble of the bedchamber. With his fingertips, he lightly touches the bloody lump near the base of his ear.

"Jesus, Karl," Britt says as he surveys the broken stones littered around him in the dark room. Dust in the air nearly causes Britt to gag. "What happened... where's Mar——" The name sticks in Britt's mouth.

The question need not have been asked... Britt now sees the delicate hand protruding from beneath a pile of huge ceiling stones.

"She was dead before those stones buried her, Britt," Krimmel says. "It was not your fault."

Salty tears are swelling in Britt's eyes. They tumble freely down his cheeks and leave clean, glistening trails in the marble dust on his skin. "Ohhh, God," he sighs softly, sorrowfully.

"Oh... God..." he repeats in tones of despair.

"Britt... Britt," Krimmel says with gentle firmness. "Maria is no longer there in that shell. It might as well be a mannequin lying under those stones." Krimmel pauses and looks at the hand that hangs cold and pale, delicate, lovely, and frail. "During the past few days you yourself know that she became convinced through you that *death* is not *dying*—that it is, rather, a birth from the womb of this crude physical existence into a far better mode of being."

Britt still sits numbly, unmoving. His eyes are focused on the hand whose softness he knew on his body only such a short time ago. "Karl..." Britt begins... but he cannot find words.

"I know... Britt... I know," the German says quietly.

"Is it worth it? Yes, Britt, it is . . . it is always worth going on, trying to make something better of this phase of human existence . . . even if we don't really know why." As he speaks, Krimmel stares out into the night . . . part of his mind is elsewhere while the tip of his index finger is lightly rubbing across a series of small marks on his wrist.

And now, for the first time, Britt notices the numbers tattooed there. For several seconds, the two men sit in silence.

Britt blinks away a tear. "Yes, Karl . . . I know that she's happier now. At least she has transitioned from this world to the Beyond with a soul at last freed of the guilt she had mistakenly felt for the past several years. To die guilt-free and at peace with one's Self—that's all that anyone can ask for . . . and it is more than most people manage. I am warmed with knowing that I was able to help her."

Slowly, unsteadily, Britt rises to his feet. "She has no doubt found her father by now, Karl—somewhere . . . perhaps a million light-years from this place . . . perhaps just down there, in the bay . . ." Something catches Britt's eye as he turns his head toward the balcony:

"What is *that*, Karl?"

XXXVIII

Britt walks out onto the dark balcony and toward an array of strange equipment that is sitting next to his communicator. The devices bear a resemblance to his own equipment.

"While you were unconscious," Karl explains, as he walks to Britt's side, "I searched through the other rooms to see if I could learn the identity of the nation for which these agents worked. I found this equipment . . . and this code book." Karl hands a small notebook to Britt.

Suddenly the castle shudders! Thick clouds of stone dust and chips of marble rain down from the sagging ceiling.

Karl glances at the ceiling and walls. "I think the struggle here tonight has weakened this structure to the point of near-collapse."

But Britt is too engrossed in the valuable contents of the notebook to tune in on what Krimmel says. "This book is really a *find*, Karl," says Britt appreciatively. *"Really a find!* There are even several unsent messages in here, Karl—apparently this group had not yet contacted their home base about us."

"Gut," says the German. Now he and Britt walk out onto the balcony. Krimmel kneels down and begins to place Britt's equipment back into the canvas sling in which Britt had brought the devices into the castle.

"Ahhh," says Britt, still paging through the book, "these messages indicate that this group was here to test a communication device similar to that which we have . . . Karl, you will make certain that this equipment is shipped back to Mero for analysis—disguise it as engine-tuning equipment like our own devices." Britt closes the notebook and jams it securely into his pocket. "With this book to break their code and with their loss of this equipment, the efforts of their group should suffer quite a setback."

Karl is working quickly now, placing the enemy communicator in a sling that he has made from his shirt. He looks up at Britt: "I battled two surgically constructed cyborgs in the courtyard, but . . ." Krimmel pauses and nods back into the bedchamber, "that man who fought you—I examined him and found *no* scar."

Britt arches an eyebrow. "He must have been a student of their school for the physiological development of natural psychics. He must have been quite proficient in the ability to affect the heart and intercostal muscles of his victims." Britt rubs his chest, his own intercostal breathing muscles are sore from the pressure of his powerful opponent. "I'm amazed that they've reached such an advanced level of sophistication so *soon*. I hope he was their only example of that psychic level."

The lanky Krimmel stands now and looks intently into Britt's eyes: "And *you*, Britt—where did *your* power come from?"

Before Britt can reply, a massive, muffled grinding noise fills his ears—the colossal castle lurches like a mortally wounded animal, and a jagged split opens between the building and the balcony on which they stand.

"Jump!!!" cries Krimmel.

At the same instant that he cries out, the agile German also swoops up the sling of alien equipment and leaps backward onto the firm bedchamber floor—but Britt slips on the tilting cinder-slick surface of the balcony and he cannot make the leap—the balcony shudders beneath Britt's feet . . . Britt stands quietly for several tense seconds . . . gradually the balcony steadies.

Slowly, carefully, Britt reaches down now and picks up the sling of Mero equipment . . . cautiously, he hands the sling to Krimmel who is waiting with an outstretched arm . . . the balcony sways! Its heavy stones grind together, and Britt—unable to push off from the shaky structure—waits out the movement once again while a thousand feet below and hidden by the darkness of the night, invisible waves roll in and hiss on the black, volcanic stones . . . now, the balcony is momentarily steady again. Krimmel has set down the Mero equipment and he is holding out his large hand to Britt . . . Britt takes the hand and, aided by a firm assist from Krimmel, steps lightly off of the tilting balcony.

Standing now on the firmer footing of the bedchamber, Britt turns toward the broken balcony: it is hanging on above the black abyss of the bay . . . hanging on like a living thing waiting for a hopeless rescue.

Britt speaks to Krimmel without turning around: "You know there is something I must do."

"*Ja*," acknowledges the German.

Britt now removes a small glass vial from his pocket. With a flick of his thumb he pops out the rubber stopper. "Give me your hand again, Karl," says Britt. Krimmel extends his long arm and Britt takes firm hold of the man's hand. Now Britt slowly, carefully, leans out over the balcony. "Keep a good hold, Karl," he says quietly. Clear acid pours down from the bottle and splatters across the surface of the bloodstained marble slab on the balcony.

Almost immediately, bubbles rise, hissing and spitting as the fluid eats into the ancient stone . . . destroying it . . . breaking down its very molecular structure.

Suddenly a shapeless, luminous form rises—rises like smoke glowing in the fading moonlight, escaping the rapidly decaying stone. And at this instant, Britt is hit by bone-chilling cold, cold as if something is drawing all the warmth of life from his flesh! But just as quickly as it came, the cold passes. The amorphous form rises rapidly up into the night, riding a moonbeam out of sight in an instant.

"Get back!!!" Karl cries.

He tugs Britt's arm just as the balcony loudly breaks loose, and, free of its centuries-long burden of sorrow, falls silently into the depths of the black bay.

"Come—*quickly*," urges Krimmel.

But Britt pulls away: "No! No . . . Maria . . . her body . . . we can't leave it here."

Now the building begins to twist. Large slivers of stone explode from the slabs under strain and fly through the dark room like deadly marble darts.

Britt looks quickly at the massive stones and rubble piled on Maria's body: *God!!! It's impossible, I know—but just maybe* . . . Before Britt can complete his thought, the side wall of the bedchamber bulges ominously. Huge stones begin falling!

KarRUMP! KarRUMP! The stones fall around!

The men look for a way out. But the balcony is gone and Britt and Krimmel must run back into the bedchamber! Running into the dusty darkness there, hoping to find a clear passage, they leap through the gap that was smashed in the back wall by the blast of Britt's psychokinetic projection! They land in a pitch-black and unfamiliar corridor of the old inner castle. The passageway's floor is littered with rubble. Showers of dust and dirt are falling from the sagging ceiling stones of the narrow black hallway! Britt and Krimmel dodge and dart, running instinctively in the near-total darkness, stumbling, striving toward a faint moonlit opening ahead. Now they reach it and find themselves in the longer corridor of the ballroom—it, too, is an obstacle course of smashed stone and air choked with dust, dust that dryly coats their mouths and lungs as Britt and Krimmel move quickly through. Before them and behind them, above and beneath, the building is splitting and tearing, stones falling, clouding the air with dry and ancient mortar dust!

Suddenly they burst out the front doorway and leap the steps! Sailing over the steps and the corpse that lies in the darkness, they land slipping and sliding on the cindery courtyard! Scrambling for speed and clutching the equipment slings, the men dodge through the splintered, strewn timbers that once were the impenetrable main gates ... and now they are out! Out onto the trembling cliffs. Onward they sprint now, across the black cinders and stones—they are straining to get clear of the castle's tall wall that is towering shakily above them in the darkness, huge and deadly ... the wall leans! It buckles!!!

... *rrrRRRWWUUUMMP!!!*

Stones from the collapsing wall thud to the earth like a shower of massive meteors!

KaruuUUMP!!!

WHUMP!!!—stones crash beside the running men!

The earth leaps under the impact of the rain of boulders from the night sky—the blocks are crashing to the ground all around Britt and Krimmel. *C'mon Luck! Stay with us!!!* Britt thinks desperately—the thud of his running feet, the beat of the blood in his veins, and slap of the sling of equipment all pound in and against his body, and as he runs ... strains ...

"Britt! Stop! *Stop!*" Krimmel calls out.

Britt's momentum carries him several steps farther before he stops completely. He turns toward the dark figure of Krimmel.

"We are clear," says the panting German. "It is over."

Britt, too, is gasping for breath. He stands like an exhausted athlete, bending forward, his hands on his knees as he inhales great gulps of air through his mouth. The pounding of his pulse fills his head!

Behind them, in the night, they watch as the huge castle continues to collapse in on itself. Its black bulk, darker than the darkness that surrounds it, appears like some strange gargantuan gargoyle thrashing in its death throes . . . and the almost-alive mass is churning and crushing the hell-fired black cindery soil from which it was born, sending up billows of dust that become faint silver smoke in the starlight . . . a cloud rising heavenward, as if the castle is at this moment giving up its own secret soul.

The black cliff now heaves sharply once more beneath Britt's feet! A sound like grinding, splitting concrete suddenly fills the air—so loud, that Britt's ears ring. Instinctively, Britt and Krimmel step back—step back just in time!

A jagged tear races across the surface of the loose, black soil and swallows a stone at the spot on which Britt stood but an instant before. The entire face of the cliff is loosening, tilting toward the opening cone of the dead volcano, toward the waters it holds in its throat.

Now, slowly, at first . . . the mountainous remains of the cursed castle begin to move . . . begin to slide . . . slide faster—and *faster!*—tumbling, rolling as the very cliff itself bows ever more deeply down toward its fate in the waiting waters a thousand feet below. A grinding, a roaring sound arises invisible in the dim starlit night . . . the sound of the quickening avalanche of monstrous stones pouring into the abyss of the bay! And at this instant the entire edge of the cliff breaks clean away—the mammoth mass plummets like a dying planet toward the waters that have waited so long . . .

. . . And now . . . now everything everywhere is strangely silent. . . .

No trace remains of the Castle of Death . . . nor of its victims.

XXXIX

"EEEEEEEEEE!!!" shrieks the huge building ahead of Britt. He stops.

Dim, warm light glows from the hundreds of small windowpanes in the giant old building. The warmth there, radiating into the rainy night, reminds Britt of the chill, the cold that stings within his feet and hands. He glances down at his shoes: they are soaked through by the rain. Looking ahead once again, Britt notices how the raindrops appear from nowhere out of the hovering dark and fall like tiny meteors lit by the light of the train station windows.

"EEEEEEEEEE!!!"

The insistent sound of the locomotive's whistle jars Britt. Wearily he resumes walking toward the station. The ferry ride from Messina to the mainland was rough and wet because of the storm chopping out in the Strait. It was the last ferry run of the night from the island and Britt had been the sole pedestrian passenger. This last run brought mainly produce trucks from the Sicilian olive orchards. The drivers sat silent and sullen in their battered vehicles, knowing that their high-speed run on the *autostrada* to Rome would be a gamble with Death because of the rainstorm.

The boat docked only five minutes ago now at the dark dock in Reggio Calabria. The distant church bells were slowly chiming midnight and no taxis were on the deserted waterfront.

Britt had tried to hitch a ride with the produce truckdrivers as they drove off the boat, but the men ignored him. So, Britt has been walking through the rain . . . through the empty, unlit streets of the ancient town . . . slugging wet and cold to catch the midnight express.

The irregular tapping of the raindrops on Britt's wet hair is suddenly exchanged for the drumming of the downpour on the high, vaulted metal roof of the train station as now Britt steps inside the building. The structure is too large for the train traffic it handles today; the building had been built by Mussolini to handle shipments of war machines, materials and men to fortify Sicily. Now, tonight—like most nights— the great station stands damp and vast and nearly deserted. Britt looks cautiously around the dim interior of the huge station. In a shadow-filled far corner, three young wanderers with knapsacks sit, talking quietly, on the long wooden benches . . . a wine-sodden derelict slumps in a phone booth. Farther away from where Britt stands at this moment, the low, hundred-yard-wide door of the building gapes: a huge mouth filled with the black of the night outside. And like strange snake tongues, silver steel sets of rail tracks lunge out of this mouth and into the station. Elevated empty concrete walkways parallel the tracks which are all empty of trains but for one set at the far side of the building. There, on that set of rails, sits a waiting six-car train. Steam is wisping, hissing softly up from the drive pistons at the front of the gray engine, and Britt can see the tiny figures of the engineer and fireman moving inside the fire-lit cab. The front coupler of the locomotive reaches just to the edge of the door . . . the headlight is shining out and crystal raindrops zip down through the beam which is burning into the deep dark of the night. Behind the patiently waiting power of the engine, four passenger and two baggage cars lie strung along the walkway. The lights are out in most of the compartments of the passenger cars, and Britt cannot see whether the compartments are occupied by sleeping passengers or whether they are empty.

All of the shops of the station are also closed and shuttered . . . except for one lone newsstand. The heels of Britt's cold shoes hit hard on the concrete as he walks toward that stand. A weathered old man sags, nearly asleep, on a stool behind the counter. Britt picks up a local newspaper and drops a fifty-*lira* bill on the counter . . . the old man looks drowzily up and nods.

"EEEEEEEEEEEE!!!"

The third and final warning whistle sounds. Britt now turns, pushes the folded newspaper up under his arm, and, carrying his traveling bag and briefcase, he jogs toward the train . . . down the walkway parallel with the compartment cars which bounce alongside in the corner of his field of vision as he runs along.

Number 14 . . . this one's mine.

Britt, briefcase in his right hand, reaches up now with the

THE MIND MASTERS [229]

least-burdened hand that holds the slim briefcase. He hooks a free finger around the cold steel and pulls down on the handle that opens the door. The train lurches slightly at this instant as Britt steps aboard. He tosses his briefcase onto the seat and slides his suitcase against the inner door. Now he turns and pulls shut the outer door behind him. The train lurches again . . . it begins to move forward slowly.

Britt sits down on the broad seat. He inhales deeply, his heart is beating rapidly from his brief run of a moment ago down the walkway. The closed compartment is quiet. Britt looks out the window . . . the station's interior is slipping silently behind—suddenly Britt is startled by the unexpected drumming of the rain on the train car roof. On the other side of the window glass, in the world that he is leaving, Britt sees the dim-lit cavern of the empty station fade and be replaced by the blackness of the stormy night.

The first, lone raindrop trickles down the window glass . . . others quickly follow. The silver streams remind Britt of the crystal tears which flowed so freely down Maria's soft cheek on that night in the shack. A wave of sorrow surges through Britt . . . pangs of loneliness and loss drain away his strength. Salty water swells up now in his eyes: the shimmering fluid breaks free, like a wave breaking over a dam, it runs quickly down his cheek and cools the corners of his lips. Without thinking, Britt automatically touches his lips with his tongue —the salty sweetness of the tears reminds him of how Maria tasted.

Come on . . . I've got to snap out of this! But what am I doing here? What happened to the life I dreamed of living as a kid in school? Was I ever that kid I remember . . . or have I always been as I am now? . . . Is there nothing else to reality but the now? Here I am, sitting on a midnight express rushing through Europe toward another date with Death and the dead . . . involved in a struggle about which only a few dozen people in the entire world even know . . . a struggle that has destroyed Gayle and Maria and so many others— and that could destroy me. Britt's Self now begins to exert its authority over this emotional outpouring from his weary soul: *No . . . no . . . this is a far better thing I do than winning the Indy 500 or becoming chairman of Bank of America. This is something important to ME, myself . . . something which needs no approval from others, no reward but that which I grant to myself.*

The self-pity passes.

Outside Britt's compartment the world whisks passed, invisible in the black of the night. Britt is staring at the window, watching his own image reflected in the dark glass, but now . . . now he turns away. Slowly, he reaches down, picks up his slim black briefcase and places it on his lap.

Lup! Lup! go the steel latches on the hard, cold case. Britt lifts the lid and takes out a long, narrow yellow paper: it is Webster's reply to the lengthy report that Britt had coded early this morning and wired back to the Ontario, California, competition parts store that serves as the Stateside cover and base for Britt's racing team. Britt has stayed in Messina all this day, first encoding his report so that it read like a race report and wiring it back to California. He sat through most of this afternoon in the *taverna* across the noisy street from the telegraph office while waiting for this reply he now holds. Greg, Krimmel, and Hollender had packed the Porsches and the equipment onto and into the transporter; then they had left on the mid-afternoon ferry with the bulk of the racing teams. The racing circus had moved on. Many were already this evening in Nurburg, West Germany, unloading their cars and equipment for next weeks *Nurburgring Ein Tousand Kilometers.* The Nurburgring 1,000 Kilometers race often attracts crowds of 300,000 or more spectators; the crowds and confusion will provide good cover for Britt's special activities . . . and those of his enemy's.

What IS that? What could it be?—the drumming of the rain on his compartment's roof reminds Britt now again of the strange interference that had prevented him from clearly communicating with the spirit last night in the castle. *I hope Adam can unscramble and identify the source of that interference from those tapes which Hollender shipped this afternoon.*

Britt shakes his head: it is an outward sign of his desire at this moment to rid his thoughts of the events of the past several days—and of last night . . . yet he knows he will never forget.

That missing factor? What can it be? His mind repeats, even as it strives hard to force these questions deep down into his soul's lower level of consciousness.

Simultaneously, Britt is struggling to command his upper level of consciousness to focus on the coded reply that he holds from Webster. Britt mentally uncodes as he reads:

"Regret failure to make definite contact," the message begins, "but am awaiting arrival of captured equipment. Encounter with alien group has apparently not compromised your cover. Evidence of enemy sophistication indicates that you must continue regardless of increasing danger of encounters.

"Your observations of your own renewed display of PK has been analyzed by Adam. Conclusion: this current event correlates positive with pattern of prior display against Pickett in hospital in Hawaii. Explanation from Adam: your innate ESP that was first reactivated by events in Vietnam is apparently the trigger for releasing subconscious PK. When your subconscious ESP picks up input of threat or evil intent, as with Pickett and enemy agent in the castle, it triggers an intense emotion of repulsion and consuming hate. The power of this hatred, sustained by release of adrenaline hormone, causes rage that inhibits function of your conscious control. PK, under control of your Id, lashes out at enemy.

"Adam's analysis of your experiences indicate that our research into reactivation, elicitation, and control of innate human psychic powers should focus now on control of emotions. This control can perhaps be accomplished electronically with modified versions of the Mood Master, chemically with artificial hormones, or psychologically through programs teaching emotional discipline. Dr. Janick is already working on the hormone investigation.

"Good luck. Be careful."

Clack, clack, click . . . clack, clack, click . . . What is it? What is it? The clacking, clicking rhythm of the wheels along the rails again brings up the insistent question from Britt's subconscious. *What caused the interference? It must be some sort of tremendous electromagnetic influence . . . what is it?*

Britt picks up the newspaper he had purchased back in the station. The banner headline tells in Italian of a new scandal in the Rome parliament, where a plot by politicians to establish a secret police force is being condemned as "an Italian Watergate" and "the resurrection of Mussolini."

But, down in the corner of the front page, Britt sees the headline that he is looking for:

EARTHQUAKE DESTROYS HISTORIC MONUMENT; ETNA
BLAMED FOR SERIES OF MINOR TREMORS.

Good, thinks Britt as he reads the article: ". . . and instruments at the University of Rome placed the disturbance between 4.3 and 4.5 on the Richter scale."

Britt tosses the paper across the compartment, onto the opposite seat. *That should do it,* he thinks with weary relief.

XXXX

God! I'm tired. Britt stretches his stiffening arms . . . he leans back wearily against the soft back of the train seat. The seat is gently rocking with the rhythm of the train along the rails. Vaguely, Britt is aware just how drained he is by the emotional and physical demands of the past week. He settles back and lets himself be lulled by the steady rhythm of the clacking, clicking wheels. His mind drifts ahead . . . to Nurburg . . .

The Nurburgring 1,000 Kilometer race is the most difficult and treacherous closed-course race in the world. Hitler himself had ordered the construction of the Nurburg track, and, like most other things that Hitler did, the track is monumental—*excessively* monumental: fourteen miles per lap. The course twists, leaps, and dives through thick, fog-shrouded German forests. Also, like most projects that bore Hitler's mark, the track included a damning error of judgment: the weather. The region in which "the Ring" is located is notorious for fogs and rains. The dampness is responsible for the thick Schwarzenwald—the famed and infamous Black Forest through whose dense hills the course was cut.

Each year, race fans from across the Continent and from England and America pilgrimage to the Ring. During practice and race day, they sit scattered around the massive track. Whole families cluster and huddle shivering beneath umbrellas and raincoats. The spectators watch brave and foolish men test their courage by driving at breakneck speeds along the rainy road and through sudden, impossible fogs—the drivers dare the dangers of the leafy arms which hang across the road . . . the forest, whose thick, gnarled trunks, black and wet, crowd to the very edge of the slick tar track, waiting to smash the unwary car and driver. And, the ancient, mossy trees do often win their dreadful wait: in 1969, World Driving Champion Jim Clark lost his life when his frail Lotus mysteriously disappeared from the track. Five minutes after he was overdue on the final lap of that race, search teams had gone out. They found Clark's body and his car lying together at the foot of a massive, silent tree. Both the car and the corpse were twisted and torn and cold, like a child's broken toy that had been left out in the rain.

If the searchers that day had been able to see through the mists that obscured the mountain which even today looms up behind the curve where Clark died, they would have noticed the ruins of *Rabenblut—Raven's Blood*. This gray, foreboding, fog-shrouded fortress had been built in 1939 by General Heinrick Weissmann.

Weissmann was a principal architect of Hitler's horrible human ovens.

During the years of the Jewish slaughter in Nazi Germany, Weissmann was known to his victims as *Todmeister—Death Master*.

Weissmann had his own personal oven built into the recreation room of his mammoth mountain retreat that overlooked the treacherous Karoussel turn of the Nurburgring. One wall of the huge, room-sized oven was made of thick, heat-resistant glass.

Young Jewish girls were regularly delivered to the castle as bottles of milk are delivered to suburban homes. There, Weissmann and his fiendish Nazi comrades raped and tortured them. And, when the men had satisfied themselves, the girls were locked in the oven, and the flames turned on and slowly up until all that remained were ashes. The Nazis would sit on couches and sip their brandy, watching the dying girls and conversing as ordinary people do around an ordinary fireplace.

The horror of *Rabenblut* ended horribly.

According to secret Allied army reports, as the victorious Russian army swept rapidly toward his hideaway, Weissmann —deserted by his staff, and alone in his monstrous building —retreated in panic to the highest of its towers, and there he hanged himself.

Strangely ... Weissmann's body was never found.

During the decades of days and nights which have withered and fallen from the calendars since that suicide, mysterious phenomena have occurred both in that house of horror and in the woods over which it once ruled.

Furious howling has periodically awakened the sleeping villagers of Lieblos, which is situated in the valley just three miles from the mountain ruins of Weissmann's evil fortress.

The village is situated near the racecourse's start–finish line. Today, the people of the village are mostly old. Lieblos had been established during Hitler's reign, and its only industry even then was to cater to the wealthy Nazis who attended the splendid races which Hitler staged at Nurburgring. Since Hitler's end, however, the track has hosted only a few races each year, and the youth of the village have left for places which offer brighter futures.

The old villagers explain to visitors today that the howling is merely wind in the thick, fog-shrouded treetops of the surrounding forest. And the fires which tourists often see mysteriously flare up and go out by themselves in the distant high tower where Weissmann hanged himself are explained away as being started by lightning and extinguished by rain.

Yet . . . racing drivers who have been lucky enough to survive the crashes which seem to occur frequently on the Karoussel curve directly below the *Todmeister*'s granite tomb —these fortunate drivers tell consistent stories of a strange, sudden pull on their steering wheels just before the crash. They report they felt they were struggling against some unseen force that was irresistibly pulling their cars off the road and toward the waiting trees. . . .

Britt can feel the hair rise on his arm. He shivers as he looks out the window into the wet, black nothingness of night. Raindrops are tracing crooked patterns down the glass.

Britt sits back again and closes his eyes. Once more, he becomes aware of the clacking, clicking of the wheels along the rails. His mind drifts again to that bothersome question of the missing factor—the factor that might help explain and eliminate the static in the communicator and at last allow man to better understand his second life.

Clack, clack, click, the wheels sound . . . *clack, clack, click*—what is it? Britt's mind repeats . . . *clack, clack, click, what is it?*

This clack and click of the wheels persist in Britt's ears, in his mind, until superseded by a sudden, startling roar! Britt jerks erect—his heart pounding!—flashing past the window are indistinguishable shapes! In an instant, however, his brain computes what they are and what is happening:

The tunnel! . . . of course . . . we must be nearing the border to Austria. He glances at his watch—speeding hours have passed since this express train left Reggio Calabria.

Amused at his fright of a split second ago, Britt now settles back again in his seat. His ears gradually grow accustomed to the roar of the train as it rockets through the narrow tunnel—the many-miles-long narrow tunnel which is buried beneath the planet-like mass of these mighty mountains—the high Alps. Like a worm in the bowels of a grave, the train is in a small black hole bored through the earth . . . a hole from which Britt will emerge to confront the undead horror of the Master of Death.

Just the beginning . . .